I0543453

Tetterbaum's Truth

Volume One in the Just Call Me Angel
Suspense Series

S.R. Claridge

Global Publishing Group LLC

Printed in the United States of America

First trade edition: February 2011

ISBN 978-0-9898467-0-7

The author would like to offer special thanks to her brilliant team of editors, whose expertise is invaluable: Cash, Jerrye, Gary, Matt and Beth

She would like to thank her family for their love and support, and to thank God for every blessing.

Tetterbaum's Truth is the first book in the Just Call Me Angel series. A complete list of books by S.R.Claridge is available at the back of this book.

For previews and information about the author, visit
www.SusanClaridge.com

For information about the publisher, visit
www.GlobalPublishGroup.com

CHAPTER ONE

Angel slid slowly out from under the sheet and lifted herself off his double bed, trying not to make any sudden movements that might wake him. She tiptoed across the hardwood floor, scanning the room for her clothes and pausing each time the floorboards creaked. Last night must have been wilder than she remembered because her clothes were strewn across the room. She was wearing one of his black t-shirts that hung almost to her knees, and her bra was missing in action. She bent down and peeked under the bed. It was possible it could have been kicked under there during their romp. Angel didn't remember taking it off, though she was certain it wasn't forced off. She'd been here before, many times, and there was no question she was a willing participant.

Too willing, she scolded herself.

She had been carrying on with Grayson for the past year, and though their relationship was unconventional and probably even unhealthy, she couldn't resist him. From the first time he strutted into Tetterbaum's pub, which she owned, she was putty in his hands. Thereafter, each time he showed up she followed him home like a bouncing puppy. He was mysterious, alluring and rendered her defenses inoperable with a mere glance from his big brown eyes and dimpled cheeks.

Making it to the bathroom without waking him, Angel exhaled a sigh of relief. She splashed cold water on her face and blotted at the mascara smudged on her cheek. Her brown eyes looked glassy, like she tied one on last night, which was only fair considering she had. Her shoulder length, dark brown hair lay flattened against her head, and she ran her fingers through it just above the ears, trying to add volume. It didn't work. She finally opted to tuck it behind her ears and let the rest fall messily over her shoulders. Standing back Angel took in her reflection and sighed. "I hope I can sneak out before he sees me," she mumbled to herself. "Talk about a turn off."

Angel was certain Grayson would wake up just as good looking as when he went to sleep, though she never stuck around long enough to find out. It wasn't because she didn't want to behold his manly glory at sunrise; it was because she didn't want the awkwardness that comes with the morning after. Everything felt easier at night when inhibitions were compromised by alcohol, expressions were hidden in darkness and there was no particular pressure to talk. At night, in Grayson's arms, Angel felt she could become anyone she wanted. She was free and open, and that spontaneous excitement was different than anything she'd ever experienced.

Tiptoeing around the bed she was able to locate her black converse tennis shoes but her bra and black t-shirt that read Tetterbaum's Pub were still MIA. She stared at the covers wadded up at the foot of the bed and surmised that her bra and shirt were probably buried in them. Deciding to attempt a quick search and rescue, she knelt down and slid her arm under the black comforter, careful not to touch his legs. Moving to the other side, she slid her arm in again, still nothing.

I'll have to go home braless and borrow his shirt, she concluded. There were no other feasible options.

As she withdrew her arm, the sheet pulled back slightly and something on his right hip caught her eye. It was a tattoo. She hadn't noticed it before, though that wasn't hard to believe since she'd never seen him naked in the light of day. Carefully she lifted the corner of the sheet just enough to view the entire tattoo. It was about two inches long and looked like a scar, like it had been burned into the skin, leaving grooves. She'd never seen anything like it. Angel fought the temptation to let her fingertips explore the grooves. She didn't like tattoos, but this one intrigued her, and she shuddered at the possibility that it could have been branded into his flesh. Cocking her head to the side, Angel narrowed her eyes and studied it. It was the letter M, but the slanted line on the left that made up the middle of the M contained tiny letters. Angel leaned closer, and silently read the letters engraved down the side. *AVGC.* She repeated the letters in her mind, trying to assign significance to the acronym.

When Grayson began to stir, Angel froze, holding her breath. *Please don't wake up. Please don't wake up,* her mind chanted and her heart raced. She didn't want him to see how horrible she looked in the morning, not to mention how weird it would be if he opened his eyes and saw her looming over him. When she was certain he was back asleep, she slowly rocked back on her heels, scooted away from the bed and made a beeline for the door.

Their relationship was perfect, she told herself as she drove to her apartment. He didn't know where she lived so she didn't have to worry about unannounced drop-ins. They'd never exchanged phone numbers, so she didn't have to obsess over whether he would call the day after sex; nor did she have to carry her phone around hoping for a text. She didn't even know his last name. In fact, they knew very little about each other outside of the bedroom. There were no strings which was exactly what she wanted, or exactly what she tried to convince herself she wanted. The truth was Angel was lonely. She turned twenty-nine last month and besides the ticking of her biological clock, her heart longed to feel loved.

Angel had experienced her share of typical teenage crushes that lasted a few months but had only been in love once and it ended badly. His name was Tony and they met as journalism students at the University of Missouri. It was love at first sight. They dated all through school, and after graduation, moved into an apartment together upon returning to Chicago. Shortly after they announced their engagement, Tony changed. As if overnight, he grew distant and began to drag his feet about setting an actual wedding date. Finally, one night, he dropped the bomb.

That memory was something Angel would like to forget, but it haunted her. He drove her to a place that had become their favorite spot outside the city. The property belonged to a friend of his parents, and Tony was allowed to use it whenever he liked, as long as he cleaned up and locked up. A gravel road led up to the enormous house, which sat a hundred yards from a small lake. The lake was surrounded by trees on all sides and Tony and Angel had gone there many times for romantic getaways, picnics, making love under the stars and the occasional spontaneous bout of skinny dipping. It was quite possibly Angel's favorite place in the entire world, though in all fairness she hadn't seen much of the world. Her travels were limited to Illinois and parts of Missouri, with the exception of one trip to New York City when she was five. Tony drove her to this special place to break the news and her heart in one fail swoop. Then he was gone.

She clung to the hope of his return for six months before denial slipped into depression. Angel's Great Aunt Olga came to her rescue, forcing her to get out of bed, to eat and shower, to go to work and to find a way to live without him. What made the breakup so painful for Angel was that she never understood why Tony left. All he said was, "We can't be together." He never explained why. He never said he didn't love her anymore or that she had done something wrong. He just vanished completely from her life. Getting over Tony had been a long, painful journey that had left her heart guarded and unable to risk desertion again.

Since then, most nights in Angel's life were uneventful. She would close up the pub and head home to her apartment in Lincoln Park. When the weather was nice, she walked since it was only a few blocks; but on stormy or snowy days, she was thankful to have her own car; even though owning a car in Chicago was actually more of a hassle and ate up a lot of money in lot fees. Still, it gave her a sense of independence, like she could hop in her car and go anywhere anytime she wanted; not that she ever did.

Every night after work, Angel would join her two cats, Midnight and Mo, on the couch for left-over bar food and a round of TV's best re-runs. Midnight was solid black and liked to lurk in small, dark places; like under the couch or in a closet. Mo was a social Calico who liked to snuggle. He had a purr so loud it sounded like a motorcycle humming in the distance. After feeding herself and the cats, she'd fall asleep on the couch, usually thinking about Grayson and wondering when he would show up again.

"Next time he shows up," she would tell Mo, "I'm not following him home. I'm going to play hard-to-get." She could see Mo didn't believe her any more than she believed herself. He'd look up with slits of mockery in his eyes, as if to say, *Who are you kidding,* and then go back to bathing himself with his sandpaper tongue. Angel knew Grayson was part of the reason there was no love interest in her life; but she resolved herself to the fact that some form of love, albeit just a physical thing, was better than none at all.

Pulling her silver Camry onto the lot and into her reserved spot, she turned off the ignition, sat for a moment, thinking about Grayson's tattoo and his nakedness. Her face flushed. *How can I date someone else,* she silently interrogated herself, *when I know the minute Grayson shows up, I'll dump the other guy for a mere night in Grayson's bed?* It was a fair question. She was stuck.

The aroma of cinnamon pancakes and maple syrup greeted her as she opened her apartment door, momentarily taking her mind off Grayson. She made her way to the kitchen and found Aunt Olga in front of the stove with big potholder gloves on both hands. Olga stood four feet, ten inches and was almost as round as she was tall. She had dark gray hair that sat on top her head in little poufy lumps like storm clouds and light brown eyes that sparkled when she smiled. She was seventy but you'd never know it because her chubby cheeks stretched out her wrinkles and she was as spry as ever; something she attributed to her daily glass of Jack Daniels. "Keeps my mind keen and my intestines clean," she always said.

Olga had her own house in the city but showed up at Angels at least three times a week, usually with a bottle of Jack and always with a hidden agenda. For some people the frequent visits may have been invasive, but Angel didn't mind. The truth was she didn't have many friends of her own. Over the years she had lost touch with high school friends and in college Tony had been her whole life. Now that he was gone, she had no one; well, no one except Olga.

Angel gave Olga a hug from behind. "Mm, you make the best cinnamon pancakes," she said, inhaling in a big whiff.

"You eat up now," Olga answered, carrying a plate over to the table. "You've got a busy day ahead."

Angel sat and shoveled in a fork full. "No, I don't."

"Angel May," Olga gasped, "no wonder you don't have a man."

Uh-oh. It was always bad when Olga used her middle name. "What?" she groaned.

"Don't talk with your mouth full. No man wants to see that. Close your lips when you chew. You don't want him to think you're disgusting do you?"

"Who?" Angel blurted, half-chewed pancakes mashing around in clear view.

Olga shook her head in disgust. "Harvey Milligan."

Angel froze with another fork full half-way to her mouth. "Harvey who?"

Olga snatched the plate from in front of Angel and stormed across the kitchen, to the sink. "I'm not done with that," Angel grabbed at the plate.

"Are you gonna go out with Harvey Milligan this morning?" Olga's question was an ultimatum in disguise. Angel watched in wide-eyed horror as she tilted the plate ever so slightly and the pancakes slid towards the disposal.

Olga was a feisty old broad and she didn't mind sticking her nose into other people's business, no matter the cost. This wasn't the first man she'd found for Angel, and she was certain it wouldn't be the last. Olga's matchmaking skills were sub-par, despite the fact that each time she met a single man she swore to Angel it was fate.

Rodney, the fireman, was the first act of fate. Olga met Rodney when she set her kitchen curtains aflame with a fondue that went awry. The oil splattered on the burner and flames shot up three feet high, singeing Olga's eyebrows and disintegrating the lace curtains altogether. Rodney was big, strong and not bad looking but he had more muscles than brains. When Angel looked into his eyes it was clear that not only were the lights on and nobody home, but nobody was ever coming home.

The next victim of fate was poor 'ol Stanley, the dentist. It took the first five minutes of their date for Angel to realize he had the personality of a doorknob.

"I don't understand," Olga wailed when Angel described what a dud Stanley was. "He's so witty when he's working on my teeth."

"That's not his wit," Angel explained, "it's the laughing gas."

While on one of her exercise kicks, Olga met Manuel, a yoga instructor. At first, Angel thought Manuel had potential. He had a great body, tan skin, chocolate brown eyes and dark hair that sat perfectly in place. He looked perfect, too perfect, which made perfect sense when Angel found out he was gay.

"No," Olga gasped at the news, "but he ogles all the ladies," she said.

"He smiles at the ladies because you're all in your seventies and you pay him," Angel replied with an undertone that said, *duh.*

Olga wasn't convinced. "Maybe he didn't like you and it was easier to lie than be up front?"

"He's not an up-front guy. Believe me, he goes in the backdoor." Angel waited for the metaphor to sink in, and then grinned as Olga giggled like a little girl.

"Oh, that's a good one. I'm gonna have to remember to tell that to Elsa at the hair salon," Olga snickered.

Then there was Clyde. Angel referred to him as Clyde the Clod. He was nice enough, but he took Angel dancing and she had yet to recover from the haunting images of him on the dance floor. He fancied himself an erotic dancer, but his five foot eight, stocky body with a beer gut bouncing up and down, and wet smelly arm pits spoke otherwise. Not to mention the profusion of sweat that dripped from his hairline onto her shoulders. Angel fought her gag reflex when he came off the floor and draped his sweaty pit around her. She let him have one goodnight kiss, out of sheer pity, then ran inside and brushed her teeth.

Angel watched as Olga tilted the plate slightly higher and one piece of pancake slopped into the sink. "Okay," she moaned, "you win. I'll go out with Harvey Milligan if you give me back my pancakes."

Olga grinned a big, rounded smile of victory. She waddled over and put the plate back down in front of Angel. "

"You're a mean old sphinx," Angel said, stuffing pancakes in her mouth.

"How do you think I've lived this long?" She sat down next to Angel and watched her eat. "Hurry. You need to shower and go."

"Where am I going and who is this Harvey guy?" Angel rolled her eyes, showing how annoyed she was by Olga's tactics. She knew Angel couldn't resist cinnamon pancakes. It wasn't a fair fight.

"Don't roll your eyes at your old aunt, it isn't proper." Angel looked over at Olga and crossed her eyes, which made Olga giggle. "You're meeting him at the Art Museum at 9:00am."

"So, he's another geek," Angel wailed.

"He's an accountant dear, very smart with the numbers and loves art. When I told him you used to work at the museum his face lit right up," she explained.

"I haven't worked at the museum for years, and I quit that job because I was bored out of my mind." Angel shoveled in the last bit of pancakes right before Olga snatched her plate and took it to the sink.

"You can't be that stranger's ho forever," Olga snapped. Angel didn't know whether to laugh at the fact that Olga just used the word ho or feel offended that she called her one. "You're not getting any younger and it's time you settle down with a real man."

Angel rolled her eyes. *Here we go again*, she thought, *the real man speech*. What constituted a real man anyway? Olga disapproved of Grayson because his ways were unconventional. He wasn't a come home and meet the family sort of guy; but he was more of a real man than any of the men Olga picked out.

"How do you think it looks being a single lady running a pub in the city all by yourself? You don't want *that* kind of reputation." Olga shook her head.

Angel hadn't thought about her reputation as a single female pub owner. True, most the night spots were owned by men, but that didn't mean a woman couldn't run a successful bar business alone. Besides, Tetterbaum's Pub was a local icon on the north side with a fabulous reputation. It was a small pub but had a quaint charm that drew in both locals and tourists. The Tetterbaum family opened the pub in 1936, shortly after the end of prohibition, and it had been in the same free-standing, corner brick building ever since. Though the building had undergone several renovations through the years, it had never lost its historic allure. There were rumors that Al Capone himself had a table at Tetterbaum's though there were no pictures to confirm the tale, just a plaque that hung over the back booth which read, "Capone's Corner." Angel was certain it was all hype to bring in tourists.

"You never should have started working at that old, nasty pub. It's no place for a woman," Olga ranted.

"It's one of the classiest pubs in the city and you know it," Angel scolded, and Olga threw up her hands.

Angel wasn't backing down because she knew she was right. Tetterbaum's Pub served the highest quality bar food on the north side, and you couldn't find a more unique ambiance. The walls were red brick with dark wooden beams running up and across the ceiling. The floors were dark wood with a natural gleam that reflected the lights from the tiny yellow lamps that sat on each table. The bar ran the entire length of the dining area and the front of it was over-laid in red brick to match the walls. The top was deep brown mahogany, surrounded by a dark brown leather bumper and tiny inset lights illumed the overhang on the outside of the bar. Each stool was covered in dark brown leather to match the bar bumper and the booths throughout the restaurant; and the stool rungs were shiny gold-plated.

Mr. Tetterbaum didn't believe in neon bar signs advertising alcohol products. He said, "The liquor speaks for itself and doesn't need a flashy sign." So, the back of the bar was simply a large mirror, surrounded by shelves made out of the same mahogany as the bar top. Bottles of every size, shape and color adorned the shelves and tiny yellow spotlights from the ceiling were intricately aimed at each shelf, highlighting their offering. It was a beautiful design, with the dim lighting creating an aura of romance and sophistication. It was unlike any pub Angel had ever seen.

"It's still no place for a single woman," Olga sputtered.

Angel sighed from the mental exhaustion of arguing with Olga. It wasn't like running a pub was her dream job. She had wanted to be a journalist, but like so many other things in her life, she just sort of stumbled into it. After Tony left, Angel started waitressing at Tetterbaum's Pub, not because she needed the money but because she needed something to force her out of her apartment every day and keep her mind off Tony. She especially liked working the evening shift because nighttime hours spent at home by herself were the loneliest. After a few months, Mr. Tetterbaum had Andrew train her to become a bartender, a challenge she found fulfilling. It somehow gave her a feeling of control, at least over one tiny aspect of her life.

"They shouldn't have sold the pub to you. They should have sold it to a man," Olga mumbled as she waddled from the sink to the stove to the table, wiping things down.

"That's sexist," Angel argued, raising an eyebrow. "There's no reason a woman can't run a pub in the city. Besides, the Tetterbaums didn't have anyone else to sell it to."

"Rubbish," Olga spat. "You mark my words missy," she said and shook her finger at Angel, "that pub is bad news."

"It is a great investment, and it gives me a sense of purpose. I was lucky to get it," Angel argued.

Less than a year after Angel started waitressing at Tetterbaums, Ernest Tetterbaum died of a sudden heart attack and his wife, Mable, offered the pub to Angel.

"I'll sell it to you for under half of what it's worth," Mable told Angel with her eyes darting around the pub in frantic, paranoid bursts.

"I've never owned a restaurant before," Angel told her, but Mable insisted.

"I don't want anyone else to have her," she said, wringing her hands together. "You were like the daughter we never had, and it should be yours." She patted Angel on the side of the cheek. "If I didn't need the money, I'd give it to you for free."

Angel used some of the inheritance money from her dad to purchase Tetterbaums. Though he left her a substantial amount, she rarely touched her dad's money. She used it to pay for college and to buy her car, but everything else was paid for by income she earned herself. It was important for her to feel independent and self-sufficient. She didn't like relying on other people because if fate had taught her anything it was that people inevitably leave. Using her dad's money to buy the pub was an investment that she felt would have met with her dad's approval. In fact, Angel felt certain that he'd have made Mable an offer on it had he still been alive.

After Angel purchased the pub, Mable wished her good luck and left. Angel hadn't seen or heard from her since.

"Humph," Olga snorted. "It isn't right."

"That pub has been nothing but good for me." Angel grinned, thinking about how she met Grayson one week after she officially became the new owner of Tetterbaums. In her mind that was icing on the cake, like a tiny kiss from fate.

"People are starting to talk," Olga said in a half-whisper.

"Wait a second," Angel blurted, catching up on the conversation, "Did you call me a ho? I'm not anyone's ho."

"Well, sure you are dear," Olga argued. "Whenever he comes to call, you go. That's a ho. He probably has a ho in every bar across town." Angel hadn't thought about that, and it made the hair on the back of her neck stand up.

"He does not," she scowled.

"How do you know?" Olga stood with her feet squared and her hands on her round, chubby hips. She gawked at Angel, waiting for an answer.

This was getting out of hand. Maybe Olga was right, and Grayson did have a girl in every bar across town, but that didn't make her a ho. That would make him a ho.

"You're wrong about him," Angel sputtered defensively, all the while searching her vocabulary for a definitive term that would paint her relationship with Grayson in a more positive light. "We're friends with benefits," she muttered. Olga threw up her hands and Angel felt infuriated. "Maybe he's MY ho," she blurted, raising her right eyebrow slightly. "Did you ever think of that?"

Olga stopped futzing around the kitchen and gasped, "A man ho, now that's a horse of a different color."

"Yep," Angel chimed in, feeling vindicated. "He's my boy toy and I keep him around to pleasure me until Mr. Right comes along."

Olga chuckled a raspy laugh; one only years of smoking could produce. "I can't wait to tell Elsa you have a man ho." Olga shuffled around the kitchen. "Maybe I should get me a man ho?"

Angel buried her face in her arms and let them drop onto the kitchen table, exhaling an exasperated sigh. "You're killing me."

CHAPTER TWO

Angel wiped down the bar and tried to wipe away the memory of her date that morning with Harvey Milligan. Talk about boring. All the while her thoughts drifted to Grayson and the tattoo. She doodled it from memory on a white cocktail napkin and slid it into her apron pocket, next to the tube of lip gloss. Business was slow due to the storm and minutes passed like hours. Angel let two waitresses go home early, leaving her with Antonio in the kitchen and Andrew helping at the bar.

Antonio looked like a full-blooded, hot Italian model. His black, thick hair hung in wavy wisps below his ears and flipped up at the nape of his neck. He had green eyes and dark tan skin and he knew his way around a kitchen. Angel hired him a week after she purchased the pub. The first time Olga came in to check out Angel's new investment, she caught a glimpse of Antonio in the kitchen and grabbed her chest.

"Merciful Heavens," she gasped, "that man just stopped my heart." She nudged Angel, "I see why you hired him."

"I hired him because he's a good chef," Angel defended, but Olga shrugged her off.

"If I were younger, I'd be ordering some of that to-go." Olga's libido was unaffected by her age, and her taste in men hadn't aged with the rest of her. She still liked them young and hot.

Angel leaned her elbows against the bar, listening to the booming thunder and downpour outside. She loved loud, crashing thunderstorms. They brought a sense of calm. She remembered very

20

few things about her dad, but one thing she recalled was how he loved to watch lightning shoot across the sky. He used to hold her on his lap, snuggled in a big, comfy blanket, and they'd watch the storm from their front porch. It was storming the day he was buried at St. John's Cemetery and Angel always thought how perfectly ironic it was, as if he were looking down from Heaven creating the storm himself, just for her.

At quarter to eleven, the front door swung open, and Grayson stepped inside, shaking the rain from his hair. Angel's jaw dropped as he sauntered over to his usual stool, third seat from the right and sat down. Two nights in a row was unprecedented and Angel could barely contain her excitement. Grayson gave Andrew a nod, and then turned his attention to Angel with a big smile. Her knees went weak and anticipation lit her face. She could feel herself glowing in his presence.

"You obviously don't need my help with this one," Andrew sarcastically spewed as he breezed by Angel, heading toward the kitchen. Angel was too wrapped up in Grayson to notice.

Grayson was a creature of habit, always arriving a little before eleven, always sitting on the same stool, always wearing a pair of faded Levi's and a black t-shirt, always ordering three shots of whiskey and an amber beer. He was predictable in every area, except when it came to sex. In the bedroom Grayson appeared to have no rules, even allowing Angel to take control at times. It seemed only fair since he got to control when and how often they saw each other. That was the one part of their relationship Angel would change if she could, but she couldn't bring herself to confront the issue. Her desire for Grayson was greater than her self-esteem.

Olga was right, when he snapped his fingers, she came running. She wanted him in a way that rendered her powerless and was drawn to him with a force too strong to fight. Despite both Olga's prodding and Andrew's warnings, Angel refused to stop seeing Grayson. "I couldn't stop if I wanted to," she told Olga. She longed to be swept up in the current of his passion and carried helplessly away.

Andrew peeked his head around the back wall and whistled for Angel's attention. Excusing herself, she walked to the back. "Don't go home with him tonight," Andrew said. Though he had made comments in the past, he had never been this direct and Angel felt her defenses flare.

She crossed her arms. "This is none of your business."

"Do you even love him?"

The question threw Angel into a tizzy and she sputtered around.

"It's not a hard question," Andrew taunted, "you either love him or you don't."

It shouldn't be a hard question, but for Angel the concept of love was something to which she could no longer relate. Ever since she was abandoned by Tony she felt incapable of love, like that piece of her had died. Love came with vulnerability and for Angel that ship had sailed. She could give her body but her heart was no longer available.

Andrew studied her eyes. "Tell me you love him, and I'll leave you alone about it." Angel exhaled an aggravated sigh and headed back to the bar. "I'll take that as a no," Andrew hollered after her.

Who was he to question her feelings for Grayson or anyone for that matter? Andrew was just a friend, not even a close friend, more like a co-worker type of friend, so what she did with another man was none of his business. *Besides*, she reminded herself, *I want to talk to Grayson about his tattoo. I'll just have one more night for the purpose of research*, she justified.

As she worked, Angel fought the desire to stare at Grayson. His dark brown hair was tussled and damp from the storm, his olive skin held a reddish tan like he'd worked all day in the sun, and his brown eyes and dark lashes were mesmerizing. They were the sort of eyes that glistened even in the dark. The muscles that bulged from beneath his black t-shirt were enough to make Angel take pause, and his sculptured jaw line and cheekbones looked like they had been crafted by Michelangelo himself.

As she moved up and down the bar, stocking items for the next day, she felt his eyes drink her in. Glancing up, she watched his stare slowly climb from her feet to her face and fix on her gaze. She knew that look. It was the sign of temptation and the vanishing of her defenses. A warm rush filled her as she gave Grayson a slight nod of acceptance for what was to come. Taking off her apron, Angel looped it around the keg handle and motioned that she would be back in a moment. She then disappeared to the back room, grabbed her purse from the desk drawer and headed to the restroom to freshen. *I deserve another night with Grayson*, she told herself, *especially after suffering through that horrible date with Harvey Milligan*. Three hours at the museum with Harvey's constant nasal-toned chatter was enough to make her head throb. He gave the term nerd a whole new meaning.

"Where in the world did you find him?" Angel asked Olga, when the date was finally over.

"He saw me struggling with my grocery sack at the market and he rushed over to help. I knew right away he was a good match for my Angel. Besides, he comes from good stock," Olga added.

Angel hit herself in the head. "Oui Ve."

"He's an honest boy. What you see is what you get."

In the case of Harvey Milligan that was not a selling point. "I didn't see much," Angel sneered and smirked.

"Maybe your standards are too high missy." Olga shook her finger at Angel. "You better start looking at real men to build a real life with."

Angel stared at her face in the mirror and replayed their conversation. She knew Olga was right, and she did need a real man in her life. But who was to say Grayson wasn't that man? Maybe she did love him, and she was just too afraid to admit it? Maybe he was Mr. Right after all? Angel flipped her head back and forth a few times to fluff her hair, and then touched up her blush and lipstick. She was taking a last-minute look in the mirror when three forceful raps on the door startled her.

"Hey boss, you in there?" Andrew hollered through the door.

"I'll be right out," she yelled back. Andrew was the only employee Angel kept on staff after buying the bar from the Tetterbaum family. Actually, he was the only employee that didn't quit when she took over and she felt grateful to have him around. He had been with Mr. Tetterbaum a few years and he knew more about the bar business than she did. Besides, he was eye candy for the female patrons with his dark brown hair, always clean-shaven skin, natural pink lips and deeply intense brown eyes. He had a cute, puppy-dog charm about him and a sweet temperament. He smiled like a little boy, but that was the only thing little about him. At six foot four Andrew served as both bartender and bouncer when needed. He was Angel's gentle giant and though he usually didn't speak much, she felt oddly close to him.

"Are you heading home?" Angel asked, opening the restroom door and walking down the hall toward Andrew, who leaned against the wall with his arms folded over his chest.

"Yep." Andrew shuffled his feet and stared at the floor. "You need a ride?"

Angel knew he wasn't really asking if she needed a ride because he knew her car was parked outside. It was his way of telling her again not to follow Grayson home.

"I'll be fine," Angel answered flatly.

"I didn't say anything about whether you'd be fine or not." Andrew shifted his weight and stared at the floor.

"You didn't have to."

Silence fell between them.

"I know it's none of my business, but how long are you going to let yourself be played by him?"

He stared directly into her eyes and Angel felt anger rising in her gut. "What makes you think I'm being played?" She crossed her arms defiantly as he looked down at her with those piercing brown eyes that made her feel the urge to squirm in her skin.

"Deep down you know I'm right. I can see it in you," he said.

"You are right," she replied, tightening her jaw. "You're right about it being none of your business."

Angel started to storm by him, but Andrew grabbed her arm and whirled her around effortlessly. She stared up at him, both angry at his words and amazed at his strength. He'd never touched her before. "Be careful," he clenched, then released his grasp and left through the back door.

She stared, speechless as the door closed behind him. She'd never seen this side of Andrew and not knowing why he repeatedly warned her about Grayson infuriated her. She liked Andrew as a friend, but a different kind of tension was growing between them, and Angel wasn't sure what to do about it.

She shook off the questions dancing in her mind and hurried to the front to find Grayson. As she stepped behind the bar, she looked out into the empty restaurant. No Grayson. She called out his name, but the emptiness only echoed back her own voice. She scurried to the men's restroom and peeked inside. Nothing. She rushed over to the front door, and stepped outside in the rain, scanning the street for his car. It wasn't there. Walking back inside, she was unaware of everything except the ache of emptiness that sank like a rock in her stomach. He was gone. This was the first time he'd left without her in tow. A wave of rejection swept over her as she locked the front door, shut off the lights and let herself out through the back door. Her eyes watered, but pride alone made her fight the urge to allow real tears, as she contemplated the only question in play. *Why did he leave without me?*

Angel sat in her car for a few moments, staring blankly at the raindrops racing down the windshield and colliding with the wipers. She drove the first few blocks down Wells Street in a complete daze, with sadness creeping in and humiliation pushing out. She turned left on Goethe and tried to tell herself that he didn't owe her an explanation, but the pep talk wasn't working.

"We have no commitment," she reminded herself. Then why did she feel so hurt? She drove slowly in the silence of her thoughts until the sting of rejection turned to anger and her car turned right on LaSalle Blvd and headed for Wacker Drive and his house on the south side.

"If he doesn't want to see me anymore," she ranted aloud, "he can at least have the decency to tell me to my face." Heavy hearted and footed, Angel sped down LaSalle to Wacker and then took Lower Wacker. Tears filled her eyes making the oncoming lights zoom by in a fluid streak as she floored the gas. By the time Angel saw him standing in the middle of her lane, it was too late. She slammed her foot on the brake and thrust the wheel to the right, forcing the front end of her car into the stone wall. His face was a flash in her mind.

"Grayson!" She screamed just as her car slammed into the wall, and the air bag smashed into her face. Angel felt the powdery white collision and then a piercing pain shot through her chest and up to her forehead. She tried to speak but darkness enveloped her.

CHAPTER THREE

Olga used her butt to push open the door and spun around to face Angel's bed. Her Northwestern Memorial Hospital room was filled with flowers and Olga was carrying in another bouquet. This one was a large bouquet of red roses that pricked her in the neck and chin as she tried to find a spot to set the vase. "Merciful Heavens," she exclaimed, putting the roses next to the window. "It looks like a funeral home in here."

Angel had arrived thirty hours ago and spent the first twenty-two hours in ICU in an induced coma. She was now conscious, but the morphine drip kept her from being able to stay awake. It was a struggle to open her eyes and almost impossible to keep them open longer than a few seconds. She was aware that she was in the hospital, but she didn't remember the accident. Hearing Olga's voice, she managed to pry her eyeballs open and see the flowers surrounding her. "Am I dead?" she groggily asked.

"Nope, just looks like it." Olga pulled the card from the roses then dropped it on the floor. "Ouch!" she gasped, shoving her index finger in her mouth. "Damn thorns." Getting on all fours she tried to retrieve the card from beneath the bed. After several grunts and words of foul nature, Olga had to take a rest.

"Don't worry about the card. I don't need the card," Angel slurred.

"We won't know who sent them." Olga argued.

"So?" Angel's eyes started to roll back in her head.

"So," Olga insisted, "how are you going to send thank you cards if you don't know who to send them to?" She stretched her arm as far as she could under the bed, finally reaching the envelope.

"I have to send thank you cards to all these people?" Angel slurred, forcing her eyes open long enough to peer around the room. "There must be a dozen bouquets."

"Seventeen, dear," Olga answered matter-of-factly, and stood up, proudly holding the tiny white envelope. "All from gentlemen callers." Olga gave Angel a wink. "I can't wait to tell Elsa you have more boyfriends than all her granddaughters put together."

If she could have, Angel would have rolled her eyes, but instead she let them roll back shut. The morphine was too strong, and Angel was too weak to fight for consciousness. "Go ahead and roll those eyes at me. I know you want to." Olga antagonized. "Come on, wake up and roll those eyes at your old aunt." Angel gave a slight grin and Olga squeezed her hand. "Don't you want to stay awake and see if these roses are from a gentleman caller too?"

Angel didn't respond and Olga sighed from exhaustion. She hadn't slept since Angel arrived at the hospital in critical condition. She suffered several broken ribs, a broken nose and head and neck injuries. Her eyes were blackened, like a raccoon, and her face and hair were matted in blood. It was a sight Olga will never forget. She feared she would lose Angel, and despite the nurse's prodding, she refused to leave her side. She left Angel's bedside only to use the restroom or pick up another flower delivery at the door. She read every card aloud to Angel, even when she was unconscious, and she talked and sang to her endlessly. "My Angel needs me," she would tell the nurses who prodded her to go home. "And I'm not leaving her."

"Well, you can sleep if you want, but I'm going to read this card." Olga sat down in the chair next to Angel's bed and opened the white envelope. "Hmmm," she muttered, "this is strange. There's only a letter on this card. The letter G." Olga flipped the card back to front but nothing else was written. Just the letter G.

Thrusting her eyes open as far as she could, Angel reached for the card. "G?" she whispered. She tried to prop herself up on her elbow but was prevented by the excruciating pain shooting through her ribcage. Her head was reeling and her whole body ached. Olga placed the card in her hand and Angel tried to focus on it. Was the G for Grayson? She wondered. All of a sudden, the memory of the accident came flooding into her head and she struggled to catch her breath. "Grayson," she whispered. "I saw Grayson."

"You saw who dear?"

There were too many thoughts and too much to explain to Olga. "It's not possible," she mumbled.

"What's not possible?"

Angel didn't answer. Her head throbbed with each thought. Had she seen Grayson in the middle of the road? Did she imagine him there because she was angry at him and heading to his house? She couldn't force the memory, but she knew she had seen someone in the road. "Aunt Olga," she whimpered, reaching for her hand, "what happened? Did I hit someone?"

Olga froze and the pinkish hue that usually filled her round cheeks, drained away. She stood up and leaned in over Angel, brushing the blood-matted hair from her forehead. "Now you listen here to your old aunt when I tell you it wasn't your fault."

Angel closed her eyes and felt a lump of agony rise in her throat. She tried to fight back sobs as each cry made her wince in pain.

"Even the police said there was nothing you could have done," Olga consoled, but it mattered little what she said. "A witness said he ran right out in front of you."

Angel's heart raced at the inconceivable horror of her having taken another life. Her chest ached and she felt like she might throw up. "What was his name?" she slurred.

"Let's not do this now Angel. Let's do this when you're healed and stronger."

"What was his name?" Angel demanded. "I want to know his name." Her voice cracked from the dryness in her throat and the sheer emotion of the despair rising within.

Olga sank into the bedside chair. "Please, my Angel, I can't bear to do this now."

"I have to know," she said quietly.

Even through the haze of heavy medication, Angel could see the agony on Olga's face as she softly uttered the name, "Grayson Galante."

A numbing sensation hit first as she realized the irony that killing him was how she learned his last name. Grayson Galante. She had seen him in the road. It hadn't been a hallucination or a nightmare. It was real. As that reality sank in, grief and anger consumed her in a fire so intense her body began to shake. Her face turned dark red and Angel screamed and moaned in deep mournful tones of sorrow. Olga leapt from the chair, plunking her round hips onto the bed, pulling Angel forward and hugging her tightly to her chest. They had both forgotten about her broken ribs as Olga rocked her back and forth in her arms. Angel no longer felt the physical pain. It was overridden by inconsolable sorrow.

"Grayson," she wept. *Grayson.*

Olga drew back and grabbed Angel's cheeks between her thick, Italian palms. "It wasn't your fault," she demanded. "It was an accident." Her words fell on empty ears as Angel crumbled into sobs.

The blood pressure monitor beeped and the nurse entered, surprised to see Angel sitting upright. "She knows," Olga bellowed, tearfully. The nurse nodded and quickly left the room, returning with Dr. Manzini and two orderlies.

"Angel," the doctor spoke loudly and deliberately, "we're going to lay you back down now. We need you to stay lying down for us." Angel continued to sob and hold Olga with a death grip. The doctor motioned for the orderlies to lay her back, while the nurse prepared the injection. As the sedative traveled down Angel's IV tube and into her arm, her sobbing quieted and her body went limp.

"Doctor," she whispered as her eyes rolled back into her forehead, "I want to see his body."

"Oh, Angel," Olga gasped.

CHAPTER FOUR

Angel sat in a wheelchair and stared out the window. She was being released from the hospital today and should feel excited to be going home, but instead she felt numb. Her mind fixated only on Grayson and she clutched the white card with the G on it between her fingers. Despite her insistent pleading with the doctor, Angel's request to see Grayson's body was denied. It had been five days since she learned of Grayson's death and the sorrow consumed her. It ached deep in her chest, and her eyes burned from too much crying. She could think nor dream of anything but Grayson.

The nurse wheeled her out the front entrance and helped her into the passenger seat of Olga's older-than-old Oldsmobile. It was like riding in a big boat. You had to push the door shut with all your might, and even then it took several attempts for it to close all the way. Everything was manual and outdated, but Olga loved it. She named her Big Brown Bessie and called it her trusted steed. Olga owned Bessie for as long as Angel could remember.

While Olga got in and situated herself behind the steering wheel, Angel reached up and lowered the visor to look in the mirror. Her nose was still bandaged and the skin around her eyes shown colors of black and purple with hints of lime green. Her eyes were bloodshot and glassed over from crying, but some of the swelling from the impact had gone down. She looked beat up but at least human again. She was adorned with a removable brace to hold her mid-section steady so the ribs could properly heal. It was tight and confining but felt better on than off. Dr. Manzini instructed Olga not to leave her alone, not only for the obvious physical challenges, but more so for the emotional trauma. He issued a prescription for a pain killer, sleeping pills and an anti-depressant.

"Killing another person is something that may take years to overcome, and some people never do," Angel overheard Dr. Manzini tell Olga. "She may need to see a therapist." He spoke of it so methodically, as if she had a disease with an improbable cure.

"Now," sighed Olga, turning the ignition, "what do you say me and Bessie take you home?" Angel nodded slightly. "Andrew will come by later to stay with you while I pick up your prescriptions, get some clothes from my house and some groceries. That Andrew sure is a sweetheart. He's called everyday to check on you and he's been running things at the pub in your absence."

Angel agreed that Andrew was sweet but her mind had room for thoughts of only one person. Grayson.

When they pulled up in front of Angel's apartment building, Andrew was already waiting outside. "I thought you might need some help unloading on this end," he said, opening Angel's door and helping her step out of Bessie. He gave her a smile, but Angel could see him swallow hard, taken aback by her awful appearance.

In the apartment, he helped Angel sit down on the couch and wedged a throw pillow behind her back to keep her up straight. "Can I get you anything?" Angel tried to lick her lips and speak but her mouth was dry and her lips felt cracked and crusty. "You need a drink of water," Andrew said and made a beeline to the kitchen, returning moments later with a tall glass of ice water.

Angel nodded a quiet thank you and sipped the water. It felt good running down her throat.

"Are you hungry?" Andrew asked.

Waddling in the front door, Olga overheard the question. "She's starving. Herself that is. The girl refuses to eat anything. Hasn't touched a bite in four days." Olga stormed off to the kitchen ranting under her breath about the importance of food in times of emotional crisis. She hollered to Andrew from the kitchen, "Maybe you can talk some sense into her."

Andrew looked at Angel but she didn't return his glance. She just stared at the coffee table in front of her.

"I'll be gone a couple hours," Olga announced, waddling back into the family room with a grocery list and prescriptions in hand. She shook her finger at them, "You two kids behave yourselves." She winked and grinned with that matchmaker twinkle in her eye as she closed the front door.

"Wow. She's a handful," Andrew said, "reminds me of my grandmother."

Angel gave a half smirk. "She's never boring if that's what you mean."

"I can see that."

An awkward silence filled the air as neither of them knew what to talk about. The accident and Grayson felt like a white elephant in the room, like it needed to be discussed, but neither wanted to bring it up.

"Your cats hate me," Andrew blurted suddenly.

This made Angel grin. "Why do you think they hate you?"

"I came over to feed them while Olga was staying at the hospital with you, and the black one..."

"Midnight," Angel interjected.

"Midnight," Andrew repeated. "He always hid from me. I tried to entice him out of the closet with some tuna, and he hissed at me and made this really weird sort of howling sound."

Angel laughed at Andrew's description. "He likes to be alone," she explained.

"And the other cat, the multi-colored one..."

"Mo," Angel said.

"He would stare at me with this really pissed off look, like he was telling me to get the hell out."

Angel giggled. "I'm sorry my cats weren't more hospitable." Andrew shrugged. "Thank you for taking care of them."

"No problem." An awkward silence filled the room again. "You're looking a lot better," Andrew complimented, breaking the tension.

"Did you see me before?"

Andrew nodded. "I came to the hospital right after the accident." He dropped his head down and fixed his gaze to the floor recalling the night it happened. "I, um, I thought you were dead."

Angel looked away from Andrew and stared at the window across the family room. "I am dead."

She felt him study her face, the bruises, the bandages, the swelling, and the tears welling in her eyes. A part of her wanted him to wrap himself around her and make the agony stop, but she knew he couldn't. No one could. The one person who could was gone.

"You're very much alive Angel." He reached over and gave her fingertips a gentle squeeze. "You're beautifully alive."

"I shouldn't be," she mumbled almost breathless.

"It just feels that way right now, but every day will get a little easier and a little better."

Andrew draped his arm around the back of the couch, resting his hand lightly on her shoulder and stroking it gently. At first, she wondered if his touch was an indication that his feelings for her were more than platonic, but quickly convinced herself he was merely being a sympathetic friend.

Angel shook her head as she began to lose the battle against tears. They flowed freely down her face and she tried to wipe them as fast as they fell, but she couldn't keep up. The awkwardness she initially felt was suddenly overcome by sorrow and replaced by the humiliation of balling in front of him. There were no words. He pulled her tenderly into his shoulder and held her as she wept. "I know you feel alone, but you're not alone." He stroked her hair. "I'm here."

When Olga returned, Angel was sound asleep on the couch and Andrew was in the kitchen making spaghetti and meatballs. The kitchen smelled of garlic and oregano and the sounds of boiling water on the stove filled the room.

Olga shuffled in, lifted the lid from the pot and took in a big whiff. "Merciful Heavens," she exclaimed, "good looking and a good cook, where have you been all my life?"

"I believe that has been my loss ma'am." Andrew dipped his head toward her and smiled. Olga chuckled, brushed him on the arm and called him a smooth talker.

"How 'bout you put those big strong arms to work and carry in my groceries while I stir your sauce?" She handed him the keys to Bessie. "I also have a couple suitcases in the backseat that need to come in." Andrew hurried out the door, returning minutes later with an armful of paper sacks. He set the bags on the kitchen table and put the keys on the counter next to the phone.

"Bessie's all locked up and your suitcases are in the guest bedroom."

"You're pretty handy to have around. You should come by more often." Olga gave him a wink and turned her attention back to the sauce. "Where'd you learn to make a delicious sauce like this?"

Andrew blushed. "It's my Italian blood. My grandma made the best sauce in the city. Besides, a bachelor like me gets tired of living on bar food."

Olga giggled with raspy delight and put her hands on her hips. "Maybe fate is bringing an end to your bachelorhood, eh?" She nodded her head toward Angel, who was sound asleep.

Andrew flustered. "I don't think she likes me much."

"Rubbish," spat Olga, "she doesn't know what she likes."

Andrew peeked at Angel on the couch, and then stepped back into the kitchen where Olga was setting the table. "I better hit the road. Please call me whenever you need something. Anything."

"Oh no you don't big fellah," Olga scolded. "You cooked this meal and you're gonna eat it with us. If the cook doesn't eat his own food, it makes a senile old lady like me think there might be poison in it." Olga tugged at Andrew's arm. "Now, help me set the table."

Andrew let out a sigh of defeat. He was smart enough to know there was no winning in an argument against Olga. "Okay, but I think my staying might make Angel feel uncomfortable."

"Maybe you staying will force her to eat something." Olga shook her head. "We need to be patient. It's going to take some time. It isn't right what fate's done to her."

Olga's comment went deeper than just the car accident and Grayson, but it wasn't the right time to go into all the details. Someday Angel would have to come to terms with the past, but until then Andrew resigned himself to be the friend she needed.

CHAPTER FIVE

Olga was still sleeping when Angel sneaked out the front door with Bessie's keys in hand. She had been trapped inside for the past ten days, with the exception of one trip to the hospital to get the bandages removed and take a precautionary x-ray of her ribs. Everything was healing nicely. Everything but her spirit. The crisp morning air felt good against her skin, which was almost back to its normal olive color. The swelling around her nose wasn't completely gone, but you had to look closely to notice it.

As she slid behind Bessie's wheel, a twinge of fear swept over her. She hadn't driven since the accident and suddenly she felt insecure. *If I crash Bessie*, she thought, *Olga will never forgive me.*

Despite her nerves, Angel turned the ignition and headed toward LaSalle Boulevard. She sat at the stoplight with her heart pounding. Turning right would lead her in the direction of the pub. Turning left would lead her toward Grayson's house and the place of her accident. The light turned green and Angel sat, torn between what she should do and what she felt compelled to do. A driver in a silver sedan laid on his horn and gestured rudely behind her, forcing Angel to choose. Impulsively she turned left and headed down LaSalle toward Wacker. Her palms were clammy and her breathing quickened as she made the right on Wacker and took Lower Wacker, where the accident occurred. Her heart beat violently in her chest as the feelings, sounds and smells of that night rushed over her.

She rolled down Bessie's window and let the cool morning air smack coldly against her skin. Up ahead she could see the exact location of the accident, marked by a paint streak left from where her silver Camry smashed into the wall and crumpled. She slowed down as flashbacks of that night played like a slideshow in her mind, followed by questions she feared would never be answered. Why did Grayson leave the pub without her? Why was he in the middle of the road? What did the flower card with the letter G on it mean and who sent it? She had no more tears, but the depth of sorrow hollowed her insides with a nauseating ache.

Angel parked Bessie across the street from the two-story brownstone where she'd spent many nights in Grayson's bed. She stared at the house, picturing all the nights he had fumbled for his keys while kissing her on the porch. Stepping out of Bessie, Angel stood for a moment, debating what to do. Grayson's house wasn't in the worst area of town, but it wasn't in the best area either. Standing on the street would certainly draw the kind of attention she didn't want. She needed to either stay in the car or sit on his porch where she would be less visible from the road. Opting for the porch, she crossed the street and walked up the steps, running her hand along the brownstone wall, and recalling the nights he pressed her body against it as passion overtook them. What she wouldn't give now for a chance to lie in his arms again, to roll around in those black sheets, to feel his body melting into hers and taste his lips.

Out of habit Angel reached out and twisted the doorknob. It was locked. She knew it was wrong but all at once she felt driven to find a way inside. She wanted to be in his house just one more time.

She wanted to feel close to him one last time. It made no logical sense, and she was sure any therapist would advise against it, but she wanted to smell his scent and feel his presence. She pulled back the welcome mat hoping to find a spare key, but there was only dirt. She lifted a small ceramic flowerpot which sat in the far corner of the porch, filled with some sort of dried-up plant that had obviously been dead a long time. There was no key under the pot and when Angel set it back down the pot tipped over and the dead plant fell out in one big clump of dirt. Angel bent down to put it back in the pot when she saw a key wedged in the bottom. Excitement leapt alive in her as she took the key from the dirt and reassembled the plant. She knew she shouldn't, but her trembling hand was already outstretched, placing the key in the lock. Her heart raced as the door clicked open and she stepped slowly onto the wood floor inside. The door closed behind her, and she turned the deadbolt.

"Hello?" she called out purely out of instinct, as one should always announce themselves when walking into someone else's home. Silence. She walked past the small family room to her left, which consisted of an old couch and a television set that looked like it hadn't worked in years. Angel never noticed this room before, understandably because she always entered at night wrapped in Grayson's arms and left in the morning, sneaking out quickly. There was a staircase to the right, but she'd never been upstairs. She walked straight back where the hallway split with the kitchen to the left and Grayson's bedroom to the right. Slowly swinging open the door and peering in the room, sadness swept over her. His black sheets were crumpled at the bottom of the bed, just as she remembered them. The smell of his cologne hung thick in the air and filled her senses, triggering memories she had come to treasure. A black t-shirt hung over the middle dresser drawer, which was opened slightly. Angel held the shirt to her face and inhaled his scent, remembering all the nights she slipped on one of his shirts and curled up on his chest to sleep. Tears streamed down her cheeks as she pulled the shirt on over her clothes. She crawled into the bed and sank into the mattress, hugging his pillow to her chest. Sobs filled her throat and Angel couldn't contain the anguish she felt. She curled into a fetal position and cried until her sides ached and the emotional exhaustion begged her sleep.

The steely barrel at her temple and the hand clenched tightly over her mouth jolted Angel awake. His voice was gruff and hard and instructed her to get up and keep her eyes closed. Angel was disoriented. She had cried herself to sleep in Grayson's bed, but she didn't know how long she had been asleep or what was happening now.

"Don't make a sound," he threatened, pushing his hand harder against her face and pulling her backwards out of bed. He bent her over the top of the bed and patted her down, running his hand quickly over her breasts and stomach and under the waistband of her jeans, then over each leg. She didn't know who he was or why he would be checking her for a weapon or a wire, but she was too afraid to ask. He pulled her up and dragged her from the bed to the wall next to the window, holding her tightly against him and keeping the gun pressed against her head.

"You make a sound and I kill you right now. You got it?"

Angel nodded her head up and down, trying desperately to breathe air in through her nose. "What are they doing here?" His voice filled with panic. "Why did you bring them here?"

She didn't know who he was talking about. He spewed obscenities and she could feel the rage in his grasp. Angel's body shook all over. "I'm going to take my hand off your mouth. If you scream or make a sound, I'll kill you."

Angel nodded and his hand lifted slightly from her face. She gasped in a full mouth of air and panted. "Why are you here?" he questioned her, holding her head back by her chin with his lips so close to her ear she could feel the air from his words against her skin. Angel was afraid to speak. "Why are you here?" he demanded, squeezing his hand around her throat.

"I don't know," Angel cried and his hand tightened around her neck. "I wanted to be close to him." Angel broke into sobs.

"You knew he was dead so why did you come here?" He dug the barrel of the gun under her jawbone. "Tell me the truth or I swear I'll kill you."

Angel's body shook violently. "I...I...loved him," she wailed, almost incoherently before she went limp. She had said it, a phrase she never again thought she'd utter. *I loved him.* He let her slide down the front of him and drop to her knees, sobbing on the floor. "Go ahead and kill me," she begged, "go ahead and kill me like I killed him." Angel buried her face in her hands and wept.

He placed the barrel on the back of her head, pushing her face to the floor. "You move or make a sound and you're dead."

The room went silent. Angel stayed motionless on the floor, with the sound of her sniffling and the rapid pounding of her heartbeat in her ears. Though he lifted the gun from her head, she could hear him breathing so she knew he was still behind her. As her sobbing subsided, she could hear the voices of two men outside the window. They were talking but she was unable to make out their words. She was certain he was listening to the men too, and that these men were the cause of his panic.

He reached down and grabbed her hair, pulling her head back. "I see you open your eyes, and I will put a bullet between them. You got that?"

Angel nodded with her eyes clenched shut as tightly as she could close them.

He crouched down next to her and whispered in her ear, "These men are looking for you. We've got to get you out of here."

Angel didn't speak but for a moment she heard a familiar tone in his voice and she instinctively opened her eyes. Was she imagining it? Did she want him so badly that her mind deceived her? She tried to muster the courage to turn her head to face him.

"I told you to keep your eyes closed," he spewed, pressing the gun back into her skull and pushing her to the floor.

"I'm sorry." Angel shut her eyes tightly. "I thought you were...you sounded like..." Her voice trailed off as her mind told her it wasn't possible. He was dead.

He pulled her from the floor and dragged her into the foyer, pushing the front of her body against the front door. "I don't want to kill you, but one wrong move and you're dead." Angel nodded. "How did you get in here?"

"I found the key in the flowerpot."

"How did you know about the key?"

"I didn't. It was just luck." The more questions he asked, the more Angel was sure of his voice and surer that he wasn't going to harm her. Her body began to relax beneath his grip.

"Why did you bring them here?"

"I didn't bring anyone here. I came alone. I don't even know who those men are."

He slammed her body against the door. "That's a lie!" Angel winced as her ribs pressed against the door.

"I'm not lying," she cried.

He grabbed her by the back of her hair and pushed her face toward the peep hole. "Look," he demanded.

Angel closed her left eye and peered through the hole with her right. She could see the men standing on the sidewalk by the steps that led to the porch. They were standing with their backs to the front door, facing Bessie. The man on the right shuffled his feet and turned slightly to the side. Angel gasped, "Andrew."

"That's right," he sputtered. "Why did you bring him here?"

"I didn't. He must have followed me." Angel couldn't figure out why Andrew would follow her. Then it hit her. "Wait. How did you know I knew Andrew?" Angel was certain now and despite the fear, she was filled with a mixture of relief and hope. There was only one way he would know she knew Andrew, and that was if he had seen them together at the pub. His grip on her hair loosened, as if he were granting her permission to turn and face him. Even though he released his hold, she remained facing the door.

He backed away from her and sat down on the staircase, lowering the gun to the floor. "This wasn't supposed to happen," he said in an undisguised voice. "Turn around Angel."

Her breathing quickened at the way he spoke her name. She turned slowly with her eyes closed and stood before him.

"Now open your eyes," he instructed.

It felt as if time stood still. Angel lifted her eyelids and saw Grayson. She shook with disbelief and fear and confusion. Tears filled her and she rushed toward him on the steps, kneeling in front of him and burying her face in his lap. "Grayson," she sobbed.

He pulled her up into his arms and held her against him. "Angel," he sighed, and the sound of his voice speaking her name was like a rush of healing. She clutched onto him as one clinging to life.

"I knew in my heart you couldn't be dead."

Grayson grabbed Angel's arms and pulled her from his neck. "You're in danger," he warned.

"Not from you. I know you won't hurt me." She couldn't stop herself from smiling and crying at the same time. Just seeing him made her heart flood with joy and she couldn't stop the happiness from pouring out.

"Not *from* me. Because of me." He shook his head. "Angel, this is bigger than I could ever make you understand."

"Try."

Grayson exhaled and hung his head. "You were supposed to believe I was dead."

"Why?"

"It was the only way to protect you."

"Protect me from what?" Angel studied Grayson's face but found no answers. She could see the fear in his eyes, but she didn't understand.

"You have to leave and never come back here." Grayson stared at her. "Do you understand?"

"No, I don't understand." Angel felt anger stirring in her stomach. "I've been living in hell, thinking I killed you…" Her voice faded as another realization sank in. If it wasn't Grayson then who did she really kill in the accident?

Grayson grabbed her cheeks in both palms and held her face steady. "I will tell you everything. I promise. But it isn't safe now. You have to go and pretend I am dead." Angel was speechless. "You can't tell anyone I'm alive, especially Andrew." Feelings of confusion and sadness and joy and anger ricocheted inside her like ping pong balls bouncing off the walls. Grayson pulled her closer and let his lips brush against hers, first upward then downward and finally pulling her into a deep kiss. She melted in his touch. "No one, Angel." He grabbed her face again and stared into her eyes. "You can't trust anyone."

"When will I see you again?" She searched his eyes.

"I'll find you when it's safe. Now go." He pushed her toward the door.

"I don't want to leave you."

"If you don't leave we will both end up dead. Now go." He disappeared up the staircase and Angel tried to gain her composure before opening the front door. She didn't want to leave. She wanted to follow him up the stairs and stay in his arms. She didn't understand the danger he was talking about or why everyone needed to believe he was dead.

Right now, it didn't matter. All that mattered was he was alive and her heart was dancing.

Stepping onto the porch, she forcefully pulled the door closed behind her to ensure it locked. Andrew immediately rushed to her side. "When Olga called and said you took Bessie, I had a feeling this was where you'd come. Are you alright?"

"I just needed to see it one last time." She looked down at the ground. "To say goodbye." Angel fought hard to conceal the smile that wanted to sneak out. She glanced up at Andrew to see if he was buying her feigned sadness. She saw only compassion in his eyes as he draped his arm around her shoulder and kissed her on top her head.

"How'd you get inside?" Andrew asked, turning her to face him. Angel suddenly felt nervous and licked her lips. She wasn't ready for questions. "Was it unlocked?"

"Yes," Angel nodded, exhaling relief, "it was unlocked."

"Is that Grayson's shirt?"

Angel forgot she was still wearing it. "Uh-huh." She nodded. "I want to keep it."

They walked toward Bessie and Andrew opened the driver's door for her. "Do you feel like you have closure now?"

Angel looked back at the house. "Yes," she lied.

CHAPTER SIX

Angel returned to work but with less enthusiasm, knowing she'd never again see Grayson saunter through the front door. At least he was alive, and she held onto his promise of contacting her when it was safe. There were so many questions harbored in her heart but no one to ask. Grayson's warning not to trust anyone, especially Andrew, made her instinctively pull away from him. She barely spoke at the pub and went straight to her bedroom after work. Olga begged her to see a therapist, but Angel refused. Depression was the best cover, and she knew how to make it look real.

Business was steady, which helped the time pass more quickly, but the nights were the hardest part. Lying in bed, she stared at the ceiling and pondered how Grayson would contact her. It had been three days since she'd seen him, and the anticipation was driving her crazy. She feared he would abandon her, like Tony, and never explain why. Her mind replayed everything until her head hurt and the few hours she actually slept were filled with dreams of the car accident and Grayson. Angel's obsession for finding answers grew with each passing day.

By the fifth day Angel decided to search for answers on her own, starting with the name of the real victim from the car accident. She pulled Bessie into the Northwestern Memorial Hospital visitor's parking lot and double-checked the name of the doctor on her paperwork. Manzini. She wasn't sure if she'd remember what he looked like, but as she approached the nurse's station, Dr. Manzini caught her eye and made a beeline for her.

"Angel, you look terrific." He had a big smile that filled his whole face. He ran his hand quickly through his dark brown and speckled gray hair and adjusted his black rimmed glasses on his nose. "How are you feeling?"

"I'm fine. Good actually."

Dr. Manzini looked at her with an expression that said he wasn't buying it and motioned her down the hall and into a private room. "Your aunt has called me every day and she's very concerned."

"I've been a little withdrawn, but it's just because I feel exhausted when I get home from work."

"That's normal," Dr. Manzini nodded, "your body endured a great deal of physical trauma. That being said, I still think you should consider talking with someone. We can fix the physical a lot easier than the emotional."

"Actually, that's why I'm here. I wanted to ask you some questions."

Dr. Manzini smiled. "What can I help you with? Do you need a referral for a therapist?"

Angel twisted her fingers nervously and began to explain to Dr. Manzini that she wasn't going to be able to overcome Grayson's death until she saw the body.

His smile quickly faded. He put his hands in the pockets of his white coat and lowered his head. "That's not possible. The body has been returned to the family and most likely cremated or buried by now."

Angel anticipated this answer and moved to phase two of her plan, making a play for his compassion. She forced tears and pretended to swallow hard, as if fighting back a lump in her throat. "Please," she cried, "I need to talk to his family to find out where he's been buried. Maybe I could visit the grave. I can't move forward without somehow being able to say goodbye." The acting came easier than she imagined, and she amazed herself when real tears streamed down her cheeks.

Dr. Manzini touched her shoulder. "I can't give out confidential contact information even if I wanted to."

"But with my permission you could give my contact information to them, right?" Angel looked at him, her eyes pleading.

Dr. Manzini paused for a second. "I'll make you a deal. You see a therapist for me, and I'll make sure Grayson's family gets your contact information. I'll even do what I can to make sure they get in touch soon."

Angel agreed and left the hospital with the name of a therapist and the assurance that Grayson's family would be in touch. Logic told her that someone else had to know Grayson was still alive and that she hadn't killed him in the accident. Someone had to be helping him with whatever trouble he was in, and she felt both determined to find that person and confident they would hold all the answers.

The next step was to dig deeper into why Grayson told her not to trust Andrew. There had to be a connection between them that went beyond the pub and her. Andrew made it clear he never liked her seeing Grayson, though he gave no details as to why, just warnings to be careful. *Careful of what?* she wondered. Did Andrew have feelings for her beyond their working relationship and his warnings were a mere manifestation of jealousy? He had never verbalized anything to allude to a romantic interest, but sometimes he looked at her with warmth that felt deeper than friendship. Maybe she was misreading his intent and he was just, as Olga said, "A true gentleman." Either way, it was clear the time had come to let Andrew get closer.

It was Sunday and the pub closed at 10:00pm. Antonio was cleaning up in the kitchen and Andrew was finishing up at the bar when Angel let the last patron out and locked the front door. She turned off the main lights, leaving only the bar and the back room illumed. When Antonio finally left, it was time to make her play on Andrew. Angel licked her lips and tried to calm her nerves as she approached the bar. She'd never blatantly come on to a guy before and all of a sudden, she felt jittery and awkward. She sat down at the bar, across from where he stood and twisted her fingers nervously.

"Um, I was wondering if you would maybe like to hang out sometime." The words came out all stutter and Andrew turned around with a grin on his face and a hint of humor in his eyes.

"Are you asking one of your employees on a date?"

Angel hadn't thought about the fact that she was technically his boss. "No, not on a date, date, but like just to hang out and talk." Angel stammered around like a scared teenager, feeling the blood rush to her face.

Andrew's grin grew bigger until it morphed into a deep chuckle and Angel dropped her head onto the bar with a thud. *This is so humiliating,* she moaned inside her mind.

"You seem flustered," he teased. "How 'bout we skip the formalities and I pour us a couple beers and we hang out right now?"

Grateful for the life raft he'd thrown her, Angel agreed and a couple beers later the awkwardness was a mere memory. They sat at the bar chatting comfortably, like two old friends. On their third beer Angel decided it was time to break the ice and confront heavier topics. "So, how do..." she paused and corrected herself. "How *did* you and Grayson know each other?"

The look on Andrew's face told her this was not something he wanted to discuss. "Let's just say our families go way back and leave it at that."

"Why didn't you like him?"

Andrew became visibly uncomfortable with the topic, spinning his stool around and leaning his back against the front of the bar. He crossed his arms over his chest and exhaled.

Angel pushed harder. "I can sense there's something you're not telling me."

"Sweetheart, there are some things better left unsaid. Skeletons that should stay in closets."

"Why?" Angel studied his face as she pried for information. "I won't tell anyone if that's what you're worried about."

Andrew spun his stool to face her. He boldly took her hands and held them inside both of his, which for a brief moment made her both nervous and somehow comfortable. "That's not what I'm worried about." Andrew released her hands, got off his stool and walked to the other side of the bar, raising the arm and ducking slightly under. He slid both mugs toward the keg and refilled their beer, then slid Angel's back to her.

"You're not going to tell me anything are you?" She took a swig from her glass.

"And you're not going to let it go, are you?"

"No." Angel stared Andrew directly in the eyes, trying to read behind them. *What was he afraid of?* she wondered. *What was he hiding?*

"You're a stubborn woman," he said. Angel shrugged her shoulders and took another sip. "Tell me about your father," Andrew said.

The question came out of left field and Angel thought it was an overly obvious attempt to change the subject, but she let it go. "I don't know much," she answered truthfully. "He died when I was five and I don't remember much about him." Angel narrowed her eyes, trying to force the memory of her dad to the front of her mind. "I remember he had dark black hair and the deepest, brownest eyes I've ever seen. He was handsome and he had a smile that lit up his whole face. My mom used to say he never smiled, but I remember him smiling all the time."

Andrew grinned as he watched Angel describe her dad, and his expression made her blush. "Maybe he only smiled around you."

"Maybe." She gulped down a big drink.

"What else do you remember about him?"

"I know he loved baseball, but not the Cubs. He hated the Cubs."

"Living in Chicago and hating the Cubs? That must have been rough."

"It was worse than rough," Angel exaggerated. "My dad was a Yankees fan. He took me to a game once in New York. That's where he was from."

"You got to go to Yankee Stadium?" Andrew obviously thought that was pretty cool because his eyebrows were raised into his forehead and his mouth was half opened.

"Uh-huh. I thought I was the luckiest girl in the world." Angel smiled at the memory.

"Your dad must have had some money to be able to fly you to New York just for a Yankees game."

She could feel Andrew's eyes studying her while she processed his question, which was phrased more as a statement of fact. She stared up at him. "I think my dad traveled there a lot on business. I just got to go that one time. It was right before he died. I think he might have had family there, but I can't remember. I was young."

"What type of work did he do?" Andrew gulped down a big drink of beer but kept his eyes on Angel's while he drank.

"I don't know," she answered slowly, as if her brain was busy contemplating something else while her lips were responding.

"How did he die?"

She lowered her chin. "He was in a car accident."

It was obvious Andrew sensed her sadness because he leaned down on the bar in front of her and changed the subject. "So, you're telling me you've never been to Wrigley Field?"

"Never," she replied. "It would be blasphemous."

"And you're still a Yankees fan?"

"Until the day I die," Angel swore, crossing her fingers over her heart.

Andrew shook his head. "That's very disappointing."

"Sorry," she answered flippantly, polishing off the remainder of her beer in one gulp and plunking the mug down with attitude.

Andrew walked back around to the front of the bar and sat on the stool next to her. "That could be a deal breaker."

She smirked sideways at him. "I wasn't aware of any deal." Angel looked at Andrew and held his stare until her heartbeat quickened and her stomach grew nervous. All at once she realized she felt something for him. She was drawn to him and afraid of him at the same time. A part of her wanted to lean forward and feel his lips enclosing on hers, and the other part wanted to run out of the pub as fast as possible.

"Sweetheart, are you flirting with me?" Andrew's teasing tone relieved the tension and Angel burst out laughing.

"Only if you were flirting with me first."

Silence fell between them, and Angel fought the desire rising within. This wasn't supposed to happen. She wasn't supposed to feel attracted to him; she was supposed to get information from him. She turned her body to face forward, trying to regain mental composure, "So, how come you didn't like Grayson?"

Andrew dropped his head and Angel could hear the disappointment in his exhale, telling her he did not want to talk about Grayson. "How come you liked him?" he rebutted.

"Why do you always answer my question with a question?"

"Because in this case your answer is more relevant than mine."

Angel narrowed her eyebrows and conceded to answer. "I liked him because he was different. He was strong and mysterious and sort of reminded me of someone I loved once." The words were barely out of her mouth and she couldn't believe what she said. Did she really just make that comparison? It must have been the beer loosening up the chains around the secret compartments of her heart because she never intended to be this open with Andrew.

"Grayson reminds you of Tony?" Andrew gawked.

Angel was shocked by the mention of Tony's name. "How do you…"

Before she could finish the question, Andrew cut her off, "Olga gave me the summed-up version."

Angel rolled her eyes. "Olga."

"She didn't tell me the details, just that he broke your heart."

"That sounds like details to me." Angel would have been more disgusted, but this was typical of Olga. For some reason Angel's love life was one topic Olga liked to broadcast to the masses.

"So, let me ask you this…" Andrew cleared his throat and spun Angel's stool to face him. He placed his legs on the footrest of her stool, wedging her knees between his. She knew she should feel uncomfortable with her legs touching his, but a part of her liked it. "Why do you want to be with a man who reminds you of someone who hurt you?"

It was a fair question and Angel knew how insane it sounded. She shrugged dismissively, "I guess that's just my type."

"Dangerous is your type?"

"Tony and Grayson aren't… *weren't* dangerous," Angel corrected herself again. "They were mysterious."

Angel smiled but Andrew didn't. His jaw was tight, and his eyes looked stern. "You keep using that word," he said, "why do you like mysterious men?"

"They're never boring," she joked, but Andrew's scowl didn't change. He continued to stare at her as if he were reading every thought that entered her mind. She grew uncomfortable and squirmed on the stool. "What's wrong?"

Andrew didn't answer. He got up and moved to the other side of the bar and stood in front of Angel.

"Are you angry about something?" she asked.

"Yes." Andrew leaned in toward Angel with his palms pressed down on top the bar.

Angel swallowed hard, feeling like a child about to be punished. "Are you going to tell me why you're angry?"

"Because you're playing with fire, and you don't even know it. Because you're not being honest with yourself. Because you have no idea how deep this goes." Andrew's hands drew up into fists of frustration.

Angel felt a rush of nerves hit her stomach. That was almost exactly what Grayson had said to her, that she didn't know how deep something went. Angel threw her hands up in the air. "How deep what goes?"

Andrew's jaw grew tighter. "Open your eyes Angel!" he hollered, and it startled her. Andrew was usually quiet spoken. She never heard him yell.

"Open my eyes to what?" she yelled back. "I don't even know what you're talking about."

Andrew slammed his hands onto the bar. "Grayson was a Galante. A Ga-lan-te."

She shook her head from side to side. "I don't know what that means."

"He was an animal." Andrew dropped his head down and breathed hard. "You, of all people, YOU should not be with a Galante."

Andrew may as well have been speaking another language because Angel didn't understand what any of this meant. Silence fell between them and confusion flood her thoughts. She spoke softly, "Grayson told me once that I shouldn't trust you." She looked up at Andrew, with her eyes pleading for the truth.

Andrew leaned down over the top of the bar and grabbed Angel's face between his palms. She thought for a moment he was going to kiss her and her breathing quickened in anticipation. "Then don't trust me," he said. "Trust you. Trust what's inside here." He touched his finger to her heart and then returned it to her face.

"You're not making sense." She searched his eyes. "I don't know what you're talking about."

Andrew slid his hands from her face. "Then find out. Start by finding out who you are."

"I know who I am."

"No, you don't." Andrew shook his head. "If that were true, you would have never been in Grayson's bed. Never."

Amid the whirlwind of confusion, Angel felt a twinge of indignation rising. "That's none of your business," she shouted.

"So you've said." Andrew walked into the back and left Angel sitting at the bar. She expected him to come back in, but he didn't. Her heart sank when she heard the backdoor open and slam closed.

The night didn't go as planned and Angel felt more confused now than before. She drove Bessie home and sat in the lot, replaying the conversation

with Andrew in her head. None of it made sense,
including her feelings. Did he have romantic feelings
for her, or was the closeness and touching merely a
manifestation of his stereotypical Italian nature?
Was her attraction to him driven by all the beer they
drank, or was it genuine? Of one thing she was
certain; she needed to find out what he meant when
he said she of all people would never be with a
Galante.

CHAPTER SEVEN

It had been two days since her conversation with Andrew and the tension at work was mounting. They hardly spoke to each other, and he seemed to go out of his way to avoid her. It wasn't an angry feeling that hung in the air between them, but an undeniable awkwardness, like they had crossed a line and couldn't go back. Admittedly she felt something for Andrew, but Grayson was still the forerunner in her heart, and waiting for him to make contact was driving her crazy. Even worse was knowing he was alive and not being able to tell anyone.

She wiped down the bar for the umpteenth time, not that it needed it. Business was slow tonight. Angel reached in her apron pocket to reapply her lip gloss and felt the white cocktail napkin which held the drawing of Grayson's tattoo. She had forgotten about it. She pulled it out and studied the drawing, trying to assign meaning to the large M and the letters that ran down one side. AVCG. She couldn't think of anything to fit that pattern. The more her eyes soaked in the tattoo drawing, the more her heart longed for Grayson.

Angel was too deep in her own thoughts to notice that Andrew had walked behind the bar and stood, peering over her shoulder.

Finally sensing his presence, she jumped and spun around to face him, with her eyes wide and her mouth half open. A gasp flew out.

"Calm down, sweetheart, it's just me." Andrew let his eyes drop from hers to the napkin, and then pulled his gaze back to meet her stare.

"You scared me."

"Sorry," he said. "I didn't realize my presence behind the bar, where I usually work, would freak you out."

Angel rolled her eyes at him and shoved the napkin back into her apron pocket. "I wasn't freaked out."

"You flailed your arms when you jumped. That's the definition of freaking out."

"Flailing is the definition of freaking out?" Angel crossed her arms and smirked.

"Look it up if you don't believe me."

"Fine, I will." She narrowed her brows and glared at him.

"Fine." He faced her and mimicked her arm crossed stance, adding on a pouty face and holding it until Angel finally broke into a smile. Then extending his right hand he said, "Peace?"

They shook and Angel felt a tiny weight had been lifted. She didn't like when things weren't right with Andrew. She felt disjointed.

The rest of the night flew by and before she knew it she said goodnight to Antonio and Andrew and began a last-minute walk-thru before locking up. She turned off the front lights and made her way to the back with the exit sign illuminating a path down the hallway to the back door. She passed the bathrooms on the left, and the entrance to the kitchen on the right, stopping momentarily in the hall to pull her purse out of the desk drawer. It was an odd place to put a desk, but Mr. Tetterbaum said it was the best location for him to hear everything that went on in the pub while he managed the receipts. It was the first thing Angel said she was going to move when she purchased the pub but had never gotten around to it. Pulling her keys from the side compartment of her purse, Angel strode toward the backdoor. Almost to the door she realized she was still wearing her white bar apron.

"Crap," she exhaled aloud, and headed back up the hall toward the bar. She knew if she wore it home it would never find its way back to the pub. She'd been down this road before, which was why there were already two aprons hanging in her coat closet at home. Somehow, she managed to wash them and hang them up, but couldn't remember to put them in the car and return them to the pub. The same breakdown occurred with video rentals and library books. She was dysfunctional at returns. The good thing was she had at least come to a place in her life where she understood her dysfunction and stopped renting videos or checking out books that would ultimately result in paying out the maximum late fee. It was a small step, but she felt proud of her progress.

Angel untied the apron, hanging it in its usual spot over the beer tab, then turned around and walked back down the hall. She was almost to the back door when a rustling noise from the storage room stopped her. She froze and listened. The silence seemed loud in her ears as she strained to hear. She inched her way toward the storage room, which sat on the left side of the hallway just before the back door. She reached her right arm in the doorway and felt for the light switch. She flipped it but the light didn't come on. This would have frightened her except it happened a lot. The wiring in the building was old and for some reason the single bulb that hung in the storage room always jiggled loose. The room had a small window in the back wall that sat six feet off the ground. It was too small for an adult to climb through and had metal bars on the outside, but light from a streetlamp trickled through, so the room wasn't pitch black.

Angel heard another rustle and yelled out, "Who's there?" She inched her way toward the window and squinted into the darkness. "Anyone there?" Her voice quivered. "Grayson?"

She tried to convince herself it was probably just a rat, but she couldn't escape the eerie feeling that she wasn't alone. She crept toward the back wall, which was lined with thick aluminum shelving. The shelves were stacked with various food products, liquors, cookware and cleaning supplies. A mop and bucket sat in the far corner between a break in the shelving. Angel took a step and felt something hard against her left leg. She instinctively jumped and squealed, then bent down and felt the object. It was the wooden mop handle that had fallen forward into the middle of the floor. Probably Antonio hadn't pushed it all the way back when he closed up. She breathed a little easier as she bent down, picked it up and secured the mop back into the bucket.

Feeling relieved, Angel turned to leave and ran right into him. It was like hitting a brick wall head on in the dark. She screamed and he pulled her forcefully into his chest.

"Shut up Angel!" he scolded in a hushed, but fierce tone.

Angel's heart beat crazily as she pulled her face from his chest and backed up. She couldn't trust her eyes in the darkness, but her ears didn't lie. She knew his voice. Squinting at the silhouette before her, Angel's mouth fell agape.

"I know you didn't expect to see me." Angel stared at him, motionless. "I don't have much time, but I needed to warn you." His breathing was short and she could see the glistening of sweat on his forehead in the moonlight. "For god's sake, say something."

Angel could barely form words as emotions of shock, fear, anger and heartache rushed through her. She stammered, "T...T...Tony?" Anger crept into her voice, and she pushed his hands away from her arms. "Who the hell do you think you are?" All of a sudden, she felt furious. You can't come in here, scare the crap out of me and then tell me to shut up and listen. You are..."

"Angel," he cut her off mid-sentence, but it didn't stop her from drudging on.

"...a selfish son of a bitch. Do you know that?"

"Please, just listen."

"No, I'm done listening to you. There is nothing you could say that would change my mind about you. Now get out of here and don't ever come back!" She tried to push by him, but he wouldn't budge.

He grabbed her arms. "You're in more danger than you know and if you don't listen to me, you're going to wind up dead."

Angel froze with her mouth still half open. She was ready to blurt out more of her mind but stopped when she heard something about winding up dead. Dead didn't sound good. She stared at Tony. "What do you mean I could wind up dead?"

"We need to leave now, and I'll fill you in."

"I'm not going anywhere with you."

"We can't talk here, babe, it's too dangerous."

Angel folded her arms and glared at him as if
to say, "I'm not budging."

Tony reached down, lifted her up and tossed
her over his left shoulder. She started to squirm and
kick but he gave her a swift swat on her ass and
told her to be quiet. Every time she made a sound,
he issued another swat until she finally hung
silently over his back. Tony was not a little guy. He
stood six foot and was built like a tank with muscles
bulging from his arms. He could easily bench press
300 lbs. so tossing around her 125lbs was not a
problem.

Once outside he carried her behind the
dumpsters and up the alley to the right. Just before
the next street was a door and he quickly whisked
Angel inside and shut it behind them. One dim light
bulb hung in the center of what looked like an old,
stone cellar. He set Angel down and bolted the door
behind them. When she started to speak, Tony
covered her mouth with his hand. "Can I trust you
to keep your mouth shut until I tell you it's okay to
talk?"

Angel nodded and Tony removed his hand.
The room was musty and dark, and she didn't
completely mind that Tony took her hand in his as
he led her down a concrete stairway into what
looked like an old wine cellar. He pulled the string
on a bulb that hung in the far corner and stood face
to face with Angel. Her heart was pounding both
from fear and the excitement of seeing Tony again.
Even though she hated him for dumping her and
disappearing from her life altogether, a part of her
missed him. His sandy brown hair wisped across
the top of his forehead and his hazel eyes sparkled
the way she remembered. He studied her face and

his lips curled into a tiny smile at the corners. "I've missed you babe."

A part of her melted but at the same time her defenses leapt alive. "Right," Angel sneered in disbelief. "You've missed me which is why I haven't heard from you since you dumped me."

"That's the past. I'm here to talk about the present." Angel lowered her eyes to the floor. *Typical Tony,* she thought. He was always able to easily move from one thing to the next with no regard to how she might be feeling.

"Babe, I don't mean it like that," Tony stammered. "It's just that we don't have a lot of time and you don't know the truth."

"I do know the truth," Angel blurted, glaring at him. "The truth is you left."

Tony grabbed Angel's arms and pulled her closer, looking deep in her eyes. "I had to leave."

Angel pushed his hands off her arms and looked away. "Why?"

"It's complicated."

"It wasn't complicated when you left me, so why is it complicated now?"

Tony tightened his lips and shook his head. "It's always been complicated but especially now. It's a matter of life and death."

"If you're trying to scare me or hurt me with your words, it isn't going to work," she said. "I don't love you anymore." Angel's voice trailed off as she fought to hide any feelings she had left. She turned her back toward him, and he pulled her in closely from behind.

"I'm not trying to hurt you, babe," he exhaled. "I never wanted to hurt you. I'm trying to tell you the truth."

Anger won the battle over sadness and Angel was glad to let it step to the plate. "So, you show up over a year later to finally give me an explanation as to why you left?" She spun around to face him, "Well, you're too late," she sneered. "I don't care why you left."

"You've got it all wrong, babe," Tony explained. "I'm not here to tell you why I left."

"Then why did you come back? she barked.

"I left you a year ago to save my ass." Tony raised his voice, "I've come back now to save yours."

"I don't need you to save me from anything. I don't need you at all." She turned and started for the stairs when Tony grabbed her arm and whipped her around to face him. His face was red with anger.

"Who is gonna save you? Grayson? You think your boyfriend is going to save you?" A flare of hatefulness flashed in his eyes.

"Grayson is dead," she yelled, faking the drama but dropping her gaze to the floor so he couldn't see she was lying.

Tony chuckled. "You've never been able to lie. You know he's alive." Tony released his grip on her arm. "For God's sake Angel, you just called out his name in the storage room."

Angel rolled her eyes. She had forgotten about calling out Grayson's name. "Then who did I hit with my car?" She was hoping Tony knew the answer.

"Some poor babbo."

"Some poor what?"

"A schmuck who was new to the game."

"But I saw Grayson's face, right before I hit him." The flashback filled her mind. It was the one thing about the accident that was driving her crazy.

If it wasn't Grayson she hit, and she knew it wasn't, then how did she see Grayson?

"Babe, who do you think pushed that schmuck in front of your car?"

"You're saying Grayson pushed someone in front of my car?"

"Now you're catching on."

Angel shook her head side to side. "No. I don't believe you. Grayson wouldn't kill someone in cold blood and risk my life at the same time."

"You're looking at this all wrong. He didn't push the guy in front of YOUR car. He threw him in front of a car that happened to be yours."

Angel continued shaking her head no.

"Babe, open your eyes." Tony's voiced raised. "You think Grayson is some knight on a white horse and he's gonna ride around saving your ass?"

"Yes," she yelled back, "Grayson would save me if I needed saving."

"C'mon Angel!" Tony hollered inches from her face. "Grayson is a wolf. A hunter. A killer. He bedded down with his prey, and it got him into trouble."

"Shut up!" Angel screamed.

Tony pushed her against the stone wall. "Why do you think he had to fake his own death? Maybe because he couldn't make his mark, and who do you think the real mark is?"

Angel's mouth went dry, and she couldn't take her eyes off Tony and the hatred in his face.

"Answer me goddamnit!" Tony grabbed her face in his hands.

"I don't know who the mark is," she loudly expelled. "I don't know what you're talking about."

Tony released her face and burst out laughing as he backed away. It wasn't the ha-hafunny kind of laugh, but rather the explosion of irony or even insanity. Angel started to back toward the stairway as Tony leaned his arms against the wall across the room, dropped his head and let out a loud sigh. "Go ahead and sneak up the stairs and leave if you want to, but if you do, you'll be dead by the end of the week."

Angel froze with one foot on the first step. Her hands were shaking and her stomach was knotted. Silence filled the empty space between them and Angel fought to decide whether to trust Tony or to run. Maybe against better judgment or maybe because of it, she sank to the step and sat down. "Tell me the truth."

Tony reached out his hand and said, "I'll do you one better, babe, I'll show you."

Hesitant for a moment, Angel placed her hand in his and followed him through a small opening that led down a long walkway and emptied into another stone room. This room was smaller than the first and the temperature was much warmer. Angel took a deep breath as the warmth overtook her. "What is this?" she asked, pointing to a table with a computer keyboard and a mouse. Wires ran through the stone wall to five monitor screens that were built into the wall and sealed behind some type of plexiglass covering. Tony didn't say anything, just pushed a few buttons and a visual of Tetterbaum's Pub appeared on one screen.

"That's the dining room at the pub," Angel gasped.

"You can see every room," he said, clicking the mouse and showing her a quick shot of each room in the pub. You can even see the bathrooms."

"Who set this up?" Angel was furious at the invasion of privacy, especially in the bathroom.

"Tetterbaum. A long time ago."

"Why?"

Tony laughed again and chills shot up Angel's back. "Are you really that naïve?" Her face flushed from embarrassment. Obviously, she was that naïve, but she didn't like him pointing it out. Tony kicked a folding chair away from the table and sat down, pulling Angel on top his knee. "You know what your trouble is, babe?"

"No, what?"

"You don't know who you are."

What did that mean? He was the second man to say that to her in the past week and it was infuriating. "I know who I am," she spewed defensively; "I'm Angel May Martin."

Tony laughed again and shook his head. "Babe, you really believe that?"

CHAPTER EIGHT

Angel lay in bed that night staring up at the ceiling. Tony gave her more questions and no answers. The most unsettling thing was that she was starting to believe she wasn't at all who she thought. The questions parading around her head made it impossible to sleep. She forcefully kicked the covers off, breathed a loud sigh and sat up on the edge of her bed. The cream-colored curtains were open just enough to let a glow of moonlight trickle in, and Angel stared outside. She wasn't going to be able to sleep until she saw Tony again and got some answers.

She slipped into her robe and began pacing back and forth across the room. Why would Tetterbaum install surveillance equipment? Why would he hide it in an underground location not even attached to the pub? How did Tony know the equipment existed? She was the new owner, and she didn't even know about it. Why did Grayson fake his death? How did Tony know Grayson was still alive? She grunted aloud and threw herself onto the bed. The questions were driving her crazy.

Angel turned as the bedroom door creaked open and Olga's silhouette filled the doorway. "I thought I heard you futzing around in here," Olga said, waddling in and plunking herself down on the bed next to Angel.

"I'm sorry. Did I wake you again?" The past few nights Angel had been up at all hours and accidentally awakened Olga.

"Not tonight dear, I was up worrying about someone." Olga nudged Angel with her elbow and winked at her.

"Anyone I know?" Angel teased. She assured Olga there was nothing to worry about, though the truth was there were a million things to worry about. The problem was Angel didn't feel she understood any of them well enough to begin an explanation. "Honestly," she said, "I'm fine."

"Merciful Heavens, you're a terrible liar." Olga patted Angel's knee. "Now, we're up at 2:00am for a reason, so you might as well tell your old aunt what's troubling you so we can both get some sleep."

Angel skipped the part about knowing Grayson was alive and decided to eliminate the part about Tony showing up at the pub. She knew the very mention of Tony's name would send Olga into a tizzy. She began by telling Olga about her conversation the other night with Andrew. When she got to the part about her dad, concern lit Olga's face.

"Angel May," Olga frowned, "if you want to know something about your father you ask me, you hear? You don't talk about him to strangers."

"Why not?" Angel blurted. "Andrew's not a stranger. Why can't I talk to Andrew about my dad?"

"Talk about what?" Olga's face flushed. "What about your dad needs to be discussed?"

"Everything!" Angel yelled, leaping to her feet. "Everything needs to be discussed because I feel like I don't know anything."

"Rubbish." Olga crossed her arms defiantly.

"I feel like everyone knows something that I don't."

Olga shook her head from side to side. "That's rubbish. You know all you need to know."

"No, Aunt Olga, I don't. I need to know the truth." Angel could sense Olga had information. She could see it in her eyes.

"You need to stay away from those Italian men and their inflated egos. All they do is stir up trouble and break hearts," Olga said.

"I thought you liked Andrew?"

"I thought he was different, but I was wrong. He's just like the rest of them."

"The rest of whom?"

"Don't you worry," Olga said, taking Angel's hand and giving it a tender pat, "Aunt Olga's gonna find you a good boy, from good stock. I promise."

Angel rolled her eyes. "This isn't about finding me a man. It's about knowing who I am."

Olga scooted herself off the bed and toward the door. "You're my Angel May. That's who you are. It's who you've always been. Now get some rest." She waddled out the door and Angel could hear her go down the hall and close her bedroom door. She plunked back down on the bed and flopped on her back. Olga was hiding something; she could feel it. *What was she hiding and why?* She stared at the ceiling exasperated. It was going to be another long night.

~ ~ ~

By the time she woke up, Olga and Bessie were gone so Angel phoned Andrew and asked him to pick her up on his way to the pub.

"No Bessie today?" Andrew asked as she climbed into the front seat of his black Eclipse.

"Nope, she was gone when I got up."

"How long has Olga had Bessie?" Andrew grimaced to indicate Bessie was ancient.

"As long as I can remember," Angel replied. "It's a miracle it still runs. I think it's possessed," she joked.

"Like Herbie the Love Bug?"

"Yeah, sort of like that. Like Bessie has this spirit that just refuses to die. I don't even know if she can still get parts for the thing if something breaks down."

"Maybe from the Smithsonian," Andrew quipped and they both laughed.

"It's an eye sore, but for some reason she loves it," Angel explained.

"Well, at least she never has to worry about anyone stealing it."

Getting the pub ready to open temporarily took Angel's mind off Grayson and Tony and the questions haunting her. By the time Antonio and two waitresses came in, Angel was ready to get out of there. She wanted to get a better look at the underground surveillance equipment Tetterbaum installed and to find out what, if anything, had been recorded. She also wanted to head back to Grayson's house to snoop around, secretly hoping he would show up.

Angel took off her white apron and slung it over the tap handle.

"You going somewhere?" Andrew's voice startled her.

"No, why?"

"You threw your apron over the tap, which is what you do whenever you're getting ready to leave."

Angel lifted it off the handle. She didn't realize she was so predictable. "Actually," she stammered, "I was going to ask you if you could drop me off at a car dealership later."

The insurance check for her totaled Camry had come in the mail, and she was desperate for her own car again. She didn't like being dependent on other people for a ride.

"Okay, but Big 'ol Bessie's gonna miss you."

"She'll survive," Angel said and smirked.

"You want to go now before the lunch rush?"

When they arrived at the dealership Andrew offered to wait and help her shop, but Angel told him to leave. "I'm driving my new car off this lot no matter how long it takes," she swore. "I'll see you back at the pub."

Angel hated shopping, with the exception of shopping for shoes. Shoes felt therapeutic. The worst kind of shopping was shopping for cars. There were too many choices, the salesman talked too much, and the paperwork was labor intensive. It took over four hours to buy her silver Camry, which was now in the automobile graveyard. She was determined to make this purchase in less than two hours, paperwork completed and all. That way she could be back at the pub before the big lunch rush hit.

Angel walked up and down the rows, staring blankly at every car. She had no idea what to choose. She just wanted a reliable vehicle to take her from point A to point B without breaking down.

"Stick shift or automatic transmission?"

She had been zoning when the salesman interrupted her stare. "Automatic," she answered, slowly coming back to reality, and turning to introduce herself.

Before she could, he extended his hand. "Markus," he said, with his chubby cheeks stretched around a bleached, pearly white smile of teeth she was certain were veneers. He had bleached blonde tussled curls and wore a white button-down shirt that looked two sizes too small. "Glad you said automatic 'cuz we don't carry many stick shifts no more. They're just not what folks here in the city like to drive; you know what I'm saying? Too much start and stop and no time for a relaxing ride. That's what they tell me, but I think it's really because nobody can text and shift at the same time."

"Angel," she said, shaking his hand, and glad he had finally stopped rambling so she could get a word in.

"I've never met no one named Angel before. You sure are as perty as an Angel if you don't mind me saying so."

She grinned at his accent. He was cute in a down home country boy kind of way, but the accent was over the top. "Where are you from?" she asked.

"Tennessee originally. Came here by way of Texas though, so my accent's a little bit of both. How'd you know I wasn't from Chicago? Was it my accent or my boots?" He put one leg on the bumper of a car and pulled up the bottom of his Levi's blue jeans, displaying the ugliest cowboy boots Angel had ever seen.

"Wow," she gasped.

"These here are genuine alligator," he proudly proclaimed, "caught by my granddaddy himself. Everyone in my family has a pair."

"That's nice," Angel raised her eyebrows and feigned interest.

"There I go rambling on about myself again. You're not here to listen to me gab; you're here to buy a car so let's get to it." He was almost too peppy for Angel. She thought he looked a little bit like a puppet, with his bouncy curls and big teeth. He was so animated she had to force herself not to laugh.

Almost an hour later they had narrowed her search to a black, automatic transmission, two door car and were ready to begin the daunting task of interior selection. With both front doors open, Angel sat down in the driver's seat and Markus stuck his head in the passenger side, leaning on one arm and pointing out all the features with the other. It all sounded like blah, blah, blah to Angel. Her needs were simple. She needed a radio, an air conditioner and a heater, and honestly those were the only features she could afford without tapping into her inheritance money.

Angel leaned her head against the back of the seat and sighed as he droned on about leather versus vinyl seats. *This is taking forever*, she mentally moaned. She closed her eyes for a split second and opened them when she heard a pop sound and felt something wet splatter across her right cheek, down her neck and all over her arm. She turned to face Markus just as his body slumped forward, half in the car and half out. Blood filled the passenger seat and gushed from a hole in the back of his head. Angel screamed and leapt from the car, sprinting three car lengths away before she stopped and looked back. Her hands were trembling and the urge to vomit was rising in her throat. She glanced wildly around the lot but saw no one. She reached in her purse to grab her cell phone just as a black Mercedes SUV sped down the row of cars and straight for her. Angel dove between two cars when the Mercedes screeched to a stop.

The passenger door thrust open and Tony yelled, "Get in!"

Angel jumped into the car as Tony floored it across the lot and into the mainstream of traffic. "There's a plastic bag in the glove compartment if you need to puke," he said, "but I can't pull over until we're further away."

Angel took the bag out just in case. "As soon as it's safe I'll get you to a gas station and we'll clean the blood off." Tony's voice was calm and matter-of-fact, like this was a regular, every- day occurrence for him. "Babe, you're shaking," he said, reaching over and squeezing her knee.

She looked at him with disbelief, knowing she was probably in shock and feeling terrified and relieved all at once. "How did you know where to find me? How were you right there to pick me up?"

"I've been following you."

"Somebody shot that guy." Angel stared at Tony. "Did you see who shot Markus?"

Tony stared straight ahead. "It's okay babe, you're safe now."

Angel rummaged through her purse. "We need to call the police," she stammered. "We need to report what happened."

Tony swerved the car across two lanes and just barely made the off ramp. His tires squealed around the ramp and Angel gripped the front of the dash. "What are you doing?" she yelled.

He pulled the car over and slammed the gear shift into park. "Give me your phone." Tony's face was flushed and hardened as he stretched out his hand for the phone. "I'm not gonna ask you again, Angel. Give me your phone." Something in his eyes told her this was no time to argue. She pulled out her phone and handed it over. He immediately lifted off the back and pulled out the battery. "Son of a bitch," he spewed.

"What?" Angel searched his face. "What's going on?" Tony jumped out of the car and smashed Angel's phone on the pavement, then threw the pieces as far as he could. "What the hell was that for?" she yelled but he didn't answer. He got back into the car and hit the gas, weaving in and out of traffic. "Where are we going?"

"Away from here," he said. His jaw was tight and his hands gripped the steering wheel with white knuckled determination.

As they ventured further outside the city, Angel could see Tony's grip relax. He pulled into a gas station, where she slipped into the bathroom and scrubbed the blood from her face, neck and arm. Thankfully she was wearing her black Tetterbaum Pub t-shirt and it hid the blood stains. One glance down made her wish she had opted for black pants today instead of her light blue jeans, now soaked with blood. When she got back in the car, Tony drove them to a run-down motel on the side of the highway, promising to answer her questions once they were safely inside.

Angel's heart paused as he slid the key into the lock and held the motel room door open for her. It had been a long time since she'd been in a bedroom with Tony and an awkward tension filled her. She slowly stepped inside and was overwhelmed by the stagnant, musty, cheap motel smell. It smelled like someone left wet towels wadded up for a year. She covered her nose and mouth with her hand until she was able to adjust to the stench. The room looked like it was decorated back in the early seventies. It had dark red shag carpet, a queen size bed, covered with a bedspread that looked like it had never seen a Laundromat and a television set that still had a turn knob for channels. The walls were dirty yellow with water-stain marks on the ceiling and the yellow and red plaid curtains were adorned with cigarette burns. There were rust stains in the shower drain and in the sink. The only bright and clean looking things in the room were the towels that had been neatly folded and stashed in the holder above the toilet.

Tony closed the door, locking the knob and the bolt. Then he pulled the curtains shut and turned to face Angel. "Take off your clothes."

She glared at him, infuriated by the very idea that she would consider sleeping with him. "You asshole," she seethed.

"Babe," he grinned, "we need to wash the blood and guts out of your clothes or they're gonna smell worse than this room."

"Oh," she said, feeling a little embarrassed that she assumed he wanted to sleep with her.

He raised his left eyebrow and smiled. "Disappointed?"

"No, I'm not disappointed." But the weird thing was a part of her, albeit a small part, was. She'd never stopped loving Tony even though she hated him for leaving. Seeing him again felt good, but she swore to herself she'd never let him know it.

"Go in the bathroom, take off your clothes and wrap in a towel. I promise I won't look."

Tony washed her clothes out in the tub and a few moments later Angel's wet shirt and blue jeans hung over the shower rod. She sat on the bed in her black bra and panties, with a towel wrapped around her torso. Uncomfortable didn't begin to describe how she felt. Tony sat down next to her, and she could tell he was trying not to smile. "It's not funny," she said.

His lips curled up at the corners, "I know," he smirked.

She felt infuriated, humiliated and freaked out, but the weirdest thing of all was the fact that somehow, amidst all those emotions, she felt comfortable with Tony.

"Someone killed Markus. Why wouldn't you let me call the police?"

"Because that someone was me."

"What?" she gasped as disbelief filled her.

"I walked up behind him and shot him in the back of the head." Tony used his hands to make a gun and motioned the shot. "Then I kept walking, got in my car and came and picked you up." It was all said so matter-of-fact.

Angel's heart pound loudly in her ears. She heard the words but then everything seemed to fall into slow motion. She lunged for the round waste can in the corner, and in the process, vomited with such force that it splattered from the can onto the wall above it. Her towel slipped, but so did her modesty and she no longer cared that her breasts were half exposed, or that her ass was in plain view.

Tony picked up the towel and wrapped it over her shoulders. "I'll get you some water."

Her temples throbbed with pulsating thoughts of fear and anger. Something inside told her Tony wasn't crazy, despite the fact that everything pointed in that direction. He was someone she lived with and loved for years. She knew him, or she thought she knew him. Now, she felt like she didn't know anything.

A few minutes later, Angel sat back on the bed and listened as Tony explained why he had killed Markus.

"So," Angel repeated with sarcastic disbelief, "Markus was not really a car salesman, he was a hit man, and I was his mark?" The whole thing sounded ridiculous.

"He was getting ready to make his move," Tony said.

"How do you know that?"

"I know Markus. I've seen his work. I know his technique. It was only a matter of minutes before he made his move on you."

"How do you know he even had a gun?" she questioned.

"He had a .22 in his boot," Tony answered with confidence. "Babe, you know I'd never lie to you."

The irony overtook Angel and she spewed a sarcastic laugh. "Oh, I see, you'll murder but you won't lie. What high moral standards you have."

"I just saved your ass and you're busting my balls about it?"

"You just murdered someone," she corrected.

"No, I protected someone." Tony tightened his jaw and Angel could tell he was pissed off. "He was going to take you out. I can prove it to you."

"How?" Angel glared at him.

"The news. The news isn't going to cover the shooting death of Markus Cullato. They're going to tell us about the murder of the real car salesman. The one Markus killed."

"If I was his so-called mark, why would Markus kill another salesman?" she asked.

"To make sure he was the one to be alone with you in the lot. So, he could privately do what he wanted with you and then kill you."

"What are you talking about?" Fear trickled into her voice.

"Markus Cullato is one of the worst thugs on the east side. He doesn't just hit his mark like your average respectable hit man. He's a mutant. A real whack-job. He has a reputation for rape and mutilation. He's called 'The Animal' because he rips his victims apart. Literally." Angel felt her stomach knot up again as Tony continued. "I could tell you stories that would have you puking in that can again."

"Are you sure that was him?"

"Markus is known for disguises and his little country boy get up was one of them. Trust me babe, that was him."

"What makes you think I was his mark?" she asked. "Why would he want to kill me? I don't even know him."

"He's a Cullato."

"I don't know what that means."

"The Cullato's are the controlling family on the east side. They don't want interference from you. None of the families do."

"I don't understand what you're talking about." Frustration rose in her. "Why would I interfere with anybody's family?"

Tony shook his head. "You really don't know anything do you?"

Angel leapt to her feet and screamed at the top of her lungs, "Anything about WHAT!" Anger overtook fear and emotion. She was tired of feeling stupid; tired of being told she didn't know anything and tired of feeling manipulated.

Tony grabbed her wrists and tugged her back down on the bed. "You don't know anything about your family."

"I don't have any family except Olga. Everyone else is either dead or gone," she said. "You know this."

Tony softened his grip, took Angel's hand and held it. "Babe, your grandfather is the Capo Di Tutti Capi."

"The what?" She used to love when Tony spoke in Italian but right now it was annoying.

"It means the boss of all bosses." When she shrugged she saw Tony droop his shoulders and exhale. It was obvious that he was as frustrated by her lack of understanding as she was. "Your grandfather is Giovanni Maratinzano."

"No, my grandfather's name was Gerry Martin and I think he's dead."

Tony shook his head. "That's what you were told."

A lump formed in Angel's throat. "I don't understand what you're saying."

"Babe," he laced his fingers between hers which she found terribly distracting, but in a good way. It had been a long time since he held her hand and she used to love how he would lace her fingers and then stroke her pinky with his. "Your grandfather, Giovanni Maratinzano, is head of the Commission. Your father, Joseph Maratinzano, was head of the Maratinzano bogata here in Chicago. He could have been the next Capo Di Tutti Capi if he hadn't been killed."

"My dad was Joe Martin and he wasn't killed. He died in a car accident when I was five," she objected.

"A car bomb is not an accident." Tony said, letting go of her hand to make quotation marks around the word accident.

The hair on the back of Angel's neck stood straight up. "A car bomb?" Tony nodded. "Why?" Questions raced through her mind. "Who would want to kill my dad?"

"Everyone," Tony blurted.

"Who's everyone?"

"The other four main Chicago families, for starters." Tony stood up and paced around the room. "The Maratinzano family was the most powerful crime family in Chicago with the added strength of having sustainable roots in New York. Your father had a lot of power."

"My dad was Joe Martin," she uttered almost to herself. "He was just a regular businessman from New York. He wasn't in the mafia."

"Babe, you've been brainwashed." Tony leaned against the far wall, crossing his arms over his chest. "Your whole life isn't real. It's all been made up, constructed, so you would be protected from the truth."

"Why?" she asked.

"I don't know," Tony said with a sigh. "Maybe your dad wanted out. Maybe he knew the hit was coming. Maybe he was trying to protect you from knowing about your mafia roots. Maybe he thought if you didn't know anything, you could have a normal life."

Silence fell between them as Angel's brain tried to put all the pieces together. "So, my last name is Maratinzano?"

"Yep."

"You said none of the families wanted me to interfere with them. What does that mean?"

Tony exhaled deeply. "You need a lesson in Mafia 101 here, babe, and I don't know if I'm the right guy for the job."

Angel stood and walked over to Tony. She uncrossed his arms, leaned in closer and rested her head against his chest. "You saved my life today, right?"

"Yeah."

"Then I think you're the perfect guy for the job."

Tony wrapped his arms around her and held her close. She wasn't sure what to think or feel, but his arms were strong around her and for a moment she felt safe.

~~~

Several hours later, Angel got out of the cab in front of Tetterbaum's pub and took a deep breath. Tony had bought her another pair of blue jeans because they couldn't get the blood stains out of hers. The jeans were stiff and uncomfortable and her black Tetterbaum t-shirt was still a little damp in places. She mentally ran through the plan one last time before opening the front door. She needed to lie and she needed to make it believable, especially to Andrew. Tony emphasized that Andrew could not be trusted, and since he was the second person to say this, she was beginning to believe it

Tony said that he destroyed her cell phone because it contained a tracking device. She needed to find out who put the device in her phone. Most of all, she needed to appear calm and collected, as if nothing unusual had taken place.

"Remember," Tony warned, "anyone not connected with one of the four families won't know Markus Cullato was killed at the dealership. The media won't release it."

"Why not?" Angel had asked.

"Let's just say there's an agreement in place to keep peace and minimize public disharmony."

Tony paused and then continued, "So anyone who knows about his death has inside connections and can't be trusted."

Angel stood in front of the pub. *You can do this,* she told herself as she swung open the front door and stepped inside. Andrew looked up from behind the bar and Angel could see a spark of knowing in his eyes. She breezed through the dining area and into the back, dropping her purse in the desk drawer and heading to the bar for her apron. She kept her eye contact with everyone brief and sporadic.

"Took longer than you thought?" Andrew muttered.

"Yes, I…uh…couldn't find anything I liked at that dealership, so I got a cab and went to another one." She delivered the line just as she'd rehearsed with Tony.

"Which one did you go to?" Andrew leaned in closer to her, and she could feel his eyes penetrating her defenses.

"A Ford dealership across town, but I didn't find anything I liked."

"That's too bad," said Andrew, "I was anxious to see your new ride."

Angel's heart was pounding rapidly in her chest as Andrew moved down the bar, chatting with patrons and filling drink orders.

"By the way," he raised his voice so she could hear him across the bar, "Olga called here several times. Said she tried to reach you on your cell phone but she said it was out of service."

It wasn't what he said that bothered Angel. It was realistic that Olga would call the pub if she couldn't catch Angel on her cell. The part that struck fear in her gut was the way he said, "out of service." It was as if he was secretly telling her he knew the tracking device had been destroyed.

She glanced up at Andrew and once again saw a flash of knowing in his eyes. Was he the one who placed the device in her phone? Is that how he knew it was gone? Was she just paranoid? She needed to hold it together and stay calm.

"Okay," she uttered almost breathless, "I'll call her in a while."

Andrew walked closer. "Is there something wrong with your phone?"

"No," she blurted, nervously. "The battery's probably dead."

Andrew's stare burned right through her. "Why don't you plug it in here so it will be re-charged by the time you need to head home?"

"I don't have my charger with me."

Andrew grinned. "It's your lucky day," he said, going to the desk and pulling out a charger. "We have the same phone and I keep a spare charger here."

Angel's heart sank into the pit of her stomach. "Great." She forced a smile and walked back to the desk, pretending to dig through her purse in search of her phone.

Andrew leaned in behind her, towering over her shoulder. "What's the matter? Can't find it?"

Angel was about to hit maximum panic mode. "I don't know where it is," she lied. "I must have dropped it when I got out of the cab."

Andrew's brown eyes shone with a knowing that both scared Angel and intrigued her. Part of her wanted to trust him and the other part feared him.

"Hmmm," he folded his arms and stared at her, "carless and now phoneless. What are we going to do with you?" His teasing tone and tender smile slightly lifted the weight of the agonizing nerves pressing her down.

"I don't know," she casually answered.

"For starters, I'll give you a ride home tonight." He winked at her and walked back behind the bar.

Angel felt all color drain from her cheeks.

CHAPTER NINE

Angel climbed in the front seat of Andrew's black Chevy Equinox and stared out the tinted window. She was certain Tony was out there somewhere, watching her. How close and from where she had no idea. Her stomach felt knotted as she wasn't sure if she was in the car of an enemy or a friend.

Andrew started up the ignition and they drove toward her apartment building in silence. Just before he was supposed to turn left into the lot, Andrew hit the gas and barreled passed it. Angel's eyes widened as terror gripped her again. "Where are we going?"

"We're being followed." Andrew glanced in the rearview mirror as he spoke. "I'm not dropping you off while we're being followed."

Angel looked in the side mirror. "I don't see anyone."

"They're there." Andrew's voice told her he was certain and there was no point in arguing. They drove for a few minutes in silence, with Andrew monitoring the mirrors and making last second impulse turns. "Since there is no reason for anyone to be following me," he broke the silence, "is there anything you want to share with me about your little excursion today?"

Her breathing quickened as she tried to think of a way to respond. He obviously knew something, but what? She needed to control the conversation, to manipulate it so she could find out what he knew without telling him anything that happened. Times like these made her wish she was a better liar. Her mind quickly devised a plan. She'd attempt a subject change first, and then proceed to denial and from there she'd have to wing it.

She glanced out the back window, "Who do you think is following us?"

Andrew didn't miss a beat. "Probably someone you were with today."

Angel swallowed hard. "I was shopping for a car, remember?"

Andrew nodded his head. "And how'd that turn out for you?"

"I survived." Angel met his gaze for a split second and looked away.

"Interesting choice of words," he noted.

The tension between them was so thick it was almost visible. Angel bit her lip, trying to come up with something to talk about. Anything to change the subject. She reached over and turned on the radio. "Can we listen to some music?"

It clicked on and the newscaster said, "Police are currently investigating the brutal murder of a salesman found dead today at the Park Meadows Honda dealership. His body was found by a co-worker. No details yet on motive or assailant."

Andrew reached over and turned off the radio. "Funny, but isn't that the dealership I dropped you off at this afternoon?" he asked.

Angel ignored the sarcastic flair in his tone. "Yeah, weird, huh."

"Huh," Andrew mimicked her.

Angel saw Andrew's grip on the wheel tighten, and he sped up again, taking turns at a velocity that prompted a death grip on the handle above her window. "Slow down!" she yelled.

"I'm going to lose this tail and then you and I are going to have a talk." He made her feel like a kid who was about to be punished for lying.

Andrew weaved around cars, heading further from her apartment and any security she felt. *Where was Tony,* she wondered. *Was he the one following them and was he keeping up?* She couldn't see anyone behind them, though Andrew swore someone was still there.

"Andrew, I want to go home. Please take me home now." She swallowed hard, trying to hide the fear in her voice.

"I can't do that. We're past that point." *What did that mean? Past what point?* Angel was afraid to ask. Andrew stared straight ahead, flooring the gas and screeching a hard right. Then a quick left down an alley, then a right onto a main thoroughfare. With all the fast turns, Angel wasn't sure what street they ended up on. He pulled into what looked like a run-down, abandoned strip mall, cut his lights and drove behind the buildings. He backed the Equinox behind one of the dumpsters and killed the engine.

The only sound Angel could hear was deafening silence and the sound of her own heart beating. Andrew looked at her and she knew he could read fear in her face, though she tried to feign braveness.

"Now we wait," he said, returning his gaze out the windshield and beyond the dumpster.

"For what?"

He didn't answer. "

Wait for what?" she repeated a little louder. Andrew didn't move and didn't answer. Angel was getting pissed off. "Fine," she spewed, "if you're not going to answer then I'm getting out." She grabbed for the door handle when the cocking sound made her freeze. She turned her eyes toward Andrew and saw the .22 pointed at her head.

"Take your hand off the handle," he said, and Angel immediately obeyed. "We're going to sit here quietly for a few minutes and then I'll tell you when it's safe to get out."

Angel nodded. The sick feeling was back in her stomach and she swallowed hard.

"The gun I'm holding is a .22 pistol," Andrew calmly explained. "You saw what it does at close range today when one of your boyfriends took out Markus right in front of you."

Angel's mouth fell open as disbelief encompassed her. "How did you know that?"

Andrew gave a half-smile. "Sweetheart, it's my job to know."

Her hands started to tremble as Tony's warning replayed in her head. *"Anyone who knows about Markus's death is from one of the four Chicago families."* She covered her face with her hands. "Oh my God," she stammered, "you're mafia."

"I don't like taking these measures," Andrew explained, "but you following my instructions is a matter of life and death; and if it takes me pulling a gun to get you to obey then so be it."

Angel didn't respond. She sat frozen, trying to think of her next move and wondering if Tony was anywhere close. If he was close, was he about to splatter Andrew's brains all over her lap just like he did with Markus?

All of a sudden Andrew lowered the gun. "You can get out of the car now."

Her whole body started to shake and tears streamed down her cheeks. "No," she blurted defiantly.

"Angel, open the door and step out of the car."

"No!" she screamed. "If I get out of the car you're going to shoot me and throw me in that dumpster." She closed her eyes tight, afraid to open them.

Andrew holstered the gun. "If I was going to kill you, you'd already be dead."

He reached into his pocket, pulled out an ID badge and held it up for Angel to read. "Open your eyes," he ordered.

She shook her head no, so Andrew reached across the seat, grabbed her left hand and placed the ID in it.

Angel opened her eyes and looked down at the badge. It read Chicago Police, Special Detective Andrew Venturini. She was certain her eyeballs were bulging out of her head like a trembling Chihuahua, as she looked up at Andrew. "You're a cop?"

He gave a slight nod of his head and Angel burst into sobs. Her mind broke down the situation in its simplest form. Andrew was a cop and cops were good guys and good guys didn't shoot innocent people, which meant she was safe. She scooted across the seat and wrapped her arms around his neck, burying her face in his shoulder. The fear she felt was suddenly overrun by relief as she clung to him.

He rubbed her back, "It's okay now," he said, running his hand down her hair and squeezing around her. "I've got you. You're safe."

When the tears subsided, Angel got out of the car with Andrew and walked into the back door of one of the strip mall shops. It was dark except for an emergency exit sign that hung overhead. They walked down a long staircase, through two sets of steel double doors and into a room filled with all sorts of equipment and weapons. The room was very sterile looking. The floor was light colored tile and the walls were concrete, painted white. Two elongated florescent bulbs hung overhead making the room uncomfortably bright. A black punching bag hung in the far corner, next to a set of weights and a black mat. A long table in the other corner was home to a number of different weapons. Several .22 and .38 caliber pistols, a couple 9 mm pistols, some automatic rifles, silencers, tasers, tear gas containers, hand cuffs, and what looked like an Uzi. On a table next to the weapons sat a computer monitor, keyboard and mouse, as well as recording devices and a GPS tracking system. In the far corner hung three Kevlar vests next to a cot with a white cotton blanket that had seen better days and no pillow.

"What is this place?" Angel asked.

"Let's just say it's my secret lair."

"Oh, like your Bat Cave."

Andrew grinned at her, "Yeah, it's my Bat Cave." Andrew went immediately to the computer and started pushing buttons, bringing up pictures and articles. "Sit," he said, pulling out a folding chair. "Read." She sat down, looked at the first screen and saw a picture of her father.

It was a newspaper article. The title read: "Mob Boss, Joseph Maratinzano: Out of Commission." The article detailed the explosion that took her dad's life. It was painful to read and Angel felt she was on an emotional rollercoaster between anger and heartache, until she got to the very last line. It read: "Joseph Maratinzano leaves behind no living relatives."

Tony was right, she thought, *my whole life has been made up.*

She clicked to the next screen and the next, reading article after article about mafia dissention, as the families fought for power after her dad's death. Murder after murder, the Maratinzano family was dismantled one by one, hit by hit, until there were no more loyal members left. Entire families linked to the Maratinzanos were brutally murdered. Anyone who survived ran for their lives, and anyone in a position of power was killed. Tears filled Angel's eyes, not from sadness, but from rage.

She looked over at Andrew. "Why couldn't the police stop this?"

"They tried. Well, the ones who weren't meat eaters tried." Andrew shook his head. "It was a dark hour for the city of Chicago. The code of ethics went by the wayside, disloyalty was rampant. Every bogata lost members, but your family was hit the hardest."

"What does eating meat have to do with anything?"

Andrew chuckled and Angel felt humiliated. "I'm sorry," he said, "I'm not laughing at you, it just sounded funny." He cleared his throat and regained his composure. "A meat eater is a corrupt cop. It's a police officer who's paid off by the mob."

Changing the subject, Andrew slid a cell phone across the table. "Try not to lose this one."

"You put the tracking device in my phone?"she asked and he nodded. "When?"

"Your first week at Tetterbaum's."

"Why?"

"I knew who you were." Andrew went on to explain how few people knew Angel even existed. "Your father went to great lengths to protect your identity. Medical records from your birth were altered so you could never be linked to the Maratinzano family."

"If everything was altered then how did you find out who I was?"

"Your father had a Compare." Angel narrowed her eyebrows and shook her head to show she didn't understand. "Sort of like a Consigliere. A counselor. A man he trusted. Only a Compare isn't a member of the bogata. He's a trusted friend on the outside." Angel nodded that she understood. "You haven't known it, but this man has been watching you and protecting you since the day your dad was killed."

"Who is he?" she asked.

Andrew paused. "He's known only as the Compare. That's all I can tell you."

"Why?"

Andrew leaned against the table next to Angel. He put his hand on her shoulder and gave a tender squeeze. "There's more you need to understand. This isn't the kind of guy you can just call and meet for coffee. He contacts you. You don't contact him."

She rolled her eyes. She was so tired of being told she didn't understand. "Why can't you just tell me what I need to know?" Angel leapt to her feet, pushing his hand off her shoulder. "Do you have any idea what I've been through today? I had someone's head blown off into my lap. I had to literally pick brains out of my hair. I found out my phone was bugged. You pull a gun on me. Then I find out you're a cop. And don't forget the small fact that my whole family, including my own father, was massacred!" Angel paced around the room. She felt this deep anger rising inside her. Her heart quickened and she kicked the folding chair and sent it hurling against the wall. She could see the surprise in Andrew's face. "Now," she panted, "you still haven't told me how you knew who I was." She crossed her arms and glared at him.

Andrew dropped his chin to his chest and exhaled. He picked up the chair she had kicked across the room and motioned for her to sit back down. He then pulled a chair across from her and sat. "What I'm about to tell you is something your father never wanted you to know about or become involved in." He shook his head, "but since there's a leak, we have no choice."

"What do you mean there's a leak?"

"Your father's Compare was the only person to know of your existence, other than your grandfather, birth mother and Aunt Olga. Up until a year ago it was as if you didn't exist to the outside world, not as a Maratinzano anyway."

"So, who found out I was a Maratinzano?"

"We don't know yet," he said and shifted in his chair.

"What does it matter if I am his daughter? I'm not an active part of the mafia and it's not like I know anything about any of them anyway."

"In the minds of some of the brotherhood, any Maratinzano is a threat." Andrew took a deep breath and exhaled loudly. "Let me back up. Have you ever heard of the AVGC Commission?"

Angel shook her head to indicate she hadn't, but her mind immediately flashed with a picture of Grayson's tattoo and the letters that ran down one side of the slanted line that made up the M. She was positive it read "AVGC."

"The AVGC," Andrew continued, "symbolized four of the five main families in the Chicago

Syndicate. Andriacchini. Venturini. Galante. Cullato. The AVGC commission was formed as an act of war against the peace-making project, that's why there's no M to represent the Maratinzano family."

"What was the project?"

"It was both a merging and splitting of territories in a manner of speaking. It was your father's idea and he based it off of the work of your grandfather, who sat on the Commission in New York. Actually, your grandfather is the Capo Di Tutti Capi."

"The boss of all bosses," Angel said, and she could tell by the grin that curled up at the corner of his lips, Andrew was impressed by her knowledge. She felt vindicated for not knowing what a meat eater was.

"Anyway, all Italian-American crime families are ruled by the Commission, even the ones here in Chicago. Your grandfather controlled them all, in a manner of speaking. There was a lot of disharmony in Chicago at the time..."

"What do you mean 'disharmony'?" Angel interrupted.

"Competition for turf and businesses led to a lot of bloodshed."

"No wonder Olga keeps telling me to stay away from Italian men." Angel rolled her eyes. "You guys are violent."

Andrew smirked. "There was also warfare between the Outfit and non-Italian-American groups."

"You mean the mafia isn't just the Italian-Americans?"

Andrew laughed. "No, Angel. Italian men are not the only violent ones."

"I didn't mean ALL Italian men are violent. Just the mafia ones."

"Not all mafia men are violent people either," he said and she could tell her questions were wearing him down.

"Go on and explain," she apologized. "I won't interrupt anymore."

Andrew shot her a glance that said he didn't believe that was true, and then continued. "The Outfit not only fought between their own families, but battled other organizations, similar to the Russian mafia and the Jamaican posses of today. There was chaos in the city, so your grandfather sent your father here to organize things." Andrew stood up and paced around the room while he talked. "Your father's idea to divide territories was a way of minimizing the disharmony between the families by giving each bogata a controlling portion of the city. Their own turf. They could handle business within their own turf however they wanted, but if they wanted to cross turf lines, they needed the collective approval of all five bosses." Andrew stopped and looked at Angel. "Are you following me?"

"I think so." She bit her lip. "So, I couldn't go onto your turf and kill you unless it was first approved by all five bosses?"

"Correct."

"Then wouldn't that mean one of the bosses would be approving a hit on his own family?" she asked.

"Yes, that meant a boss would be approving a hit on his own family at times. A hit here and there with due cause was an acceptable price to pay for overall peace between families. More importantly, minimizing warfare would keep the police from breathing down everybody's necks."

"With the exception of the murdering part, that sounds like a good plan to me," Angel noted.

"Four of the five bosses found the terms acceptable, and the one who did not, mysteriously disappeared. Probably buried next to Hoffa," Andrew joked. "The underboss took control of that family and accused your father of putting out the contract on their boss."

"Did my dad do that?" Angel's eyes widened with horror.

Andrew shrugged. "I don't know, sweetheart, but he got blamed for it. The underboss sought revenge. Not only was he upset about his boss's murder, he didn't like how the project limited his power and gave the Outfit control over the family's actions."

"You keep using that word, what's the Outfit?" Angel lowered her eyebrows and scrunched up her face.

"Sorry, mob lingo. It's another name for the Chicago Syndicate."

She nodded, taking a moment to process the information. Then she asked, "Which family are we talking about?"

Andrew sat back in the chair next to Angel. "The Galante family," he said, and raised his eyebrows at her. She knew he was making sure she made the connection to Grayson.

Angel put her hands up to her mouth and gasped as the realization settled in. "That's why you said I, of all people, should never be with a Galante." Andrew nodded. "Because the Galantes killed my dad."

Andrew nodded again.

"Why didn't the original Galante boss like the peace project idea? Did they lose a bunch of territory or something?" she asked.

"The Galantes were power hungry. They still are. They have an upper level of administration, but the rest of their family is primarily made up of cugines."

Angel threw up her hands and made a face at the use of the word cugines. "If you want me to follow you, you're going to have to use words I understand."

"Sorry," Andrew said with a smirk. "A cugine is like a younger, tough guy who's waiting to be made. He's lower-ranking, works on the crew, takes orders from the boss, but he's not a button yet."

"A button?" Angel frowned.

"A button is a sworn in member of the family. Someone who has taken the Omerta. The code of silence."

"Wait a second," Angel blurted, "so family members aren't blood relatives?"

Andrew shook his head. "Some are, but most are not. The Chicago bogatas have had other members in the upper echelons of their administration for decades. Most are of Italian or Polish ethnicity, but not all. They come in as cugines or associates until they prove their loyalty and are made. It's necessary for building a large powerful family."

"Then how do you know who's mafia and who's not?"

Andrew grinned. "Those in it know. It becomes instinct."

"So, the rest of us are just screwed. Nice." Angel rolled her eyes.

"Can I get back to the story please?" Angel nodded and Andrew leaned backward in the chair and exhaled. "As I was saying, the Galante family started what became one of the bloodiest massacres in Syndicate history."

"Couldn't the other families stop them?" Indignation rose in Angel's voice.

"It got messy quick. No one knew who to trust, not even in their own bogatas. There was no way to identify who was loyal and who was a commissioned member of the AVGC, with the exception of a branded mark on their body; but by the time anyone would get close enough to see the mark, it was lights out." Andrew held up his hand in a gun shape and pretended to pull the trigger.

Angel pictured Grayson's tattoo in her mind.

"The AVGC's commission was first to take out anyone in the Maratinzano family. Next, take out all sympathizers of the peace project from any of the other families. Your father was their first mark."

"So, they branded the initials of all the main families, except Maratinzano, in their own flesh?" she asked just to clarify.

Andrew lowered his chin and his brows. "There's an M to represent the Maratinzano bogata and the AVGC is carved into the M. You've seen this tattoo because you drew it from memory on a napkin and put it in your apron pocket."

Angel exhaled and let her shoulders slump over, nodding her head in the process.

"The tattoo was to serve as a permanent reminder that the Maratinzano family were traitors. If the initial was imbedded in member's skin, it would never be forgotten."

"Do they still tattoo members today?"

"Some do, but most don't. The tension died down for a long time, but it's escalating again."

Angel grimaced. "Here's what I don't get," she said, "all of this happened twenty-four years ago. What does it have to do with me now?"

"That's where the leak comes into play. The commission of the AVGC is still alive today, though not nearly as active as they once were. Somehow, they have found out you exist, and you've become the mark. If they take you out, the rightful bloodline of the Maratinzano family disappears and they've achieved the ultimate revenge."

This thought was more than unsettling. In fact, Angel wasn't sure whether she wanted to cry or throw up. The only thing she felt for certain was a deep anger growing inside her, unlike anything she'd experienced before. Her jaw clenched tight and, for a brief second, she thought she understood the desire to kill someone in a moment of rage.

Andrew must have seen it in her eyes because he got up, pulled her out of the chair and held her close to him, resting his hand on the back of her head. "Sweetheart," he said, stroking her hair, "this has been too much in too short a period of time. Let's stop discussing it and I'll take you home."

She lifted her head from his chest. "I want to read for a little longer." She sat back down and skimmed articles on the computer until her eyes felt like they were burning. It was page after page of victims and hit men, jail time and funerals. She rubbed her eyes and squinted across the room at Andrew.

"You ready to go home?"

"I'm starving," she moaned. "Can we get something to eat?"

Andrew looked surprised. "Most women wouldn't feel like eating after a day of picking brains out of their hair," he said.

Angel rolled her eyes. "That was hours ago; and, evidently, I'm not most women."

"You got that right." Andrew gave her a wink. "Come on, we'll hit a drive-thru on the way to your apartment."

As they pulled into the small lot outside her apartment building, Angel noted that Bessie wasn't there. "I guess Olga is still upset with me," she said.

"Why? What happened?" Andrew asked.

"I told her about our conversation at the pub and she flipped out, telling me not to talk to you or anyone about my dad."

Andrew glanced over at Angel and raised his eyebrows. "Now you understand why."

Angel nodded. "She's trying to protect me."

"So, cut her some slack. She's been living with secrets for a long time."

"It amazes me that she can keep all this stuff secret and yet, she feels the need to tell everyone she meets about my love life."

Andrew chuckled.

He walked to her apartment door, took her keys, unlocked the door and pulled out his .22 as he entered. "Stay behind me," he ordered. After a quick walk-thru he told Angel she could turn on some lights and they sat at the kitchen table and ate the cheeseburgers and fries they picked up at the drive-thru. Angel inhaled hers. She knew it was probably from the stress, but she felt like she hadn't eaten in days. "Whoa," Andrew joked, "you didn't even chew."

Angel felt her face flush with embarrassment. "I told you I was starving."

"I believe you," he laughed.

It was 3:00am when they finished eating and Angel threw away the fast-food wrappings. Andrew said he was sleeping over and gave Angel no choice in the matter. Normally she would have argued, but tonight she didn't mind the protection. She brought him a pillow and blanket for the couch and said goodnight.

"Those mean cats of yours won't try and get me during the night, right?"

"Well, Mo might want to snuggle with you," Angel grinned.

"Great," Andrew mumbled under his breath. "A cat lover and a Yankees fan; this is definitely a deal breaker."

Angel peered over the top of the couch, "We don't have a deal," she said and smirked.

"Thank God for that," he replied with a wink.

Angel walked down the hall toward her bedroom, stopping once to glance over her shoulder. She saw Andrew peering over the back of the couch, smiling like a little kid.

"What?" she asked.

"Nothing," he grinned. "You have a cute walk."

Angel blushed, said goodnight again, and dashed down the hall into her bedroom. She closed the door and locked it.

"Not to mention a nice ass," Andrew murmured to himself, "a very nice ass."

CHAPTER TEN

The last time she glanced at the clock it was 4:30am. After that she must have finally fallen asleep. Angel woke up with the sun illuminating her bedroom and questions igniting her mind. How was it that Andrew was a cop but still worked for her at the pub? Andrew's name was Venturini, which was one of the five main families in Chicago; so, was he mafia or not? If Grayson was a member of the AVGC commission, why didn't he kill her when he had the chance? And the ever-present question still taunting her heart, why did Tony leave her?

She stumbled tiredly down the hall and found Olga in the kitchen making cinnamon pancakes and Andrew at the table drinking coffee.

"Merciful Heavens," exclaimed Olga, wheeling around on her heels and facing Angel, "you look plum awful, like you haven't slept in days."

Angel winced, "Thank you for pointing out the obvious." She gave Olga a tight hug and an unspoken understanding solidified between them. Angel was glad she had returned and Olga was glad to be back.

Olga gave her a wink and patted her cheek. "Dios Mio," she exhaled, making the sign of the cross over her body with her spatula.

"Good morning," Andrew interjected and jumped up to get her a cup of coffee.

Angel opened the cabinet to get a mug but Andrew beat her to it. He snatched the mug and had it filled before she got the cabinet door shut again. "I can get my own coffee," she blurted.

"Angel May," Olga gasped, "when a gentleman fetches you coffee, you say thank you; you don't sass him."

"Yeah, don't sass me," Andrew said, obviously holding back a laugh.

Angel rolled her eyes at Olga, and then looked over at Andrew. She batted her lashes, placed her hand delicately against her cheek and spoke with overly dramatic, southern belle flair. "Why Andrew, I'm just pleased as punch you gone and fetched me coffee this here bright and cheery morning."

Olga scrunched up her face at Angel and waved her spatula in the air, while Andrew laughed. "Nice accent," he said, "but I don't see prim and proper, southern belle coming from you."

Angel narrowed her eyes at him and Olga burst into a low, raspy chuckle. "He sure pegged you there."

Shortly after breakfast Andrew left and Angel cleaned up the dishes while Olga excused herself to the guest bedroom to lie down. She told Angel she was awake most of the night and needed forty winks to re-charge. Forty-winks was Olga-speak for a two-hour nap. When the dishes were done, Angel hopped in a quick shower to help her fully wake up. She had showered right before falling into bed last night, making sure all the blood was out of her hair and symbolically scrubbing away the scent of death, but she felt she needed another hosing down this morning. Once out of the shower, she threw on a pair of blue jeans and a black t-shirt, pulled her hair back into a ponytail and sat down in front of her computer. It was time to conduct some research.

She studied the territories of the five main Chicago bogatas. Andriacchini controlled the west side. Venturini controlled the north side. Cullato controlled the east side. Galante controlled the south side, the worst area of town. Her father, Maratinzano, controlled Rush Street, by far one of the most lucrative of sections due to the large number of businesses. She grabbed her notebook and jotted down a couple of questions:

> *Who took control of Rush Street after the Maratinzano massacre? Who has control now?*

Her next search was for Grayson Galante. The only information she found was an obituary stating he died in a car accident the same night as her accident, which was obviously not true. She leaned forward in her chair and rest her elbows on the desk. It was clear searching for answers on the computer was frivolous. Any information she found on particular mafia members would probably be tainted. She needed to talk to real people if she wanted the truth. Even if she could get an audience with mafia members, she knew she'd encounter lies as she would bump into the Omerta, their sworn code of silence, punishable by death. So how could she find out the truth about her father, her family and her own identity?

She knew of only two people who might be able to fill in the blanks. One was asleep in her spare bedroom. Angel considered telling Olga everything that happened, but she feared Olga would worry herself right into her grave. Someday she would tell her everything, but that time wasn't now. The other person was her father's Compare, the one man he trusted with her identity. The man who, according to Andrew, had been watching and protecting her since her father's death. She jotted down another question:

> *Who is dad's Compare and how do I find him?*

Angel slipped on her black converse tennis shoes, grabbed her purse and shoved her new cell phone in the back pocket of her jeans. She left a note to tell Olga she had borrowed Bessie and headed out the door. She wanted to get a better look at the surveillance room Tony showed her the other night, and before the pub opened was the perfect time to snoop around. If anyone saw Bessie parked on the street, they'd just assume she had gone to work early.

She parked Bessie outside the back door of the pub and hurried past the dumpster and down the alley to the right. She was carrying a crowbar she had found in Bessie's trunk, expecting to have to break the lock on the door, but when she got there the door was already unlocked. She slipped quietly inside and made her way toward the stone staircase. She kept the crowbar gripped tightly in her right hand; in case she needed a weapon.

The room was just as she remembered from the other night, except now it felt cold, damp and more eerie. The staircase was dark and Angel ran her fingers down the side of the stone walls as she crept along. It grew darker with every step and she began to second-guess whether this was such a good idea. By the time she reached the last step it was pitch black. She strained to see anything but her vision was lost in darkness. She followed the feel of the wall toward the opposite side of the cellar where she remembered seeing Tony turn on a single bulb with a pull string. She inched slowly along, despite fear trying to immobilize her.

With only a few feet to go, Angel's toes bumped against something on the floor, startling her and causing her to jolt forward into another step. This time her foot landed on top of something and she stumbled forward, scraping her right shoulder and right cheek against the back wall and sending her crashing to the floor. The crowbar went airborne, and Angel heard it land with a clang across the room. She felt the warmth of wetness seep through her jeans and onto her knees, and then realized her left hand was in something wet and sticky. She stretched her arm out and felt the floor, searching for whatever it was that had sent her hurling to the ground. She felt something soft and ran her fingers across it. It felt like cloth. She continued to follow the cloth-like material until her fingers met up with a fleshy surface. Her heart stalled as realization sank in. She was touching a man's fleshy but firm, hairy arm. She felt panic rising as she scrambled to her feet and inched away from the body, telling herself to exhale and remain calm. It was too late, fear-driven adrenaline kicked in and she began frantically swinging her arms in the darkness, in search of the hanging light string.

When she finally found it, she tugged hard and was momentarily blinded by the brightness. She squinted, letting her eyes adjust and then gasped at the sight. On the floor lay her chef from the pub, Antonio, his Tetterbaum apron clutched in his right hand. He was face down and it looked like half his head was missing. Angel instinctively put her hands up to cover her mouth and realized her left hand was covered in blood, as were her knees and feet. Tears streamed down her cheeks. She hadn't known Antonio well, but no one deserved to be gunned down like this. Her hands were trembling as she reached into her pocket and pulled out the brand-new cell phone Andrew had given her. When he answered she tried to control the shaking in her voice.

"Andrew," she quivered, "I need you to come get me right now. I don't think I can move." Angel's feet were glued to the floor with fear.

"What happened? Where are you?"

Angel described the alley behind the dumpster and the wooden door to the right. "Please hurry," she begged, "there's a body here."

"A body?"

She started to cry. "It's Antonio. Somebody shot him."

"Did you see who shot him?"

"No, he was dead when I got here."

"Angel, listen to me carefully, are you alone?"

Angel's eyes frantically darted about the room. "I think so." But she wasn't certain and the thought that the killer was still there pushed her closer toward panic.

"Do you have a weapon, something to defend yourself with?"

"I have a crowbar," she sputtered and dashed to where it lay on the floor.

"Don't move," Andrew ordered, "I'm only a few minutes away."

Angel positioned herself in the opposite corner with her back against the stone wall. She tried not to look at Antonio, but she couldn't help it. Fighting the urge to vomit, she decided she needed to get out of that room and away from the body. She inched her way toward the hallway that led to the surveillance room. She could see the equipment

lights from the hall and moved quickly toward them.
The further she got from Antonio's body the easier
she could breathe, though her pulse was still
hammering in her ears.

Reaching the surveillance room, Angel sat in
the folding chair and tried to calm herself by putting
her head between her knees and taking several deep
breaths. When her pulse began to slow and the
nausea subsided, she looked up and noticed the
monitor in front of her. She could see the empty bar
and dining room area of the pub. She reached over
and clicked the mouse and it displayed the kitchen.
She clicked again and saw the hallway, and then
the women's bathroom. She clicked one last time
and couldn't believe her eyes. Grayson was in the
men's bathroom, washing his hands in the sink.
She jumped to her feet, her eyes bulging at the
screen. How did he get in? Was he looking for her?
"He probably saw Bessie parked outside and
thought I was inside," she uttered under her breath.

"Angel?" Andrew hollered from somewhere
above her and she jumped. She clicked the monitor
screen one more time and the picture went back to
the dining room. She hurried toward the hallway.
She couldn't let Andrew know Grayson was alive.
Even after all she'd learned about the Galante
family, the fact was Grayson didn't kill her when he
easily could have, which told her there was more to
the story. She needed to talk to him.

Andrew met her in the hallway and wrapped
his arms around her. Concern lit his face as he saw
the scrape on the side of her cheek and the blood all
over her hands and knees. "Sweetheart, are you
okay?" Angel nodded yes but felt that no was
probably the appropriate answer. "There are going

to be a lot of cops crawling around here in about three minutes, so I need to get you out of here now."

"Won't they need to talk to me since I was the one who found Antonio?"

"Eventually, they'll talk to you because Antonio worked for you, but they don't need to know you were here." He looked at Angel with a stern glare, "You were never here, you understand that? You don't even know this place exists."

She nodded and they hurried past the body and up the stairs. Andrew peered out the wooden door into the alley. "I want you to hurry down the alley, get into Bessie and go straight home and get cleaned up. Put your bloody clothes in a trash bag and I'll get rid of them later."

Angel nodded, "Okay."

"I'll come over and pick you up as soon as I take care of everything here."

Angel followed Andrew's instructions, except the part about getting into Bessie and heading straight home. When she got to the back door of the pub she couldn't help but wonder if Grayson was still inside, maybe even waiting for her to show up. Instead of getting into Bessie, she unlocked the back door of the pub and stepped inside.

Angel moved slowly past the storage room door and up the hallway. She peered into the kitchen and glanced in the dining room from the back of the bar. "Grayson," she whispered, "are you still here?" She stepped closer to the men's bathroom door. "If you're still here you've got to get out of here because it's under surveillance."

She slowly pushed open the men's bathroom door and called his name, but there was no answer. Turning around to head back down the hallway, Angel felt a jolt of intense pain run through her body and all of her muscles tightened at once. She fell straight to the ground, unable to move her arms to catch herself.

She must have blacked out because when she woke up she was in the backseat of a moving car, with duct tape around her ankles and her wrists and covering her eyes. There was a buzzing in her head, probably from hitting the floor and her whole body ached. She didn't know how long she'd been unconscious or how far from the pub she had been driven. She started to squirm against the tape.

"Lay still and keep your head down," he ordered. "I don't want to tase you again."

"Grayson?" she asked, but she already knew it was his voice. "Why am I taped up and why the hell did you tase me?" Anger began to boil in her belly. "That hurt!"

"Sorry beautiful," he snickered, "it had to be done."

"Why?" Angel demanded. "I came into the pub to warn you."

"You're beautiful but you're not too smart, are you?"

Now Angel was just plain pissed off. On the one hand, it was the first time Grayson had ever called her beautiful, outside the bedroom; and it sent a warm fuzzy feeling dancing up her neck. On the other hand, she was tired of feeling stupid and wearing thin of Grayson, Tony and Andrew's macho guy Italian egos. "Aunt Olga was right," she blurted, "I need to find me a nice, normal, boring guy, who won't tase me and tape me up."

Grayson let out a short chuckle. "You gave me no choice."

"I gave you no choice?" Her mouth fell open in shock. "I'm unarmed, half your size and I gave you no choice?"

"I had to get you out of there fast," he defended.

"Oh, I'm so impressed by the big, strong, hot Italian guy who tased me!" she spewed sarcasm as she ranted. "How macho of you. Do you feel like a real man now?"

Angel felt the car come to an abrupt stop, which sent her bouncing forward and slamming back into the seat. Grayson reached back and grabbed her taped wrists, jerking her up into a sitting position. He ripped the tape off her eyes, and she winced, pretty sure she'd just lost every eyebrow hair she had.

"I should have taped up your mouth instead of your eyes," he said.

She watched him pull out a pocketknife that looked large enough to be a hunting knife and slice quickly through the tape around her ankles. She held up her wrists expecting him to cut the tape off, but he stared at her.

"I don't think so," he sneered. "Not yet."

"Why not?" She lowered what was left of her eyebrows.

"I don't trust you to behave." He closed the knife and stuck it back into his jacket pocket.

"YOU don't trust me!" Angel burst, then exhaled loudly and kicked her feet against the back of his seat, jolting him forward. "Who just tasered who?"

Grayson grinned, with his dimples dipping into the sides of each cheek. "I've never seen this sassy side of you," he said. "I like it."

Angel rolled her eyes and let her body sink against the back of the seat. She was tired of being manhandled. He was infuriating and yet, so hot she could barely stand it. Even now, after being tasered and taped and covered in someone else's blood, she wanted to kiss him. She wanted to feel the weight of his body on top of her. Her heartbeat quickened as naked images flashed through her mind, and she felt the flush of passion race up her body and flood her cheeks.

Grayson met her gaze and chuckled. "I know what you're thinking about."

"No, you don't." She licked her lips and tried to push the thoughts away.

"You've got fuck me eyes." He smiled.

"I do not," she sputtered, defensively. "I don't get fuck me eyes for someone who zaps me with electricity, blindfolds me and ties me up."

Grayson laughed as he got out of the car, walked around and opened the back-passenger door. He reached in, gripping the tape around her wrists and pulled her out of the car, dragging her so close that her nose almost touched his chin. He looked down at her. "Let's just call this foreplay."

He held her wrists by the tape and led her to the back of a building that looked like it was condemned years ago. Most the windows were broken. Some were taped up and some didn't have any glass left in them at all. A rusted fire escape climbed up the building but looked like it would crumble into pieces if anyone stepped onto it. Walking in the door, Angel gasped at the overwhelming stench of urine. Grayson released her wrists so she could raise her hands up to cover her nose and mouth and gripped the waist of her blue jeans instead. There was an elevator on the ground floor, but it had a giant X across it made out of duct tape. Grayson pulled Angel up two flights of steps to a landing with six apartment doors, three on each side. They entered the farthest door on the left.

Once inside, Grayson released his hold on her waistband and bolted the door shut with four different locks. The room was almost pitch black. He turned to face Angel who stared at him, a mixture of emotion running through her.

"It isn't much," he said, walking from the door to the middle of the room, "but its home." He flipped on a large flashlight and lit several candles which sat at various spots in the room: one in each of the corners and one on the countertop.

"This is where you live?" Angel did a quick assessment of the tiny apartment. It had a small kitchenette which sat to the immediate left of the door. It consisted of an old, once white but now yellowed refrigerator, and a two-burner stove with no oven. There was a small sink with two cabinets overhead. The family room was the bedroom with one window that would have looked out over the fire escape, had it not been covered with black paint. A door to a small bathroom sat to the right and a coat closet with no door was next to the bathroom. Grayson's furniture consisted of a double mattress thrown on the floor and a cardboard box, flipped over and used as a nightstand.

"Welcome to my humble hideout," he said. Pulling the knife from his jacket pocket, he sliced the tape off her wrists. "Make yourself comfortable."

That seemed like an oxymoron in such an uncomfortable place, but Angel walked to the edge of the mattress and lowered herself to a sitting position, crossing her legs Indian style.

"I'd offer you coffee, but I don't have any," he said and then paused and shrugged. "How 'bout a beer?" He pulled two bottles from the fridge and when Angel reached out to take the bottle, they both became undeniably aware of the dried blood on her left hand and arm.

Grayson pursed his lips and inhaled. "Would you like to get cleaned up?"

Angel looked at her arms and felt the blood drying on her knees. "Yes, I would. Thank you."

After she showered, she sat down next to Grayson on the edge of the mattress. "Thanks for letting me borrow your shorts." She tried to wash the blood out of her jeans but knew from previous experience, they were toast.

Grayson handed her a beer. "Wish I looked that good in those shorts," he teased.

Angel took a swig of the beer, then another, followed by a long gulp. She didn't normally drink in the morning, but the events of today not only justified alcohol, they required it.

It went down smooth and Angel made a loud "ah" sound when she finally came up for air.

Grayson eyed her and grinned. "You sure know how to pound it."

"I was thirsty." She blushed.

"Yeah, being tasered will do that." He smiled at her.

Angel finished her beer and tried to decide what her first question should be. She could open with, *Why did you tase me?* Always a good question. *Why were you in the pub and how did you get in the pub?* Two more decent questions. After a moment she boldly asked, "How come you didn't kill me when I came to your house?"

His eyes widened and she could tell of all of the questions he anticipated, this was not one of them. He leaned back on one elbow, resting on his right side. "What makes you think I would want to kill you?"

"You're a Galante," she answered flatly. Angel set her empty beer bottle on the floor and leaned back on her left side, propping her head up on her arm and facing Grayson. She could see him study her and she held his stare, allowing him to read her eyes.

He took a big swig, and then set his beer to the side of the mattress. "When did you find out who you were?"

"Yesterday."

"Who told you?"

"Andrew." Angel saw Grayson's jaw tighten at the mention of Andrew's name. She still didn't understand their connection, but she was determined to find out.

"You can't believe everything you're told," he said, reaching over and tucking a piece of hair behind her ear. It had escaped her ponytail holder.

"Can I believe *you?*" Angel studied his face as his expression morphed from anger to concern to regret.

He exhaled. "No." Grayson started to sit up, but Angel slipped her hand inside his and tugged slightly to indicate she didn't want him to move away. He slumped back down.

"Why didn't you kill me?" she asked again. This time her tone was more direct and purposeful.

"Because I didn't want to kill you." She could tell he was growing agitated. He rolled on his back and put his hands up to this forehead, exhaling loudly.

"Why not?" she pushed.

"Because I …" his voiced tapered off.

"You what?" Angel pressed harder. "Because you what?"

Grayson abruptly sat up, resting his arms on his knees and shaking his head. "Because I felt something for you, okay? I felt something and I didn't think it was right that you should die when you didn't even know why."

Angel sat up next to him. "And now?"

"Now what?"

She touched his arm and pulled until he turned his head and his eyes met hers. "Do you think I should die now that I know why?"

Grayson looked away without answering and Angel wasn't sure whether or not she should be afraid of him. After all, he could conceivably kill her in this apartment and no one would find her for a very long time, if ever.

"It's complicated," he whispered.

"Then explain it to me and maybe I can help un-complicate it."

Grayson laughed sardonically. "You have no idea what you're dealing with."

"I understand more than you think," she rebutted.

He laughed harder. "No, you don't." His eyes filled with rage and he clenched his fists. "You don't know anything."

That was her hot button and Angel jumped to her feet and grunted in frustration. "I'm not stupid," she demanded, anger rising within. "I know about your tattoo and I know you're a commissioned member of the AVGC. I know your family murdered my father and I know YOUR family started the massacre of all Maratinzanos." She paced back and forth in front of Grayson, stomping and pointing and flailing her arms like every good Italian communicator. "I know you're made up of a bunch of unsophisticated, classless, trigger-happy cugines who probably don't know their own ass from a hole in the ground!" Angel stopped to suck in a breath when Grayson leapt to his feet, grabbed her by the shoulders and threw her onto the mattress.

Before she could speak his lips were on hers and their tongues danced wildly. It was anger. It was passion. It was fear. It was wanting so deep she couldn't harness it. Grayson pulled off his shirt, revealing his muscular chest and bulging arms. She gripped them and let the arousal from his strength rush through her. His caress sent chills of excitement up her back, as he ran his hands behind her neck and pulled out her ponytail holder. Her hair fell messily on her shoulders. For a brief moment it seemed the world stood still, as their bodies conversed in a language only lovers speak, and Angel felt the fear melt away.

When the ecstasy faded, Grayson lay next to her, draping his left arm around her breast and pulling her close. He took a deep breath and then spoke, "I was commissioned as a member of the AVGC because I'm a Galante. Every Galante holds that commission. It's part of our Omerta." He rolled up onto his side and looked in her eyes. "When I met you, I didn't know who you were." He rolled onto his back and laced his fingers behind his head.

"And when you found out, you were supposed to kill me, right?"

"Technically."

She rolled over and laid her chin on top his chest. "But you didn't."

"I couldn't so I promised myself I would stop seeing you, but I couldn't do that either."

Angel smiled. "I'm glad you couldn't, on both counts." She kissed his lips. "So, did you fake your death just to get away from me or were you running from someone else?" She was half teasing, but his expression told her she was onto something. Angel pushed herself up from his chest and looked in his eyes. "Did someone in your family find out about me?"

"They didn't find out," Grayson spewed. "I was ratted out."

"By who?" Grayson shook his head and didn't answer. "The man you pushed in front of my car that night was from your own family, wasn't he?" Grayson's eyes stared away. "He was sent to kill you, wasn't he?" It was all beginning to make sense. "You must have found out you were his mark so you killed him and then went into hiding."

Grayson looked at her with a smirk and brushed aside the hair that had fallen in her face, tucking it behind her left ear. "You've got part of it right."

"Which part is wrong?" She shifted to a sitting position, putting her knees to her chest to hide her breasts.

He sat up next to her but took no precaution toward modesty. "I made the mistake of thinking that piece of rat-shit was the only one who knew." He ran his hands through his hair. "He was a cugine who nobody liked. He was never going to be sworn in and he knew it. So, I figured he probably kept the information to himself, planning to take me out first and then tell the boss. That way his actions would be viewed as an act of loyalty to the family and he would be made."

"So, you took him out thinking you could return to your life as normal and no one would ever know."

"Not exactly." Grayson got up and walked across the room to the refrigerator. He was naked and Angel couldn't force herself to look away. His muscles were firm and the very sight of him warmed places in her that liked to be warm. "You want another beer?"

"Please," she said.

He walked back toward her with his full glory in plain view and Angel thought her toes might curl just seeing it.

Grayson chuckled as he handed her the beer. "You're beautiful when you have that horny glow."

Angel rolled her eyes and took a big gulp. Grayson sat back down and explained how his goal was never to return to normal life, but to use the situation to his advantage and start over. "I wanted out," he said. "I killed the babbo and paid off Dr. Manzini to forge a death certificate for me instead."

I knew it! Thought Angel, but she didn't say it out loud. She knew Dr. Manzini was hiding something. She could sense it.

Grayson continued. "That way if anybody had known anything it wouldn't matter anymore because everyone would think I was dead. I hid out for a couple weeks and kept watch on my house to see if anyone from the family found out what I'd done. When I thought I was in the clear I went inside to pack up my stuff, and that's when you showed up, being followed by that scum meat eater." Angel could hear the anger rise in his voice.

"I only came there to get closure," she defended. "I thought I killed you. Besides, on some level you must have wanted me to know you were alive or you wouldn't have sent the roses with the card that read: G."

Grayson stared at her with his brows narrowed. "I didn't send you roses."

"Who else would send me a card with the letter G on it?"

"That's a good question." It was obvious by his inflection that this disturbed him.

Angel took a sip of her beer and then what Grayson had said sank in and she turned to face him, shock lighting her eyes. "What do you mean I showed up with that scum meat eater following me?" She studied his face for an answer. "Andrew followed me to your house that day. Andrew isn't a meat eater. Is he?"

"He's a Venturini first and a cop second. He's on the Venturini payroll. There's no bigger meat eater on the force than Special Detective Venturini." Grayson's words dripped with sarcasm.

"I had no idea." Angel sat genuinely stunned.

"Why do you think he works at the pub?" His tone indicated that she should already know this answer, but she obviously didn't.

"I don't know." Angel crossed her arms over her knees and rested her chin on her forearms. "I guess I thought he was there to protect me."

Grayson burst out laughing. "Boy, you really are naïve."

There was that feeling again. That indignation rising within. That anger that caused her to want to defend herself. She scooted her body further from him and faced him. "Since you're so smart, why don't you tell me why he works at the pub?"

Grayson didn't miss a beat. "He wants the Tetterbaum tapes."

She stared blankly. "Tetterbaum has tapes?"

"Yeah, surveillance tapes."

"Where are they?"

"Nobody knows and everybody wants them."

"Why? What's on the tapes that's so important?"

Grayson swigged his beer. "I don't know

"So, every family is after the recordings Tetterbaum made?"

"Yep. That's why Andrew started working there. He convinced the police to put him undercover, under the guise of spying on the mob; but really the Venturini family put him in there to find the Tetterbaum tapes."

"How do you know all this?"

"Everybody knows about the tapes. Why do you think Antonio Cullato worked there?"

Angel's heartbeat quickened and she had that all too familiar surreal feeling of everything moving in slow motion around her. It was one word that struck fear into her heart. The word *worked*. Grayson used the word in the past tense, indicating he knew Antonio no longer worked there. How would he know Antonio no longer worked there unless he knew he was dead? And how would he know he was dead unless he was the one who killed him? Come to think of it, Grayson never asked whose blood was on her arm and clothes. It stood to reason that he didn't ask where it came from because he already knew. Angel tried to slow her pulse and stifle the urge to panic. She rose slowly from the mattress and began to gather her clothes from the floor. She tried to conceal the fact that her hands were starting to tremble.

She picked up her panties and his shorts, and then reached over for her bra; but Grayson snatched it first. "Why the sudden urge to get dressed?"

Angel shrugged. "Just feeling modest." She stood with her back to Grayson and slid on her panties and his shorts. The shorts were way too big and clung around her hips just enough to keep them up. Without turning around, she reached her arm back and asked for her bra.

"No," he answered flatly.

"Why not?"

"Because I walked across the room naked for you, now it's your turn." She froze, trying to control her breathing. Grayson stood up behind her and pulled her shorts and panties down, letting them drop to the floor. "I gave you the full show," he said, "I want the same."

"I should really be getting back to the pub before I'm missed." Her body was trembling on the inside and she wasn't sure whether or not he could see her shaking outwardly.

"Walk across the room and turn around and face me." Angel should have downed that second beer while she had the chance. Maybe it would have helped her relax. She walked slowly across the room and turned to face him. He licked his lips and she could almost hear the deliciously dirty thoughts dancing through his head. She tried not to focus on the fact that she was not only totally naked but completely vulnerable. He smiled a big, dimpled grin.

She started to walk toward him and her clothing when he held up his hand and motioned her to stop. "What?" She held her hands up, "Why do I have to stop?"

"Because you have a question to ask me."
His tone was playful, but in an eerie sort of way.

Angel shook her head, "No I don't."

Grayson stood up and walked toward her
with a smirk on his face. "As you can see you have
my fullest attention. Now ask me."

"Ask you what?" Angel moaned.

"Ask me why I killed Antonio."

Angel closed her eyes. She was right and
now, more than ever, she wished she had been
wrong. Grayson inched his way closer and Angel
instinctively backed away. "Don't touch me," she
whispered.

He didn't listen. Instead, he scooped her up,
carried her to the mattress and laid her down. She
flipped to her side and buried her face in the pillow,
fighting back tears. Grayson lifted the far corner of
the mattress and slid his .38 pistol from beneath it.

"This is the gun I used," he said, "which is
why it was messier than normal. I prefer to use my
.22 for close range but I don't have it anymore."

Angel peeked up from the pillow and saw the
gun. "Are you going to kill me, too?"

Grayson shook his head, leaned over and
placed the gun next to her on the mattress. "You
don't get it do you? I killed him because he was
going to take you out."

Angel rolled over. "Why would Antonio want
to kill me?"

"He's a commissioned member of the AVGC.
Antonio Cullato."

"How do you know he was going to take me
out?"

"My contact learned you were Antonio's mark
and sent me to stop him."

"Who is your contact?"

"Your father's Compare."

Angel bolted up excitedly. "So, you were hired by the same man as Andrew to protect me."

"No."

"Yes," Angel demanded. "Andrew was commissioned by my dad's Compare, too."

"Andrew may be commissioned for something, but it is only for the benefit of one person, himself."

"You're wrong about him. He's protecting me."

Grayson lay down on his left side. "Has he told you your real name?"

"Yes, Maratinzano."

"No, your first name." Grayson leaned up and kissed her tenderly on the lips. "Michelangela," he whispered and the sound of the name ran chills up her arms, all the way to her chin. It was familiar, though she couldn't remember how she knew it. She scooted back just enough to look Grayson in the eyes. "In Italian it means one who is like God, a Messenger or Angel." He emphasized the word Angel and chills danced once more up her spine.

"That's why my dad called me Angel," she said softly.

Grayson pulled her down onto his chest. "Michelangela May Maratinzano," he sighed, "my Angel."

Angel's pulse had just returned to normal and her body started to relax when Grayson bolted off the mattress, grabbing the .38 and rushing to the door. He smashed his ear against it. "Son of a bitch," he spewed in a hushed, but intense tone. "How did someone find us?" He dashed across the room, sliding into his shorts and peering out a tiny hole in the black paint. "No cop cars," he said aloud, heading back to the apartment door.

"Who is it?" The question no sooner left her lips when she remembered her cell phone. She put her hands to her mouth. "Omigod Grayson, it's my cell phone. There's a tracking device inside my phone. When I didn't drive Bessie home, he probably started looking for me."

"Who's tracking you?'

"Andrew."

Grayson's jaw tightened and his eyes filled with a wild rage. He aimed the .38 at Angel's head. "You lying bitch! You set me up."

"No!"

"You and Andrew saw me in the pub, and he sent you in there so he could follow me."

"No, I swear it was nothing like that. Andrew didn't even know I went in the pub. I saw you on the surveillance screen and I came to warn you."

"You liar," he spewed.

Angel's whole body shook as she tried to tell Grayson she had forgotten about her phone, and that it wasn't a set up. She pleaded with him to believe her.

"Turn around," he ordered. "Face the wall."

"No, Grayson, please, you don't understand," Angel begged.

"Shut up and turn around."

"No!" she screamed. "You'll shoot me just like you shot Antonio."

He grabbed her up by one arm, spun her around and smashed her face-first against the wall. He placed his foot in the small of her back and kept her pinned. "Don't move," he ordered.

Her whole body shook uncontrollably as she tried to think of what to say to convince him. Tears streamed down her cheeks and rolled around her chin, dripping to her chest. Her mind clouded with the most unusual of thoughts. Aunt Olga calling her, "my Angel." Sitting on her dad's lap and watching lightning fill the sky. Kissing Tony by the lake. Then it settled on one thought, the Lord's Prayer. Angel began to recite it in her mind and mouth it with her lips. "Our Father, who art in Heaven, hallowed by Thy name…"

"Shut up!" He kicked his foot harder into her back.

"Thy kingdom come, Thy will be done on Earth as it is in Heaven…"

"I said shut up," he interrupted.

Despite his threats, Angel kept praying quietly. It was the only thing she knew to do. She continued to pray until she heard a voice outside the apartment door. It was Andrew and he was banging on doors. It sounded like Andrew was a couple doors down the hall, as he banged and hollered, "Police. Open the door."

"Keep your mouth shut," Grayson threatened.

Angel thought to cry out for help, but what good would it do. By the time she would make a sound, Grayson would pull the trigger and send a bullet into her brain. Andrew pounded on Grayson's door. "Police! Open up."

"Please," Angel whispered in sobs.

Andrew pounded on the door a second time.

"I'm sorry Angel," Grayson said, this time his voice filled with regret. He pulled the trigger.

CHAPTER ELEVEN

When Angel opened her eyes Dr. Manzini was standing over her, holding a tiny flashlight and shining it in each eye. He looked back at Olga and Andrew, both standing at the foot of the bed. "She's waking up and her pupils look good."

"Merciful Heavens, thank you Lord Jesus." Olga rushed to the side of the bed, praying aloud. She took Angel's hand in hers and held it to her heart.

"Not too much chatter now," Dr. Manzini scolded, "she's going to feel weak for a while and have quite a headache."

"Now that she's awake, how long will she have to stay here," Andrew asked.

Dr. Manzini adjusted his glasses and patted his lips together. "Let's give her another thirty minutes and we'll check her vitals again."

The doctor was right, Angel's head was pounding. It was the worst headache she'd ever had. It felt like an ice pick at each temple with piercing pains shooting up the back and over the top of her head. She looked at Olga and mumbled. "I thought it was over," her lip quivering, "and I could see your face and hear you calling me 'your Angel.'"

Olga, who seldom showed emotion outwardly, with the exception of anger and disgust, welled up but stifled it back. She plunked down on the side of the bed, squishing part of Angel's left leg with her rounded hips. "You are my Angel," she said and squeezed her hand, "and you always will be."

Angel grabbed her forehead and winced from the throbbing. She was certain Grayson shot her in the head and she felt around for missing hair and stitches. "How long have I been here?"

"About an hour dear," Olga patted her hand.

"An hour?" Angel's eyes widened with surprise. Then she justified in her mind that Olga must have meant she had been in recovery for an hour. She felt around her head for bandages. "How many days have I been here?"

"Just today." Olga smiled at Angel. "You must still be disoriented."

Angel narrowed her brows. It wasn't making sense. No bandages. No stitches. No shaved section of hair. "Did he shoot me in the head?" she blurted louder then she intended. Her eyes looked to Andrew for the answer, but Olga jumped in.

"Shoot you? Oh, merciful heavens, no child. You weren't shot, you were zapped."

"Tasered by an X26," Andrew clarified. Angel slumped back in the bed. She'd never been tasered before and now it happened twice in one day. What were the odds?

She replayed it in her mind, trying to recall exactly what happened after Grayson said he was sorry. She said to Andrew, "I know I heard the gun shot."

"He shot into the wall next to your left ear." Andrew's eyes locked with Angel's. "He then jolted you probably within a half second or so."

"Why?" Angel shook her head. "Why wouldn't he just kill me?"

"Good heavens child, why would anyone want to kill you?" Olga made an attempt at innocent ignorance but Angel saw through it. She was done with the façade. She no longer had the mental or the emotional energy to pretend to be something or someone she wasn't and it was time for Olga to stop pretending too.

"Because I'm Michelangela May Maratinzano," she said in a half-whisper, staring at Olga.

Big tears instantly filled Olga's eyes and dripped down her cheeks. "Oh no, no, no," she shook her head, gripping Angel's hand and putting it up to her lips. "Not my Angel," she spattered, kissing Angel's fingertips. "They're not getting my Angel." Defiance rose in Olga's tone and her body stiffened as she pushed herself off the bed and faced Andrew. "You did this," she spewed, "you told her who she was."

Andrew hung his head. "No, ma'am, not exactly."

Olga spat at him and mumbled something in Italian, as she waddled angrily out of the room.

Angel sat up, quickly realizing she was draped in a hospital gown that wasn't tied in the back. She pulled the two sides together as best she could and looked up at Andrew. "So, where is Grayson now?"

"He went down the fire escape," he said.

"I don't suppose he dressed me before he ran off?"

She could see Andrew fighting back a smile, as the corners of his mouth curled up slightly. "Nope."

"So, you rushed into the apartment and found me..." her voice tapered off.

"Totally naked," he beamed.

She felt her face flush. "And when you brought me here I was..." her voice tapered off again.

"I wrapped you in a sheet," he said.

She breathed a sigh of relief. It was bad enough Andrew had seen her utterly exposed, but to think that the hospital personnel and other patients were gawking as he carried her into the emergency room buck naked was too much to handle. Sure, doctors and nurses were used to seeing nudity, and probably desensitized to it, but Angel wasn't. She was highly sensitive about the whole being seen naked thing.

"I guess I owe you one," she said sheepishly.

"Seeing you naked was payment enough," he said and grinned. "For now."

She swallowed hard, unsure of what the 'for now' meant. All she knew was she desperately needed to change the subject from the topic of her nudity; either that or she needed to crawl in a hole and hide from the humiliation.

"So, why am I at the hospital if I was only tasered?"

"By the time I shot through the door and got to you, you were convulsing pretty hard," Andrew explained. "Grayson didn't hit you in drive stun mode; he blasted you at close range with the electrodes. People twice your size have suffered serious injury and even died from that kind of jolt."

"But he didn't shoot me," she said more to herself than to him. She gnawed on her bottom lip. "Why didn't he shoot me?"

Andrew tightened his jaw and glared at her. "Don't fool yourself into thinking he has the capacity for sympathy."

"He could have killed me and he chose not to."

Andrew stared at her with anger pouring out his eyes. "You want to know why he didn't put a bullet in the back of your head. He didn't kill you because he had to use you as a diversion to stop me from getting to him."

"What?" Angel didn't understand.

"If he killed you, I would have come through the door, seen you were dead and gone right after him." Andrew shook his head. "By incapacitating you, he bought himself time to get away." Angel could hear a mixture of frustration and anger building in Andrew's tone.

"Oh." She dropped her eyes to the bed.

"He didn't save you. He used you. Again."

She was certain the confusion she felt shone in her face. She didn't know which one to believe. Was Grayson right and Andrew was a dirty cop? Was Andrew right and Grayson really was an animal like the Galantes who killed her father?

Andrew's hands drew up into fists of frustration and he leaned down in Angel's face. "This guy has almost killed you twice now. What's it gonna take for you to believe me?" Angel started to speak but Andrew interrupted. "I can't believe you left with him instead of following my instructions, and what I really can't believe is what you did with him in that apartment." Andrew's voice escalated to a yell, which brought Dr. Manzini to the room.

"Everything okay in here?" He stared at them with his eyebrows raised above the rim of his glasses.

Andrew grunted and stormed out of the room.

"Guess I chased them both off," Angel mumbled.

Dr. Manzini walked to the edge of her bed, placing the blood pressure slip around her arm and pumping it tight. He stared at Angel's eyes the whole time he counted which began to make her feel uncomfortable. She glanced away and shifted her eyeballs around, but his stare remained intensely stern.

"You never talked to the therapist," he said, slipping the cuff off her arm.

Angel looked at him. "I misplaced the name you gave me," she lied.

He pulled a prescription pad from his pocket and scribbled down a name. He folded the paper in half and handed it to Angel. "Book an appointment. It's not optional."

"I don't think a therapist is what I need."

Dr. Manzini's expression turned cold and the glow that normally shone in his eyes grew dark. He lowered his voice and spoke poignantly. "Michelangela, make the appointment."

Before Angel could suck in a breath Dr. Manzini was gone. She unfolded the prescription and read the name, Venito Barone.

~ ~ ~

It had been two days since she was zapped by Grayson and her body was feeling back to normal, but her mind was still whirling. Andrew was barely speaking to her. The only full sentence he'd uttered to her in days was, "Here's a new phone, try to hang onto it."

Olga, now refusing to leave her alone in her apartment, spent half of her time sobbing and the other half baking. That's what Olga did when she was upset, she baked. Sometimes she made homemade cheesecake which was so moist and rich you could gain ten pounds just smelling it. The past couple days, though, she made homemade Cannoli, which were Angel's favorite. She called them little tubes of heaven. Whether she was baking or crying Olga was constantly ranting under her breath in

Italian and gesturing with her hands. It was like two days of one run-on sentence that Angel couldn't understand. She wasn't sure which environment housed more tension, her apartment with Olga or the pub with Andrew.

She'd spent all of yesterday interviewing potential chefs to replace Antonio and trying to find information on Venito Barone. She searched him online, but the name came up empty. If he was a therapist, he was working under an alias. She called Dr. Manzini's office, wanting to get a number for Venito Barone and talk with him about Grayson. After all, he was the one who forged Grayson's death certificate the night of the accident, leading Angel to assume he was somehow linked to all of this and must have answers. She also wanted to know how he knew her real name.

The receptionist at Dr. Manzini's office informed Angel that Dr. Manzini had moved and she was unable to give her a forwarding address or number.

"What about an email address?" Angel pried.

"I'm sorry," the receptionist answered, "I have no way of contacting him."

She got the same run-around from the hospital. It was as if, within the last forty-eight hours, he just disappeared.

The more dead ends she hit, the more driven she felt to find the truth. She stared at her computer screen, out of ideas for what to search next. Galante. Cullato. Andriacchini. Venturini. Maratinzano. Venito Barone. Dr. Manzini. Andrew. Grayson. Tony. Antonio. She'd run all their names through every search engine. Nothing gave her a clue as to whom, if any of them, she could trust. She slumped in her chair and rubbed her eyes, which were dry and bloodshot from staring at the monitor too long.

"Why aren't you at the pub?" Olga's voice startled her, and she jumped, flailing her arm and smacking her computer mouse across the desk.

Olga belted out a raspy chuckle. "Merciful heavens, I've never seen such bug eyes."

"You scared me," Angel said. "My eyes bulge when I get alarmed." She retrieved her mouse from the floor and set it back on the pad.

"They didn't just bulge," Olga giggled, "they almost came out of your head."

"I guess I'm a little jumpy," she admitted.

"Seems we're all a bit jumpy these days." Olga waddled over from the desk to the bed and sat down. She patted the mattress, indicating Angel should sit next to her, which she did.

"Seems we can't undo what's already been done, so we're just going to get through this together." Olga took Angel's hand in hers and gave it a squeeze. Angel could tell this was a conversation Olga never planned on having. She looked at Angel the way a mother gazes at her newborn baby. "My Angel," she sighed, pursing her lips to stop the quivering and swallowing hard. "Your father, God rest his soul, he did his best to protect you."

"Why?" Angel knew she interrupted Olga's thought process, but she needed to know her dad's reason behind the façade.

"You were his little girl, his princess, his most prized possession; there was nothing more important or more special in his life than you." Olga's eyes welled up again. "He didn't want the bogata life for you. He wanted you to have a normal life. He wanted you to have security, real friends and a husband who wouldn't get killed in the middle of the night and leave you widowed. He wanted you to have everything he could never have."

"He never had a normal life?"

"Merciful heavens, no." Olga shook her head. "His father, my brother, Giovanni, was the Capo Di Tutti Capi…"

"The boss of all bosses," they said in unison and smiled at each other.

"You've been doing your homework," Olga said. "Your father was to be the future Capo Di Tutti Capi someday, except he didn't ever want the position. He felt it would be too dangerous for you."

"Why did he think it was so dangerous?"

Olga sighed with heavy sadness. "Your father saw more death than anyone should." Angel shrugged her shoulders and shook her head at Olga, indicating she had no idea what Olga was talking about. Olga lowered her eyes and mumbled something in Italian. Angel didn't understand the words, but knew it meant the topic was burdensome. "Your father saw his only sister blown up in a car bomb that was meant for Giovanni. She was sixteen years old and had just gotten her driver's license." Olga's eyes moistened with the memory. "I remember she was so anxious to drive that she begged Giovanni every day. Finally, he conceded to allow her to drive up and down the driveway for practice. When she got in the car and started the ignition it blew up." Anguish poured from Olga's words. "It was the worst funeral I have attended in all my years."

"How old was my dad?"

"Twelve at the time. He was going to ride with her, but it was a rainy day and his mother made him put on his shoes before going outside." Olga made the sign of the cross with her hand over her body, "Thank the Lord for those shoes; otherwise, your father would have been in the car when it blew up."

Angel felt anger rising at the injustice. She grit her teeth. "What did Giovanni do?"

"He waged war and pledged to avenge her death with more death." Olga shook her head and wiped a tear with her fingers before it fell from her chin. "He never recovered from losing her."

"Did he find whoever killed her?" Angel asked.

Olga nodded. "Oh, yes."

"And?" Angel was on the edge of her seat, literally, soaking in every word and frustrated that Olga's words weren't coming fast enough.

Olga broke into sobs and her raspy voice cracked as she spoke, "And he killed him."

"Good," Angel blurted.

Olga gasped, "No Angel May, murder is never good."

"I don't mean good, as in right. But it was justified," Angel defended.

Olga hung her head and shook it back and forth. "Merciful heavens child, you have your father's high sense of justice." Olga took a deep breath and continued. "The problem was Giovanni's revenge went beyond justice and he ordered the man's wife and daughter to be killed as well."

He evened the score, Angel thought and then couldn't believe she was thinking it. It was heartless and cold, and it was the same blood running through her veins. It was in her and she could feel it.

"The problem is there are rules, an unspoken honor among families that women and children are

143

left alone," Olga explained. "Giovanni broke that code."

"They broke it first," protested Angel, "when they killed his daughter."

"That was an accident," Olga explained. "The bomb was meant for Giovanni. He retaliated and killed the man's wife and daughter on purpose. It caused a great disrespect for him, and it created more violence, as others then showed a blatant disregard for the code of ethics, justifying it because the Capo Di Tutti Capi had done it."

"So, what happened?" Angel asked.

"A year later," Olga spoke softly, "your father saw his own mother gunned down in front of a bakery, where they had gone to get pastries." Olga drew in a deep breath. "It was a miracle your father wasn't hit, but he was blocked by two men who took the bullets instead."

Angel was glued to Olga's every word. "What did Giovanni do?" she asked, both curious and afraid to hear the answer.

Olga threw up her hands and let them fall onto her lap, exhaling something in Italian. "Giovanni went crazy with revenge. He went on a murderous rampage and drove everyone who loved him out of his life, including your father and me."

"Is that why dad left New York and came to Chicago?"

"Yes, it was years later, after you were born. He and your grandfather agreed their relationship would be better with some distance, so your father came to Chicago to run operations here."

"So, where was I born?"

"In New York, but your records have been changed to read Chicago. You father brought you and your mother here when you were only a few months old."

They moved into the kitchen and talked for the next couple hours, in between bites of Olga's homemade Cannoli and sips of coffee. Olga confirmed everything Andrew told her about the chaos between bogatas over territory and her father's peace project. She also answered questions Angel had about her mom, and for the first time Angel began to understand why her mom behaved the way she did.

"Your father refused to marry her," Olga explained, "even after you were born."

"Why?" Angel asked.

"In his mind she and you were safer if you weren't legally his."

It made sense. Even after her mom was widowed the fear from the bogata lifestyle never went away. Angel now understood that her mother had run away from the fear, not away from her.

"Your mother loved you very much," Olga told her, "but believe me, it isn't easy living in a cave, always looking over your shoulder, wondering who you can trust and fearful each day may be your last. She had to break free and start her life over."

"She didn't have to leave my life completely," Angel said. "I haven't heard from her since I was eighteen."

Olga reached across the table and gave Angel's hand a squeeze. She stared in her eyes, deliberately emphasizing each word. "Your mother left to protect you from ever being identified so that you would never have to live in fear."

Angel shook her head. "That seems to be a reoccurring theme in my life, people leaving to protect me." Angel used her fingers to make quotations around the word protect.

"Angel May," Olga smacked her fingertips, "you stop this selfishness right now." Olga's face grew stern, and her brows lowered until her eyes looked like tiny slits. "People have given their whole lives to hide you and protect you. We've changed our own identities, left behind all we knew and vowed to leave you rather than risk your exposure."

"What do you mean 'we?'"

Olga threw her hands in the air and mumbled in Italian.

"You said 'WE changed our own identities.'" Angel's voice grew louder. "What do you mean WE?"

Olga lifted herself from the chair and shuffled her way across the kitchen to the coffee pot. "Would you like more coffee dear?" she asked, avoiding the question.

"Damnit Olga!" Angel yelled, slamming her hands onto the table. She'd never raised her voice at Olga before, but frustration was quickly turning to anger. "Who is WE?"

Olga carried her cup back to the table and sat down, turning toward Angel with deep sadness on her face. "When Giovanni went crazy with revenge, my husband, Lorenzo, and I took your father in. We were worried for his safety. His mother and sister had already been killed and we feared they would kill your father next. Lorenzo tried to talk sense into Giovanni but it was no use." Olga broke down into sobs and Angel watched as the woman who always seemed solid as a rock, crumbled before her. "Giovanni accused us of kidnapping Joseph and he had my Lorenzo killed."

Angel reached Olga's hand and held it in hers, stroking the top with one hand and squeezing her fingers with the other.

"It was terrible to have my husband murdered by my own brother."

Tears filled Angel's eyes as she watched the agony of that awful memory etch itself across Olga's face.

"Your father was returned to Giovanni and I left in the middle of the night. I feared for my life, so I went up north and hid until things settled down. Then I contacted the one man I thought could help me."

"Who?"

"Lorenzo's brother, Venito."

Angel's mouth went instantly dry at the mention of the name Venito. Though it was a typical Italian name and there were probably thousands of men named Venito, her stomach writhed with an instinctive knowing. There was a connection.

"Aunt Olga," Angel spoke calmly, though her insides were somersaulting. "What was Lorenzo and Venito's last name?"

"Barone." Angel sat back in her chair, stunned as Olga continued to speak. "My real name is Lucia Maria Maratinzano. When I married Lorenzo, I became Lucia Maria Maratinzano Barone." Olga broke into sobs again. "After Lorenzo was killed, Venito helped me change my name to Olga Bartanovic and I escaped to Chicago and started a new life."

"Giovanni wouldn't have killed you. You are his sister."

Olga shook her head. "He became a madman, and I didn't know what he was capable of, so I fled."

"Did my father come here with you?"

"No, he was taken back to Giovanni. I didn't see him again until years later, when he moved you and your mother here."

"How did you find him?" Angel asked.

"Merciful heavens child, a Maratinzano of your father's rank in the administration was not hard to find. Venito set up the meeting. Your father instantly received me with love and asked me to be your keeper since my new identity outside the bogata was secure. You and your mother came to live with me shortly thereafter."

"How did you know you could trust Venito?"

Olga's lips twitched. "You never know for sure who can be trusted in bogata life." She shook her head and lowered her eyes. "There is so much corruption; but Venito was my brother-in-law, and he was also known for fixing problems among bogatas. They called him "the therapist."

The therapist. Angel repeated it in her mind. Another confirmation that Dr. Manzini was somehow connected. "Where is Venito now?"

Olga sighed. "Goodness dear, I have no idea. I haven't had contact with him since he set up the meeting with me and your father all those years ago."

Angel's mind was a whirlwind of thought and Olga looked exhausted from the emotional download. Olga blotted her eyes with her napkin, and then looked over at Angel with a smile. "It feels good to have you know the truth."

"Thank you," Angel spoke softly, "for everything you've done and all you've sacrificed."

Olga patted Angel's hand. "I wouldn't change what I did, not for anything." She gave Angel a wink, and then took a sip of her coffee. Angel understood the magnitude of that statement. Olga lost her husband and left behind her whole life to protect Angel's father and ultimately her. In the process she lost her only family, Giovanni, who went crazy with revenge. Her life was filled with death and fear, and yet she seemed so stoic and strong. Angel admired the strength she saw in Olga.

Clearing her throat, Angel asked, "I don't have to call you Lucia now, do I?"

Olga chuckled, "No, and I'm not calling you Michelangela either."

"Deal," Angel said.

A few minutes later Angel swallowed the last bite of her third cannoli and slurped down her coffee, letting out a big sigh of contentment. There was nothing like Olga's cannoli.

"It makes me happy to see you eating again," Olga uttered.

"You know I can't resist your cannoli. You should make some as a special dessert at the pub. We could advertise the first Tuesday of every month as Cannoli Tuesday, or something like that." The idea sounded better in her mind than when it came out her mouth.

Olga shook her head, "Merciful Heavens child, I want nothing to do with that pub." She drew in a deep breath, shaking her finger at Angel. "You shouldn't want anything to do with it either."

"I *own* it," she said and rolled her eyes as if to say "duh."

"Well, UN-own it."

Angel deflated. She really liked owning the pub. "Even if I sell it, I'd still have to run it until it sells."

"You're not running it today."

"Andrew is handling it today. We're sort of working in shifts so we don't have to work together." Angel lowered her eyes, "He's still mad at me."

"Well, let Andrew handle it every day until it sells," Olga said.

"I never said I was going to sell." Angel's defenses rose and Olga sat back and threw her hands in the air.

"Mable should have sold it to one of the other bogatas when they made her the offer. But no, she HAD to sell it to you and for dirt cheap." Olga was off on a rant, but at least this one was in English so Angel could follow along.

"Wait a second," Angel blurted, "you mean Mable had offers on the pub and she didn't sell?"

"You betcha she had offers. Five offers in all according to Elsa Lieberstern down at the hair salon."

"Then why did she sell it to me?" The question was rhetorical though Olga started spewing out theories. Angel tuned her out. She was contemplating a theory of her own. If four of the offers were from each of the main bogatas, then who made the fifth offer? Each bogata had incentive to buy the pub to get their hands on the Tetterbaum tapes, but what incentive did the fifth person have? Her mind played devil's advocate, telling her it could have been an entrepreneur or an astute restaurant guru who knew Tetterbaums was a wise investment; but her gut told her otherwise. The fifth buyer was most likely after the tapes as well; but why?

Angel looked at Olga, who was still ranting and raving about the pub. She grabbed her hand. "Does Elsa Lieberstern know who the five offers came from?"

Olga shrugged. "It's possible. Elsa has an uncanny way of getting information. It just sort of falls in her lap, but I guess that's what happens in the salon business. Hairdressers and priests get all the good dirt." She took another nibble of her cannoli.

Angel jumped up and grabbed the phone from the kitchen counter, handing it to Olga. "Call her."

She set the phone on the table. "I'll see her at the hair salon on Saturday." Olga finished chewing. "You know I go in every Saturday for my washing and style."

"I need to know who the five potential buyers were," Angel said and pushed the phone toward Olga. "I need to know now."

"I can't call her and start asking those kinds of questions." Olga folded her arms.

"Fine." Angel knew she was right. It would look suspicious. Angel cut a cannoli in half and stuffed it into her mouth. Then she jumped up and made a dash to her bedroom. Throwing on a pair of boots, she grabbed her purse and headed back down the hall toward the kitchen, stopping only to snatch Olga's purse from the spare bedroom dresser. She set Olga's purse on the table in front of her and grabbed Bessie's keys from the counter.

"Why did you bring me my handbag?" Olga asked, taking another nibble.

Angel held up Bessie's keys and jingled them in front of Olga. "I need to have my hair done and you're coming with me."

Olga chuckled and shook her finger, "You are a sneaky little thing."

"I've learned from the best," Angel said, giving Olga a teasing nudge.

"Good heavens, you're just full of sass."

Angel locked the apartment door on the way out and double checked it. Then she helped Olga down the two flights of steps and across the lot to Bessie. After Olga was in and situated, Angel ran around to get in the passenger side when a thought hit her brain like a bolt of lightning. She reached into her purse, pulled out her cell phone, jogged across the lot and threw it into the trash can that sat at the base of the stairs.

When she finally got into Bessie, Olga asked, "What were you futzing around with out there?"

"I was losing a tail," Angel said. "This adventure is for our eyes and ears only."

CHAPTER TWELVE

The trip to the salon turned out to be just that, an adventure, especially for her hair. Angel got into the passenger side of Bessie and lowered the visor mirror, staring at her reflection with terror. *Never let a bunch of seventy-year-old women pick out a hairstyle for you*, she scolded herself. Her dark brown hair was teased higher than people wore it in the eighties. She looked like a cross between Jackie O and Elvira. At least her split ends got a good trimming, though she was pretty sure Elsa had split a bunch more with all the teasing.

Despite the fact that she didn't want anyone to see the way she looked, Angel asked Olga to drop her off at the pub. She was desperate to find a new chef and needed to review any new applications that had come in. "I'll have Andrew bring me home later," she promised.

"Merciful heavens, child, don't walk home," Olga warned as Angel pushed open the door to exit Bessie.

She rolled her eyes, "I'll be fine."

"I know you'll be fine," Olga said. "I'm just worried you'll be picked up for prostitution with that hairdo." She chuckled low and raspy.

"You're not helping," Angel scowled.

"I can't help it," she laughed, "I've never seen hair so high. You've got hooker hair."

Angel pushed down on it with the palm of both hands. "I can't get it to go down," she grunted, which made Olga burst into a full-on belly laugh. "This is your fault," Angel said, pointing her finger at Olga. "Your friends did this to me."

Olga's eyes were watering from the laughter, "Oh goodness," she said, "Elsa didn't mean it. She's not used to working on anyone with long hair."

"What was your first clue?" Angel blurted sarcastically, pointing at her poufy do.

"We old ladies all have short hair so when you tease it up it gives us just the right amount of body." Olga drove off laughing, and Angel tried to flatten her hair one more time before walking inside the pub.

She entered the dining room and was relieved to see it empty. Empty was bad for business but good for no one seeing her hair. Then Andrew came around the corner of the bar and was barely able to stifle a laugh. "Omigod," he exclaimed, "did you get tasered again?"

She pursed her lips and narrowed her eyes.

"Seriously, what happened to your hair?" He couldn't keep a straight face and, despite the humiliation, Angel thought this might be the comic relief they needed to break the tension between them.

"I went to Olga's hair salon to do some research."

"What were you researching? The effects of too much mousse?" He covered his mouth with his hands to try and hide the fact that he couldn't stop grinning.

"Oh, this isn't mousse," she ranted. "We're talking old school here."

"Old school?" Andrew grimaced.

She nodded and her poufy hair jiggled, causing Andrew to break into a chuckle. "It's not funny. They actually teased and sprayed it up this high and I don't know if it will ever come back down."

"I hear they're holding auditions for Hair Spray downtown," Andrew teased.

Angel gave him an un-amused glare. "Are you going to help me or not?"

A few minutes later Angel's head was in the slop sink in the back of the kitchen and Andrew was hosing down her hair. "Is it working?" she yelled over the sound of the water.

"I don't know, it's pretty matted underneath." Angel moaned and Andrew laughed harder. When the washing was done, Angel flipped her hair up and back and then wrapped it in a white dish towel.

"After all this trouble, I hope you found whatever information you were looking for."

Angel sighed and leaned against the stainless-steel counter. "I got gossip on half the city, but I didn't get what I was looking for." Elsa confirmed that each bogata made an offer on the pub, but she didn't know who made the fifth offer, which was the one tidbit of information Angel really wanted.

Sitting at the desk, she dug through more chef applications while Andrew tended bar to the few patrons who ventured in. The absence of food was hurting business. People weren't satisfied with only peanuts, pretzels and chips and salsa. They wanted the usual fare, standard to the Tetterbaum tradition. After scheduling several chef interviews for tomorrow morning, Angel used the hand dryer in the bathroom to blow her hair semi-dry, then grabbed her apron and went to the bar to help Andrew. The happy hour crowd would be arriving soon and since they cared more about drink specials than food, she anticipated the usual rush. When she approached the bar, Andrew was leaning over the top, engaged in what looked like a serious conversation with another man. They spoke in hushed tones, and though she tried, she couldn't make out any words.

When his eyes darted from Andrew to her, she smiled a quiet hello, and the man gave her a single nod of acknowledgment. Then he put his fedora atop his head and made a quick exit out the front door.

"Sorry to chase off your mob friend," Angel said to Andrew, as soon as the front door closed.

Andrew crossed his arms and leaned against the bar. "So, you think your instincts are honed enough that you can spot the mob now?" His tone held just enough sarcasm to piss her off.

"Yes, I do," she said with a smirk of confidence.

He shuffled his feet and nodded his head. "And you trust those instincts?"

"Yep," she quipped arrogantly.

"Well, don't," he spat, and her ego popped like an over-inflated balloon. "He's not mob, he's a detective."

"I thought those were one in the same," she quipped sarcastically.

Andrew dropped his head and shook it. "I don't get you," he said. "You trust men you know are murderers more than you trust me." He exhaled and walked out of the bar area, down the hall toward the kitchen.

Guilt rushed over her. He was right, she did trust Tony and Grayson more than him and she wasn't even sure why. Maybe it was because Grayson said he was a meat eater. Maybe it was because Tony said he couldn't be trusted. Maybe it was simply that there were too many unknowns about him.

The happy hour rush came and went but the tension between Andrew and Angel hung heavy in the air. At 11:00pm she locked the front door and walked back to the kitchen to find him. He was leaning against the stainless-steel island that sat in the middle of the kitchen. His arms were crossed, and it was obvious his thoughts were someplace far away.

Angel stepped closer to him, calling out, "Earth to Andrew," waving her hands in front of his face. He lowered his eyes to hers but didn't alter his expression nor speak. "Are you pouting?" she teased, trying to lighten the mood by sticking her lower lip out and inching her way closer.

She never saw his hand move but suddenly felt it grab the back of her hair and neck and pull her closer. Before his strength could register in her mind, his lips were on hers. They were soft but the power behind them, forceful. For a fleeting moment, she thought to squirm free, but that notion was quickly replaced by a desire to let his kiss linger. His grip on her neck loosened as she voluntarily leaned her body closer into him. As passion infused, his hands explored her back and brushed up her sides. She became undeniably aware of how different his touch was from that of Grayson. There was warmth in Andrew's fingers; tenderness she hadn't felt since before Tony left.

Just as her inhibitions began to lower and give way to passion, Andrew took her by the shoulders and pulled her away from his chest. He cleared his throat. "We should get you home before Olga starts to worry." Confusion swept her heart. "Besides," he added, "we're on surveillance here."

"Not in the storage room," she said. Andrew looked at her with questioning eyes. "The storage room isn't under surveillance," she repeated, inching closer. "We could continue this in there."

"How do you know it's not under surveillance?" Andrew held her at bay with both hands on her shoulders and a concentrated stare.

"I clicked through all the screens the day I found Antonio. There is no camera set up to survey the storage room."

Andrew immediately released her shoulders and made a beeline for the hallway. She could see he was in cop mode now and the mood was broken. Just when she was so close, too. She followed him down the hall and into the storage room, blinking to adjust her eyes as the light bulb flickered on and off a couple times before steadily illuminating. Andrew started on the right side of the room, staring intently at the stone walls and running his fingertips across it.

"I know something else you can run your fingers over," Angel taunted in her flirtiest tone, but Andrew didn't flinch. She moved closer and tried again. "Since we're not on surveillance in here, do you want to pick up where we left off in the kitchen?"

Andrew stopped analyzing the wall and turned to face Angel. There was an all-knowing sprinkle of irony in his eyes as he walked closer to her. "You know," he said, licking his lips and taking a deep breath, "when I kissed you earlier it wasn't because I wanted something from you. It was because I've wanted to kiss you for a long time."

"Then kiss me," she smiled.

Placing both hands gently on her face, he leaned down. "No."

Angel opened her eyes. "What?" She was shocked. "No?"

"Yep," he said. "No."

"But you just… why did you kiss me in the kitchen if you didn't want to…" her voice trailed off.

"Don't get on a high horse, sweetheart. The only person using anyone in this room is you." Andrew turned his back and started inspecting the stone wall again.

"You think I'm using you?" Angel was furious and stunned at the same time.

"Ah, yep."

She flailed her arms and raised her voice. "How could I possibly be using you?"

He turned to face her and this time there was no sarcasm in his voice. "You were willing to sleep with me just to find out if I bear the AVGC tattoo, and that tells me two things about you. First, your desperation is clouding your judgment. Second, you have no real feelings for me whatsoever." He turned back to the wall.

Angel stormed out of the storage room in a huff. She went into the bathroom and kicked all three stall doors as hard as she could. He was right and she hated when he was right. She was trying to seduce him so she could see if he had the tattoo, but could he blame her? Was it so wrong to want to know if she could trust him? Anger dug a pit in her stomach and humiliation sat in it. She'd just thrown herself at him and he pushed her away. He was right about her judgment being clouded; but he was wrong about her not having romantic feelings. She did feel something for Andrew, but she didn't know how to identify it. Whatever the feeling was, it was irritatingly there, eating away at her.

Grabbing her purse from the desk drawer, Angel strutted down the hall and out the back door without saying goodbye. She decided to walk home as opposed to groveling to Andrew for a ride. There was only so much humiliation a girl could take in one day and she'd had her fill.

She was two blocks from the pub when she saw the illumed taxi sign and her arm instinctively jumped up. She wasn't in the mood for a walk. The driver pulled over and two men jumped out, one from the passenger seat and one from the backseat. In a matter of seconds her mouth and wrists were duct taped, and a dark pillowcase put over her head. She tried to scream, but the sound was muffled by the tape. She kicked her legs wildly and bucked up and down as they grabbed her and lifted her into the trunk. She bunny-footed the hood of the trunk and stopped them from closing it several times before they were finally able to slam it shut. She heard two doors slam as each man got back into the cab and then felt the taxi speed off. Despite the terrible stench in the trunk, Angel tried to breathe in deeply through her nose and calm herself. Though her wrists were taped together, she used her fingers to search for a crowbar or anything sharp to cut the tape. There was nothing. To get her mind off the fact that it was hard to breathe, she forced herself to concentrate on the direction the cab was going. They were headed south, toward Galante turf.

Now she wished she hadn't thrown her cell phone in the trash.

CHAPTER THIRTEEN

Two men lifted Angel from the trunk, one placing his hands under her armpits and the other holding her legs. She squirmed but quickly realized their grip tightened with every movement, so she tried to relax her muscles and hang quietly while they walked. She heard the trunk slam shut, the shuffling of footsteps and then what sounded like a heavy, steel door open and close with a clang. They had entered a building and Angel listened for sounds and sniffed the air, searching for an identifiable odor that would give a clue as to her whereabouts. Nothing was familiar. Another door opened and closed, and she was placed in a chair with her ankles duct taped to the chair legs. She heard the opening and closing of the door one last time, then silence. She strained to hear the sound of breathing in the room, but she could only hear her own. Feeling secure in the fact that she was alone, Angel wiggled her feet and twisted her ankles, but she was powerless against the strength of the tape. If it could hold a wing on an airplane in flight, it could certainly keep her strapped to a chair.

The old Angel Martin would have been paralyzed by fear, but if the past several weeks had taught her anything, it was not to panic. She'd had a near death collision, had brains in her lap, trudged through a pool of blood in the darkness, been tasered twice, had a gun pressed to her head more times than she could count, and she was still in one piece. A little worse for wear perhaps, but alive and kicking, nonetheless. *Just keep breathing*, she told herself. In the silence she forced her mind to log in everything she could remember. She estimated she'd been in the trunk about twenty minutes, give or take a few, and that they'd consistently driven in a direction south of the pub.

When she heard the door open, Angel jumped. She wasn't riddled with fear, but her nerves were certainly on raw end. Her pulse quickened as she listened to the movement of people entering the room. They were speaking in hushed tones and for the most part, in Italian. Though she couldn't understand the words, she repeated them in her head, hoping maybe Olga could translate when or if she ever made it out of here. She determined there were two men talking with a third man. The third man sounded older than the others, having a deeper voice and a gruffer tone. His words came out slowly and dripped with authority.

"Quite la cobertura de la cabeza," the older man uttered, and Angel heard someone approaching her.

Her mind searched for the meaning of la cabeza. She'd heard it before, maybe in Spanish class in college. *La cabeza*, her brain chanted over and over. *What the hell does that mean?* The answer came swiftly, right as the pillowcase was yanked from her head. La cabeza meant head in Spanish. Obviously, it meant the same thing in Italian. The older man had instructed them to remove the covering from her head.

She let out a small squeal from the pain of having her hair pulled and squinted from the light. Her eyes frantically darted around the room, making mental notes. It was a small room with no windows and one door. A thin dark brown carpet covered the floor, and the walls were painted tan with no pictures or art of any kind. She would have guessed it was a hotel room, except there was no bed, no dresser, no television or mirror and no bathroom. She was in a chair that looked like something seen in hotel conference rooms, with a tweed cloth seat and brass coated metal legs. A round table stood next to her with an empty chair and a dark brown leather couch sat against the far wall. Two floor lamps illumed the room. Angel's eyes finally adjusted to the light and settled in on the older man.

His 5' 10" posture was slumped from age, but his stature and character were powerful. He wore a dark suit, covered by a long dark overcoat, and shoes shiny enough to render a clear reflection of anything above them. A small gold cross hung around his neck and when he met eyes with Angel, he gripped it in his crocked fingers and kissed it, mumbling in Italian what Angel thought sounded like a prayer. He moved slowly across the room toward her, never taking his eyes away.

Motioning toward the two men standing by the door, he waved his arm and grunted, "Lasciare la stanza." Angel guessed it must have meant leave because both men immediately turned and exited.

She studied his face as he pulled the empty chair toward her and lowered himself into it. He looked and moved like he was in his mid-seventies, with white gray hair slicked back from his forehead. He had olive skin and deep brown eyes, jowls that drooped on either side of his face, age spots around his jaw line and thin lips.

"La mia bella Michelangela," he spoke softly, raising both of his hands, thumbs on fingertips, to his lips and kissing them. Tenderness filled his eyes and almost instantly Angel realized the man sitting across from her was the Capo Di Tutti Capi, her grandfather, Giovanni Maratinzano.

She swallowed hard against the duct taped pressed to her lips. Disbelief and awe overran her thoughts as she stared at him. No one said Giovanni was dead, but somehow in all of her conversations with Olga, Tony and Andrew, she had assumed it.

"Do you know who I am?" His Italian accent was thick and when he spoke his facial expressions and the raspy tone of his throat resembled Olga.

Angel nodded her head to indicate yes.

She could see a smile fill his eyes, as if he felt proud to know she had been told of him.

"Then you know who you are?"

Again, Angel nodded.

Giovanni turned his face toward the door and raised his voice, "Entrare!"

Two men entered immediately: one remaining by the door and the other approaching Giovanni, awaiting instruction.

"Rimuovere il nastro," Giovanni said and pointed at Angel. A cold sweat enveloped her, as the man approached and placed the palm of his left hand on her forehead. She closed her eyes and winced as he ripped the tape from her mouth, then she gasped in a deep breath of air. By nature, she was a mouth breather, so the whole tape over the lips thing, forcing her to breathe through her nose, was a challenge that required additional mental focus.

Giovanni gestured toward Angel again and said, "Le mani libere." This time the man pulled out a large knife from his pocket, reached behind her and cut the duct tape from her wrists. "Ci lasciano ora." Giovanni waved his arm and both men departed the room.

He looked at Angel and spoke more delicately than he spoke to the men. "Does that feel better?"

"Yes," she answered, clearing her throat. "Thank you."

"Thank you is Grazie," he instructed.

She repeated, "Grazie."

"You should speak Italian and communicate with your family in their language." He spoke as if this was not a suggestion but a requirement.

"I have family?" Angel asked.

"Si."

She knew what "si" meant. Everybody knew what "si" meant. She was pretty sure it was yes in all the romance languages. Yes, she had family. Angel felt strangely excited at the prospect of having actual relatives. For her entire life the only relative she knew was Olga.

Giovanni let a smile crease his face for the first time and Angel was overwhelmed by the resemblance he bore to Olga. It was as if she were staring at a masculine version of her. The same rounded cheeks, the same shape of nose and the same twinkle in the eyes.

"You look like your sister," she told him.

"You look like your father," he replied and though he grinned, a sense of sadness filled his face. "He was a good man, Michelangela." He shook his head, "A very good man." He took in a laboring breath and mumbled as he exhaled, "It isn't right what they did to him."

Angel felt a sudden awkwardness. She didn't know what to say so she sat in silence, staring down at the carpet and picking at remnants of duct tape on her wrists.

"I have come to finish this business, re-establish our family here and avenge your father's death." Angel's eyes jumped quickly from the floor to Giovanni. "I know you feel the anger in your belly. It

165

boils in your blood like it does in mine," his voice raised. "There has been much betrayal in our history, ah, but much loyalty as well." He cleared his throat and sat straighter in the chair. "We have been quiet for many years, watching and waiting for the hour to come, and now it is time."

Angel licked her lips. "I don't know what you're talking about." She picked at the tape on her wrists and nervously bounced her right knee up and down.

Giovanni took her hand in his and patted the top. "You will in time."

"I don't even know who to trust." She rolled her eyes, "I mean, even my own grandfather has me taped up and thrown in a trunk."

Giovanni smiled again and Angel wasn't sure if her nervous twitching amused him, or if he simply liked the fact that she called him grandfather. Either way, his face softened when he smiled and she felt more at ease.

"The tape and trunk were necessary this first meeting. I am sure you understand my whereabouts must remain private. A man in my position cannot afford to take unnecessary risk. I believed you could be trusted but needed to see for myself."

"And?" Angel boldly questioned. "Now that you've seen me can you remove the restraints?" Angel motioned down to her duct taped legs.

Giovanni chuckled a deep, raspy laugh in the back of his throat and nodded his head up and down. "When I find your loyalty adequate you will no longer be taped to that chair."

Angel looked down at her ankles. "That's ironic," she exhaled under her breath, "I'm the only one in the room who hasn't murdered family members and MY loyalty is in question."

Giovanni slammed his fist onto the table and Angel jumped. His cheeks flushed with an angry redness and his jaw tightened. "Your aunt has tainted your mind. I am not a murderer; I am a protector of my family. Loyalty comes with great responsibility."

"With all due respect, you killed Olga's husband."

"Lucia does not know all the facts. Lorenzo was a traitor." Giovanni exhaled and the tension in his face softened again. "I will raise my family back up," he said, lifting both hands off the table, palms up. "And you will help me."

"Is this an offer I can't refuse?" Angel's tone held more sarcasm than she meant to convey, but she couldn't help it. There was a hot indignation rising inside her. "And what if I don't help you? Are you going to kill me like you killed Lorenzo?"

Giovanni dropped his head and rose slowly from the chair. Angel could see the disappointment on his face as he moved toward the door. "Child, you possess an unjustified hatred of me. It isn't your fault. Your mind has been tainted by other's anger. I feared it was so."

She watched him move toward the door, slumped over as if every hope left alive in him had been dashed. A rush of guilt ran through her. She didn't even know this man, yet that didn't seem to matter. There was a deeper connection and it tugged at her from within. Angel sighed, "Grandfather, please wait."

Giovanni stopped and turned his gaze on her.

"What kind of help do you need from me?" Even as the words fell from her mouth, she could scarcely believe she was asking this question. A part of her didn't want to be involved at all. It wanted to go back to being boring Angel Martin, who lived alone in a two-bedroom apartment with her two cats. But she couldn't deny a bigger part of her knew it was too late to turn back. Her soul ached to become who she was meant to be and to take her rightful place in the Maratinzano family.

"I need the Tetterbaum tapes."

"Why?" What's on the tapes that is so important?"

Giovanni stared at her with his jaw tight. "The identity of the man who killed your father."

"I thought the Galante underboss put out the contract on my dad?"

"Where did you acquire that information?" He narrowed his brow.

"I don't know. I think I overheard it at the pub," she lied. Andrew was the one who told her, but she suddenly became afraid to mention his name, or anyone's name for that matter. After what Olga said about Giovanni's revengeful killing spree, Angel wasn't sure how much he could be trusted.

"The Galante underboss arranged the hit, but the contract came from someone else," Giovanni said.

"Someone higher up than the underboss?" Angel shook her head. "The only ones higher would be the bosses from the other families, right?" Angel narrowed her eyes, "And wouldn't they have to collectively approve a hit like that?"

"Si."

"What makes you think the person who put the contract out on my dad is actually on the Tetterbaum tapes?"

"I don't think. I know. So, did someone else because they took out Tetterbaum before he could give me the tapes," he explained.

Angel sat stunned, with a raw angst rumbling in her gut. The pieces were starting to fall into place; at least some of them. Tetterbaum had proof of who killed her father and was going to give the tapes to Giovanni, probably for a good price, but before he could do it someone killed him, which was why Mable wanted to unload the pub so quickly and get out of dodge. Mable must have known what was on the tapes, too. *Poor Mable*, thought Angel. She must have known her husband didn't really die of a heart attack and was too afraid to say anything. Was it possible that she knew who Angel really was, and that's why she sold the pub to her instead of one of the other families, or the fifth mystery buyer? Was it a sideways attempt to get the tapes to Giovanni after all? Her brain was crowded with speculation, and she couldn't help but wonder if the fifth buyer was actually her father's killer trying to conceal his own identity?

Giovanni moved closer to the door. "Giovanni, I have more questions." She didn't want him to leave. She wanted to understand what happened in the past and how it connected to the present. She wanted the truth and she had to believe Giovanni, with all his resources as head of the Commission, knew more than anyone else.

He dipped his head in silent acknowledgment of what she said, and then turned back to the door. "Aprire la porta," he ordered, and the door immediately opened. He spoke to the men in a low tone, too low for Angel to make out and then he was gone.

A few moments later, the men entered, one bringing a glass of water for Angel and the other cutting the tape from around her ankles. "You can get up and stretch your legs," he said. "Giovanni will join you for supper in a while."

"Supper? It's like midnight, isn't it?"

"Yes."

"You speak fluent English, and you don't even have an Italian accent," Angel noted aloud. "Why do you only speak Italian with my grandfather?"

The two men shot each other a glance. "He prefers things to be as they have always been. He is rich in tradition."

It wasn't what he said that stuck in her gut, but how he said it. There was fear behind his words, as if Giovanni was unchangeably rooted in the past. A past filled with violence and vengeance. Angel wondered if, like her, they worried that Giovanni's drive for revenge would result in another blood bath for the bogatas.

~~~

Angel was resting on the couch when Giovanni returned with a bottle of red wine, which his men served with linguini Alfredo and warm bread. He swirled his glass, inhaled its bouquet and then sipped the wine. "Nowadays they say to serve vino blanco, white wine, with Alfredo sauce, but I like the red better." He took another sip. "Growing up in Italia we had red wine no matter what color sauce."

Angel smiled. "I don't even like white wine," she said, rolling the linguini around her fork and stuffing it in her mouth.

"You have your papa's appetite," he said and shook his finger at her and grinned, "that's good."

Her heart warmed at the sound of the word papa. She was only five when her dad had died and time had a way of eroding memories of him; but did nothing to take away the feeling that something was missing. There had been a hole in her heart for twenty-four years and somehow Giovanni filled a part of that emptiness. Regardless of the fact that she feared his powerful need for revenge, she couldn't deny that on some level she understood it. The desire to avenge her father's death burned in her as well, as did a yearning to be a part of a real family. She thought about the past and wondered if she, too, would have become a vengeful monster after the unjust killing of a daughter and a spouse. As she watched him eat, she pondered what Giovanni was like before those killings.

Was he a playful father and a tender husband? Had fate been as cruel to him as it was to her father?

Over linguini and wine, the black and white lines of right and wrong began to blur into a gray shade of loyalty, where murderer and protector became eerily synonymous.

CHAPTER FOURTEEN

Andrew felt bad about what happened at the pub and stopped by Angel's apartment on his way home. Although he still believed her judgment was clouded by desperation, he felt a twinge of guilt for the quipped sarcasm he'd used and was ready to render an apology.

Olga answered the door, obviously shocked Angel wasn't with him. "Where is she?" Olga asked. "She said you would bring her home."

Andrew slammed his fist into the outside of the door and cursed. "She walked and she left well over an hour ago."

"Merciful heavens," Olga gasped, "she should have been here by now." She made the sign of the cross over her body, touching her forehead, then chest, then shoulder to shoulder.

Olga motioned Andrew inside. "We may as well worry together."

She warmed some water on the stove for tea and pulled a freshly baked cheesecake from the refrigerator, while Andrew sat at the kitchen table, fiddling with his iPhone. Olga peered over his shoulder. "That's one of those fancy phones I've seen on TV."

Andrew grinned. "4G."

Olga flipped her hands in the air and let them flop into her lap as she sat down. "I have no idea what you just said."

"Four gigahertz," Andrew explained as Olga cut the cheesecake and placed a piece on each plate in front of them.

"My giga hurts too," Olga joked and then giggled as she cracked herself up.

Andrew smirked. "I see where Angel gets her sense of humor." Olga sighed at the mention of Angel and Andrew could see worry fill her eyes. "And her stubbornness," he added.

"Oh no," she shook her finger at him, "she doesn't get her stubbornness from me. That goes all the way back to her grandfather." Olga stopped abruptly and Andrew knew she had caught herself from saying too much.

"I have heard that about Giovanni." They locked eyes. Each one knew more about the other than they'd ever let on, and Andrew believed now was as good a time as any to lay the cards on the table. "I know you are Giovanni's sister, Lucia," he admitted.

"And I know you are Joe Venturini's son," she said. Joe Venturini was as decent a man as a mob boss could be. He did his share of money laundering and racketeering, but he never ran drugs and he had a reputation for keeping the streets clean. The riff raff couldn't survive on Venturini turf, literally. The only black mark against him was that he openly opposed the Maratinzano peace project and was rumored to have secretly enlisted some of his own men as AVGC members, set out to massacre the Maratinzano bogata and its supporters.

"I was only nine when the massacre occurred," Andrew defended. "I am more a cop trying to protect someone I care about, than I am a Venturini."

"And I am more a great aunt trying to protect the niece I love than I am a Maratinzano."

Andrew nodded. "It sounds like we're on the same side."

Olga took a bite of her cheesecake and motioned for Andrew to eat, which he did. Each time he put his fork down, Olga's expression nudged him to take another bite, and another, until he had cleaned off the whole slice. "Would you like another piece?" she asked.

"No," Andrew made a bulging cheek face, "it was delicious, but I'm stuffed."

"Just one more," she pushed, placing another slice on his plate.

"Are you sure Angel doesn't get her stubbornness from you?" he teased.

"Oh no," Olga waved the pie slicer in the air, "there is no more stubborn, pig-headed a man on the face of this earth than Giovanni."

Her face showed anger and emotion as she spoke of her brother. It was clear she hated him. Andrew reached across the table and gave her hand a squeeze. "I am sorry for your loss," he said. It was common knowledge in mafia circles that Giovanni put a hit on his brother-in-law all those years ago and that Lucia disappeared shortly thereafter.

"It's the past." She forced a smile, patted the top of his hand and shrugged off the moment.

Andrew didn't let it go. "When Giovanni killed your husband, Lorenzo, you must have wanted revenge?"

Olga set her stare on Andrew in a stern way. "How is it you think you know all about me all of a sudden, and think you have a right to come in here and disrespect me by bringing up a painful memory?" Her face flushed and she shook her finger at him. "You know nothing about my Lorenzo. Nothing," she spat.

"I know he was killed for kidnapping Giovanni's son, and for conspiring to use the son as leverage."

Olga slammed her fork on the table. "That is a lie!" she yelled. "We took Joseph because Giovanni became a madman with revenge. He'd already lost his wife and daughter. It was only a matter of time before Joseph was killed, too."

"Is it possible that Lorenzo lied to you about the reason he was taking Joseph?" Andrew asked.

"No." Olga shook her head forcefully. "No. Lorenzo never lied to me. He was a good man."

Despite her words of denial, Andrew saw doubt behind her eyes. There was a piece of her, albeit small, that recognized an element of truth in Andrew's theory. Lorenzo Barone was known as "The Negotiator." Any major changes in structure between bogatas was agreed upon in the presence of a third-party negotiator. His legal services were used by all the New York families, and he had a highly respected reputation for being fair. He was in tight with all the bosses until the day he married Olga. The talk around town was because he had married Giovanni's sister, he could no longer be trusted as a neutral advisory. His business literally tanked overnight. Not one family would hire him. Rumor had it he kidnapped Giovanni's son to prove he was not loyal to the Maratinzanos.

Andrew studied Olga. "Going from having the inside track on all the families, holding their trust like no one else, to being instantly shut out must have been hard on Lorenzo."

Olga gave him a steely glare. "My Lorenzo did what he thought was best." She breathed in and exhaled slowly. "We did what we thought was best."

"What about Venito?"

Venito helped me escape Giovanni and start a new life. He is a good man."

"Why would he help you escape?" It was a curt question but Andrew knew the deep implication it made. Why would Venito, the brother of the man Giovanni killed, help Giovanni's sister? Unless the sister was perhaps working with Venito? The widow and the brother plotting revenge? It was feasible.

Olga shook her head and mumbled under her breath. "What business is this of yours?"

"I'll tell you what business it is of mine," Andrew said and leaned in close to Olga. "Near as I can tell, Angel's identity wasn't compromised until after she announced her engagement to Tony Andriachinni." He stared Olga directly in the eyes. "Now, I have to ask myself, who wouldn't want Angel to marry an Andriachinni and why?" He leaned back in the chair and folded his arms across his chest. "Then I remembered Angel commenting that you never liked Tony and have since gone out of your way to introduce her to every geek within a ten-mile radius."

Olga took a bite of her cheesecake and chewed it slowly.

"I think you leaked her identity to the Andriachinnis because you thought it would drive Tony away. You knew any respectable bogata member would not marry a Maratinzano. Even if he loved her, his own family would put enough pressure on him that he'd have to go away."

"Pish," Olga blurted, "that's an absurd tale."

Andrew leaned forward again. "You didn't think it through, did you? And now you're in way over your head." Olga put her fork down and dropped her eyes to the floor. "I know you didn't mean to put her life at risk…"

Olga slammed her palm on the table, cutting Andrew off mid-sentence. "Rubbish!" she scowled. "I protected her from being sucked into bogata life. Had she become Mrs. Tony Andriachinni she would be forever branded with murders and immoral men who defend their killing with family honor, even against their own members." Olga had risen to her feet and her hands were trembling. "When I got rid of Tony, I protected my Angel." She was breathing heavily and Andrew stood, afraid she might wobble over. "I protected her," she mumbled, lowering herself back into the chair and shaking her head.

Andrew took Olga's hand in his. "I understand," he said tenderly. "I won't tell Angel, but I need to know who you spoke with about Tony. I know you didn't mean it, but you started the leak and the only way I can stop it is to trace it."

Olga stared at Andrew as if she were trying to decide whether to tell him or not. "Venito," she exhaled, "I spoke to Venito and he said he would take care of it."

~~~

Angel's key in the front door startled both Olga and Andrew from their seats. Andrew drew his .22 and approached the door, motioning for Olga to stay back.

Angel shrieked when she opened the door and saw the gun.

"Where the hell have you been?" Andrew blurted.

Angel closed the door. "I went for a walk."

"For three hours? You left the pub a little after 11:00pm and now its 2:00am." Andrew's irritation was obvious by his elevated tone, tightened jaw line and narrowed brows.

"If you were that concerned you would have come after me the minute I walked out the back door," Angel rebutted.

"I didn't hear you leave," he said.

"That's weird, considering the back door is right next to the storage room where you were standing when I SLAMMED it." A few seconds of silence fell between them, then Angel added, "And how do you know I left a little after 11:00pm if you didn't hear me leave?"

She smirked at him with snide glee, knowing his evident speechlessness was proof she had won that part of the argument.

His jaw clenched as he saddled his .22 back into the waistband of his jeans. "So where were you all this time?"

"I took a cab downtown. I needed some time to think," she lied.

"I thought you said you took a walk?" Andrew was obviously going to hold her accountable for every syllable that fell from her lips.

"I took a walk and then I took a cab," she clarified. "What's the big deal?"

Olga piped in, "The big deal is that we've been worried sick." She shook her finger at Angel. "You can't go gallivanting around the city by yourself, not anymore."

Olga stood with her hands on her hips and Andrew folded his arms across his chest. They were a united front, and it was annoyingly clear they were not going to accept her vague detailing of the night's events. She softened her approach and directed her focus to Olga. "I'm sorry I had you worried. I was feeling upset and thought some time alone would do me good."

Andrew exhaled a "tsk," and grinned as if amused by her. Well," he said to Olga, "she came home with her clothes on so that tells us she wasn't with Grayson." Olga gave a chuckle and swatted his arm with her napkin.

Angel narrowed her eyes dramatically and stuck out her tongue at him.

"Don't take that tongue out unless you intend to use it." Andrew's eyes flickered with sarcastic flirtation, and it pissed Angel off.

"Don't worry," she replied, "I have no intention of using it." She breezed past him toward the kitchen, turning around once to add insult to injury. "Ever."

"You want some cheesecake dear?" Olga asked, getting a plate and fork out before Angel even answered. She sat at the table next to Olga and dug into the cheesecake. She felt a rush of humiliation which was quickly replaced by anger. How dare he flirt with her after she threw herself at him and he turned her down flat? It was unconscionable. How dare he pretend to care about her in front of Olga when he didn't even bother to follow her when she left the pub? Angel didn't realize while mulling through her angry thoughts she had inadvertently chopped her cheesecake to smithereens with her fork.

"Merciful heavens, you've made a mush of it," Olga gasped. "I'll cut you another slice."

"Feeling tense, are we?" Andrew sneered.

Angel threw her fork across the table, bouncing it off the wall and leaving a trail of cheesecake mush. "Why don't you leave," she seethed at Andrew.

"Angel May," Olga scolded, "that is no way to treat a guest."

"He's not a guest, not in my home." She stood up, walked toward the door and opened it.

Andrew followed her. "You want me to leave and I want to know where you were tonight." He put his hand on the top of the door and pushed it closed. "I guess we're both going to be disappointed."

Angel stormed back into the kitchen where Olga was cleaning up the cheesecake mush and placing a new slice on a clean plate. "What is your problem?" she yelled at Andrew.

"I don't like being lied to," he replied calmly. Then he sat down, reached over and took the clean plate and fresh slice of cheesecake which sat in front of Angel. He snatched the fork from her hand, cut off a big bite and then turned to Olga and said, "You make the most delicious cheesecake I've ever tasted."

"I don't like to brag, but you're right, I do," she chuckled. "It's a secret family recipe."

"Is there anything about our family that's NOT a secret?" Angel scowled, crossing her arms.

"Your love life," Andrew blurted and Olga busted a gut. She laughed so hard her face turned bright red and tears ran down her chubby cheeks.

Angel stood up. "I'm going to bed," she announced and started down the hall.

"Angel?" Andrew hollered after her. "You might want to use some rubbing alcohol to get the duct tape marks off your wrists and your face before you go to bed. Otherwise, you'll wake up in the morning with your hair matted to it."

His sentence halted her. How did he know she had been taped? A quick glance at her wrists answered the question. There were duct tape marks.

She ran her fingers around the sides of her mouth and could feel tape remnants left on her skin. *How humiliating,* she thought. She'd been sitting there the whole time with remnants of sticky duct tape around her mouth like a beard. She exhaled and walked back toward the kitchen. *Might as well face the music since there was ultimately no way of avoiding it,* she told herself.

She poked her head in the kitchen. "Would you believe I was trying a new form of hair removal?" She raised her eyebrows and grinned, but Olga and Andrew weren't amused.

Olga's eyebrows narrowed. "Tell me you weren't with that Grayson fella who tasered you. You know I never trusted that one. I told you from the beginning he was bad news and he's worse news now."

Angel rolled her eyes and exhaled as she walked back to the table and sat down. Olga was off on another rant, and she knew there was no point in even trying to get a word in edgewise.

Olga shook her finger at Angel. "I knew the minute he sent those roses to the hospital with just a "G" on the card that he was a real disturbed guy. All the other flowers came with actual names, but not his. Who signs with just an initial anyway? It isn't proper to sign with just an initial."

Angel crossed her arms and sat quiet. Olga's rants were always filled with rhetorical questions so there was no need to expend the energy of trying to jump in with an answer.

"I've only known one other person to sign with an initial and he was more disturbed…"

All of a sudden Olga's voice trailed off and the color drained from her face. She immediately rose from the chair, excused herself to her bedroom and waddled hastily down the hall. Then it hit Angel. She knew what Olga was thinking. The roses weren't from Grayson, they were from Giovanni. He had been watching her all along.

Andrew looked at Angel. "A card with a 'G'?"

Angel shook her head and closed her eyes. "I wasn't with Grayson tonight. I promise."

"Then who taped you up?"

"I don't know. Just some thugs," she lied. "They thought I had the Tetterbaum tapes, but I convinced them I didn't, and they let me go."

Andrew stared at her and his expression alone was evidence he did not believe her story. "Who did these thugs work for?"

"I don't know," she lied again, "they didn't say."

"Can you give me a description of them?"

"No. There was a pillowcase over my head."

Andrew gnawed on his bottom lip, and then finally spoke, "Let me see if I can fill in the blanks for you since you seem to display a tendency to overlook minor details of truth." It was a long-winded way of saying he knew she was lying. "Some thugs taped your mouth and wrists, blindfolded you with a pillowcase, and what the heck, let's go all out and say they threw you in a trunk because they didn't want you to know where they were taking you."

"How do you know that?"

"It's standard operating procedure around these parts, sweetheart." Andrew leaned back in the chair, folding his arms over his chest and staring Angel down. "Where'd they take you?"

She shrugged.

"C'mon, you must remember something. Which direction were you headed? How long were you in the trunk? A sound? A smell? Anything at all?"

Angel shook her head no.

"In other words, you're not going to tell me," Andrew noted.

"I don't have anything to tell. I don't know anything." Angel wished she were a better liar. She wished her palms didn't get all sweaty and her face didn't flush, and her voice didn't quiver whenever she lied.

Andrew lowered his eyes to the table, rubbed his fingertips against it and nodded his head up and down. "Most people who see the inside of a trunk end up at the bottom of a lake."

"That would never happen." Angel dismissed the possibility with an eye roll.

"You're right," Andrew oozed sarcasm, "there's never been a Maratinzano whacked by the mob in downtown Chicago in the middle of the night." He raised his eyebrows, "So, I guess you've got nothing to worry about."

"It isn't like that."

Andrew got up and moved toward the door and Angel followed to walk him out. Before she reached the doorknob, he took both her hands and leaned her backwards against the coat closet. His face was a mere two inches away and she felt her heart quicken at the thought of his lips on hers. He leaned his mouth next to her ear and whispered, "Let me tell you something sweetheart, it IS like that. It's exactly like that. If a brother can kill his sister's husband, he can kill his granddaughter, too." He pulled his mouth away and stared deeply in her eyes. "You think about that." Then he left.

~~~

183

At 6:00am a knock on the door woke Angel. She crept down the hall and peered through the peep hole, but no one was there. She placed her ear against the door and strained to hear if anyone was hiding to the sides, out of peep hole range. She couldn't hear anything, so she slowly cracked the door open. A manila envelope lodged in the side of the door dropped to the ground. Angel picked it up and noticed there was nothing written on the outside of the envelope, no postage and no address. Whatever it was, it had been hand delivered.

She closed the door and locked it, then sat down on the couch and opened the envelope, dumping the contents on the coffee table. Out fell a set of keys, one large key with the Chrysler emblem on it, attached to a keyless entry module; another silver key resembling what would be used to open a regular door; and a small brass key that looked like it would open a lock box of some sort. She reached in the envelope and pulled out a plain white 3 x 5 note card with only one thing written on it. The letter "G."

CHAPTER FIFTEEN

At 9:00am Angel found herself seated in the driver's seat of her brand new, black Chrysler Town & Country with tinted windows and tan leather interior. She had never owned a car so beautiful. This made her silver Camry look like a hunk of junk. Hoisting Olga up and into the passenger seat was an act of comedy and at one point Angel doubled over, gripping her aching sides from laughing so hard.

Finally, in the seat, Olga looked down at the ground before pulling the passenger door shut. "Merciful heavens," she panted, "why do they make it so high? A person needs a step ladder just to get in." Angel laughed and Olga shot her a glance and shook her finger. "You just wait 'til you're my age, missy."

Angel ran her hands over the seat and gripped the steering wheel. It felt good. Olga wasn't enjoying the car as much as Angel because she couldn't get past the fact that it had come from "G," who she now suspected was Giovanni. Angel hadn't told her about seeing Giovanni face-to-face yet, nor that he was in Chicago. She felt Olga was on a need-to-know basis and for now, the mere speculation that the roses and the car were from Giovanni was stressful enough for her.

"Please don't start the engine," Olga said, "for all we know it's rigged to blow." She made the sign of the cross over her body.

Angel rolled her eyes. "It's not going to blow."

"Don't accept this car Angel May," Olga begged. "You can have my Bessie."

There was obviously no comparison between the two. Bessie was an antique, but Angel knew what an offering of love Olga had just made. She took Olga's hand in hers and gave it a tender squeeze. "He won't hurt me," she reassured her. "I'm his granddaughter."

"Men like Giovanni don't give fancy gifts without expecting something in return. I do a favor for you and then you do a favor for me. That's how they work." Olga shook her head, "And do you know what happens if you don't do whatever they ask?"

"It isn't like that," she tried to explain. "I already know what he wants from me." Angel sighed, debating how much she should tell Olga. "He wants the Tetterbaum tapes."

"Merciful heavens child, may God help us all if he gets his hands on those tapes."

~~~

After the last chef interviewee left the pub, Angel sat in the back booth and jotted down notes. Her mind was a running list of things she needed to research, and questions she wanted to ask Giovanni. Andrew approached and slid into the booth across from her.

"See you got a sweet new ride," he said.

"It's a rental," Angel answered without looking up from her papers.

"Really," he tapped his fingers against the table. "Why did you feel you needed a rental?"

"I'm not crazy about hailing another cab anytime soon and I haven't had a chance to go and buy a car yet." Her answers were curt and her tone, aloof.

"Worried you'll see the inside of another trunk?"

"Yep."

Andrew nodded his head up and down and made a popping sound with his lips. "So, where'd you rent it from?"

Angel looked up, "What is this, twenty questions?" She rolled her eyes. "Why does it matter where I rented it?"

Andrew laced his fingers together on the table. "I was just curious because I don't know of any rental places that offer vehicles with bullet resistant windows and multi-layered nylon armor." Angel looked up and locked eyes with Andrew. "I realize you probably didn't notice the polycarbonate layers between the sections of glass in your windows. And you probably didn't think to look under the vehicle's carpet for nylon armor that creates a ballistic defense against bomb fragmentation." He leaned back in the booth and crossed his arms over his chest. "I bet it never occurred to you to look and see if the fuel tank was wrapped in anti-explosive material, or that your new RENTAL contains an anti-ballistic battery similar to what they use in military tanks."

Angel sat speechless; her mouth half opened.

"You've been outfitted for war, sweetheart. I hope you're ready." Andrew slid out of the booth, leaving Angel in stunned silence.

~~~

Climbing into her new Town & Country, aka "the Tank," Angel was a mixture of emotion. She left the pub without telling Andrew goodbye, embarrassed that she had once again been caught in a lie. As she drove, she felt an adrenaline rush behind the wheel of what she now respected as a military machine and not just a fancy SUV. She secretly wondered if there were machine guns behind her headlights and at the press of a button the lights would roll back, guns elongate and pepper anything that stood in her path. Behind the Rambo power rush, lay fear, as she asked herself why had Giovanni outfitted her with such a defensive machine? It was probably his way of ensuring she had adequate protection; but what worried her was the fact that he would assume she needed military grade protection.

A mere two months ago, Angel would have never left the pub in the middle of the day when the afternoon rush was about to start. But now, she wasn't concerned about the pub, the patrons or the fact that she still hadn't hired a chef. She didn't care that business was starting to dwindle and the Tetterbaum reputation was sinking. She only cared about one thing, finding the Tetterbaum tapes. Those tapes held the answers to the past and the key to her future.

She had no idea where she was headed; she just drove, allowing thoughts to float in and out of her mind at will. Instinctively she got onto the freeway and headed out of the city, toward the lake she and Tony used to visit. Faces flashed in her brain as she analyzed each person in her life. What did they mean to her? What was their motive? Could they be trusted? If only the answers came as easily as the questions and were defined in black and white instead of multiple shades of gray.

A ringing from her purse startled her back to reality and she reached inside and felt for a phone. She pushed talk and held it to her ear.

"Where are you headed?" Andrew asked.

"None of your business," she quipped. "And stop putting phones with tracking devices in my purse."

"Then stop losing them," he replied.

Angel hung up, rolled down the window and threw the phone out. "Humph," she snapped, feeling a tiny twinge of guilt but allowing anger to push it aside. Andrew infuriated her and what made it worse, she wasn't sure how she felt about him. She wanted to kiss him and punch him at the same time. It made no sense. The most awful part about it was she didn't know if he could be trusted. What if Grayson and Tony were right and Andrew was a meat-eater, secretly using her to try and get the Tetterbaum tapes? If he got his hands on the tapes first, would he kill her? Would she suddenly become disposable to him? The fact was, all three of them had a chance to kill her and they didn't, which meant, to some degree, all of them could be trusted.

She sighed aloud, "And they're all mob so to some degree they can't be trusted," she said aloud. This thought sent chills of irony through her, knowing, though she hadn't been actively raised in a bogata, there was no truer mafia blood than what flowed through her own veins.

Angel turned left onto a gravel road that led through trees and to an opening by a lake. This was the place where Tony proposed to her and the place where he later dumped her. Memories moved in and out of her head as she got out of the tank and walked toward the lake. The weeds were high, but it was still easy to find the large flat rock at the edge of the water, where she and Tony had shared many late-night picnics. Thoughts of him pushed everything else from her brain and she wondered why he hadn't made contact with her again. She missed his face, and she missed the fun they used to have; most of all she missed the time when life was easier.

The sky was overcast but every so often the sun peeked out from between the clouds and reflected off the lake. Angel picked up tiny rocks and tried to skip them across the water, a skill Tony had taught her; but she wasn't very good at it. Most of her rocks sank with a loud splash. The sun peeked out again and Angel closed her eyes, basking in the warmth. The fresh air and the sunshine felt good against her skin.

When she opened her eyes a shiny reflection on the other side of the lake caught her attention. It looked like a tiny bright light near the edge of the water. Curiosity won over exhaustion and Angel began the trek to the other side to investigate. When she got to where she thought she had seen the shiny object, she stopped and scanned the water. Whatever it was, it didn't exhibit the same bright reflection from this side of the lake.

Angel continued to walk slowly, gazing intently at the water when suddenly her knees went weak, and her stomach knotted. She dropped to her knees to get a closer look at the shiny silver watch just barely sticking out of the water. It was attached to a wrist, and she forced her unwilling eyes to move up the wrist to the arm and the shoulder and finally to settle on the bloated face of a man staring back at her through dead eyes. His body was lodged on a rock, which kept his head upright. His forehead contained a single, black bullet-hole and Angel suddenly became aware of the air being laden with the stench of death. Instinct told her to run, to get away from this unbelievable horror but shock forbid her limbs to cooperate. She tried to stand but stumbled backwards falling into the mud where she puked repeatedly.

When Angel finally managed to stand, she took only a few steps before collapsing into a heap. An agonizing scream escaped her as she clinched her eyelids tightly trying to block out the horror before her. Even through closed eyes, she still saw the image of Grayson's dead stare and knew she always would.

CHAPTER SIXTEEN

It was a long time before Angel was able to sit up and even consider trying to walk back to her car. The weight of nauseating sorrow pushed down on her. Flashes of being naked in Grayson's arms filled her mind and a lump formed in her throat. He was dead, this time for real. She would never again feel his touch or slip into one of his black t-shirts and snuggle against his chest. She would never feel the excitement and anticipation of wondering when and where he would show up. Tears fell as the shock gave way to sadness. Grayson was gone forever.

Angel started to stand when she heard voices approaching and instinctively lowered herself into the weeds and listened. A black town car had pulled around to the side of the lake near Grayson's body and two men stood next to it. Angel hadn't even heard the engine of the car, and now wondered how long it had been there and if they had seen her. The men walked closer to the lake and began skimming the water, obviously searching for Grayson's body.

"Are you sure you threw him in here?" the taller man asked.

"I think so," the shorter guy said and shrugged. "It was pitch black out here in the boonies. I put a rock on top to hold 'em down."

The taller man was perturbed and cursed several times at the shorter man. "Go to the trunk and get the tarp," he ordered, and the shorter man scurried away.

"I don't know why we gotta move him anyway. It's stupid," the shorter man griped over his shoulder, as he trudged through the weeds to the car and returned dragging a long, black piece of plastic tarp. It made a loud crinkle sound and made eavesdropping on their conversation that much more difficult. Angel strained to listen.

"You were stupid for putting him here in the first place," the taller man said.

"Hey," rebutted the shorter man. "We was told to dump the body and that's what we did."

The taller man shook his head. "You jamook. You don't dump on other people's turf. We got places for that."

"Nobody said nothin' about particular places," the shorter man argued, raising his voice. "Whose turf is this anyway?"

"This belongs to the Therapist."

"Right. Venito Barone's place. I thought we was supposed to leave the body here."

"Not THIS body." The taller man scowled and shook his head. "Just find the body and let's get this done."

Angel followed in the weeds, quietly listening and peering through whenever it was safe. She didn't recognize either man. They were both dressed in dark suits, way too nice to be trudging through mud and weeds and hauling a body out of a lake. Their accents didn't sound Italian, but more like they were from Brooklyn. They both had dark hair and the taller one wore sunglasses. She watched intently as they approached Grayson's body.

The taller man shook his head, "You didn't even clip him right."

"He's dead ain't he," the shorter man said sarcastically. "Then I done it right."

"Your instructions were to do a message job." The shorter man shrugged and the taller man continued, "To shoot him through the eye so it sends a message to the Galantes that we're watching."

"I'm new to all this shit," the shorter man explained.

"You keep screwing shit up and you're gonna be the next one in the lake." The taller man pulled a gun from beneath his jacket and aimed it at Grayson.

"What the hell are you doin'?" the shorter man yelled.

"I oughta shoot you in the head for being such a moron," he answered, "but instead I'm gonna' fix your screw up." He fired a shot into Grayson's right eye. Angel muffled a gasp and felt every muscle in her body tense. She lay low in the weeds and watched as they waded into the water and pulled his body up, letting it slam down onto the black plastic tarp. They wrapped the sides around his body and lifted it from the ground, half-dragging and half-carrying it back toward their car.

Once Grayson's body was in the trunk, both men took out a cigarette and lit up.

"Now my fuckin' suit is ruined," the taller man cursed, looking down at his pant legs and shaking them off.

"So, where we takin' him?"

"Galante turf on the south side," the taller man answered. "We want the Galantes to find him so they know Giovanni is watching."

Angel's heart stalled at the mention of Giovanni. These were his men which meant he must have been the one who had Grayson killed. But why? The front of her forehead throbbed, and her heartbeat pounded against each temple. She had to remain calm and stay hidden until they were gone, she told herself. The best thing she could do was slow her breathing and listen and retain as much information as she could.

As soon as the town car drove off, Angel made a dash through the weeds toward the tank. With shaky fingers she fumbled to get the keys in the ignition and start it up. By the time she got back on the freeway, she was wishing she had a cell phone and promising herself she would never again get rid of one of Andrew's phones.

Several exits down, Angel pulled off at a gas station and used a pay phone to call Andrew at the pub. Despite his initial anger that she had destroyed yet another phone and tracking device, his tone was sympathetic, and he gave her explicit instructions where to meet him. This time, she followed his directions carefully.

"Don't stop anywhere along the way," he told her. "Go to the Streetside Diner and get a booth and wait for me. Don't leave. I'll be there soon."

It was 4:00pm by the time Andrew walked into the Streetside Diner on the North side of town and slid into the booth across from Angel.

"What took you so long?" Angel's voice quivered and she glanced around nervously. "People are staring at me."

Andrew grabbed a napkin, dipped the edge of it in Angel's water glass and handed it to her. "That's because you've got mud caked on your right cheek."

"Oh," she said. She had gone to the restroom right when she arrived at the diner and tried to clean the mud and puke off her clothes. She'd been so focused on getting her shirt clean, she'd forgotten about her face.

Andrew reached across the table and took hold of her fingertips, giving them a tender squeeze.

"I had to shut down the pub. I put a sign on the door that said, 'Temporarily Closed. Will Re-Open Soon.'"

"That should get people talking," Angel mumbled. "I'm already a terrible business owner, and a ho." Andrew gave her a look that said he wasn't tracking with her and she rolled her eyes. "That's what Olga told me."

"Ah," Andrew nodded. "Well, sweetheart, at this point, do you really care what people think?"

Angel shook her head. "I guess not."

The waitress came over and Andrew ordered a cup of coffee and a refill on Angel's. "I need you to tell me everything you can remember."

It was like the floodgates opened and all the emotion that fear had kept penned up, now released. Tears flowed as she replayed the afternoon at the lake for Andrew. She could see the wheels in his mind turning.

"Why did you drive to that particular spot?"

Angel exhaled a frustrated sigh. "You're missing the point of the story. Grayson is dead."

Andrew put his finger to his lips, signaling her to keep her voice down. "Out of all the places you could have driven, why did you go there?"

Angel snapped, "Why is that relevant?"

"I'm trying to understand what happened and how it was that you found his body."

"I'm trying to understand too." He was infuriating and she could feel her blood beginning to boil. "You're focusing on irrelevant details."

Andrew leaned back in the booth. "When you got in your car and left the pub, what caused you to drive to that particular spot? Did you get a call from someone to meet him there? Did you get an anonymous tip to go there for an unknown reason?"

Angel shook her head. "No, I wasn't meeting anyone, and I didn't get a call." She dropped her head. "I was thinking about Tony and that was our spot."

Andrew shot forward in the booth. "What do you mean that was your spot?"

"His family has friends that own the land and Tony was allowed to use the house whenever he wanted. So, that sort of became our special hideaway spot." Angel fiddled with her fingers on the table. "It was where he asked me to marry him."

"When was the last time you saw Tony?"

"The day you dropped me off at the dealership to buy a car."

Angel could see Andrew's mind swarming with theories. "So, it was Tony, not Grayson, who killed Markus Cullato."

Angel nodded. She wasn't sure if telling Andrew was the right thing or the wrong thing, but her options at this point were growing evermore limited. Even if Andrew was a meat-eater, it didn't mean he couldn't be trusted to help her.

"You said earlier that these men by the lake shot Grayson through the right eye?"

Angel nodded. "They said it was a message job to send a signal to the Galantes that they were watching."

"And these men implied there would be another body left on Venito Barone's land?" Angel nodded. "And you're certain they work for Giovanni." Angel nodded again and this time her face scrunched up into a sob and she hid it with both hands. "Don't cry, sweetheart," Andrew said, "we'll get this figured out."

Andrew rapped his fingers against the table and chewed on his bottom lip. "We have to assume from this that Giovanni himself is either in town or on his way in." Angel lowered her gaze to the table and she could feel Andrew's scrutinizing eyes upon her. Andrew leaned in with his forearms on the table, lowering his face and trying to make contact. "You have anything to add to that theory?" She shook her head side to side, avoiding eye contact. He reached up and took her chin in his fingers. "Angel," he spoke with emphasis, "have you seen your grandfather?"

Angel didn't answer but tears filled her eyes.

"I'm going to take that as a yes." Andrew released her chin and sat back in the booth. "You know he's here for revenge and can turn this city into streets of blood. Literally."

Angel sat silent.

"He killed Grayson because he's a Galante. He'll kill other Galantes. Even ones who had nothing to do with your father's murder."

Angel shook her head and uttered, "No."

Andrew threw his hands up. "What the hell do you mean 'no'?"

She grabbed a napkin from the dispenser on the table and wiped her eyes. "I mean, he didn't kill Grayson because he was a Galante. If he killed him, he did it because of me." She shook her head and pursed her lips. "It had to be to protect me."

"You don't know what this man is capable of." Andrew's jaw tightened. "You don't know him."

"Neither do you." She glared at Andrew and felt anger churning in her stomach. "He may want to avenge my father's death, but that doesn't mean he wants to kill a bunch of innocent people."

"He's already killed Grayson, and he had nothing to do with your father's death," Andrew rebutted.

"But maybe he found out that Grayson was supposed to kill me?" Tears ran down around her chin.

Andrew leaned back in the booth and crossed his arms over his chest. He exhaled long and hard and stared at her with concern in his eyes. "I can't convince you so I'm not going to try. Unless you tell me otherwise, I'm going to assume your vehicle came from Giovanni and since he outfitted you for war, I think it's time we get you some weapons training."

This was not what Angel expected to hear. "Weapons training? I've never even held a gun."

Andrew nodded and motioned to the waitress for the check. "There's a first time for everything, sweetheart."

After leaving the diner, they took the long way around town, leaving the tank at an old run-down motel on the south side. If there was a tracking device in her car, and Andrew told her there probably was, then it would appear Angel was somewhere on Galante turf, which would keep Giovanni's boys busy searching. Finally arriving at the vacant strip mall where Andrew had taken her the night they were being followed, he pulled behind the dumpster and turned off the ignition. They sat in silence for a minute while Andrew surveyed the area and made sure they hadn't been followed.

"I'm sorry about Grayson," Andrew said, breaking the silence. "I know he meant something to you." Angel didn't say anything; she just stared blankly at the floorboard. "What I mean is I know you loved him." Andrew stared out the driver's side window as raindrops started to bounce off his car and run down the glass.

"I didn't love him," Angel spoke quietly. "I mean, I think I thought I loved him once." She rolled her eyes and sighed. "I loved how he made me feel and the excitement of being spontaneous. He made me feel wanted and that felt really good." She met eyes with Andrew and then lowered hers back down. "I don't know if that makes sense."

Andrew nodded. "It makes a lot of sense."

She looked up and gave a half smile. There was that all-too-familiar awkward tension growing in her stomach, as a desire to fall into his arms battled against the fear of not knowing beyond a shadow of a doubt if she could trust him.

"Let's make a run for the door," Andrew said, breaking the tension by opening his door and dashing out into the downpour. By the time he got his key in the lock and they made it through the first set of doors, they were soaked. Andrew stopped inside the doors and chained them from the inside.

"Do you really think we need to chain the doors?" Angel was suddenly feeling a flush of claustrophobia, like a rat trapped in a cage. She didn't like the idea of not being able to escape.

"I'm taking extra precautions. We don't know who's following you." Andrew finished locking the chains and proceeded down the concrete steps toward the second set of doors and the room Angel had teasingly called his bat cave.

"Why do you think someone is following me?" she asked nervously. "Did you see someone tailing us?"

Andrew turned and placed both hands on her shoulders. "Sweetheart," he smiled softly, "the Capo Di Tutti Capi outfitted you with a military grade, anti-ballistic vehicle. I have to assume he has men following you." Andrew raised his eyebrows and

200

Angel's heart sank. It never crossed her mind that Giovanni would be tracking her every move.

"That means he knows I was at the lake?" Panic filled her voice.

"Not necessarily." Andrew unlocked the bat cave and motioned Angel inside. "We'll eventually figure out what kind of device he's using and then be able to see how detailed it is."

"But we left the tank across town so he can't find us now." It was a half-statement, half-question laced with underlying concern.

Andrew ushered her into the room. "I don't think we were followed. I'm just being cautious."

The room looked exactly as it had before. Plain white walls, weapons on a table in the corner, a computer and GPS tracking equipment, a small cot in the back corner and Kevlar vests that hung on hooks in the wall. Angel made a beeline to the weapon table and picked up a .22 caliber pistol.

"What's this one called?" she asked, whirling around and facing Andrew with it.

He quickly pushed her hands down and aimed the gun at the floor. "First, you never point a gun at someone unless you intend to shoot them."

"You pointed a gun at me the first night you brought me here. Were you going to shoot me?"

"That was only because you weren't listening to my instructions." He took the gun from her hand. "And, no, I wasn't going to shoot you."

Andrew pushed a full clip into the gun and handed it back to Angel. "It's loaded, so keep it pointed down." Andrew grabbed several guns and ammunition from the table. "We're going to see how well you shoot. Follow me."

They walked outside the bat cave, turned right at the end of the hallway and went through a door on the left. It opened up into a large room with three, fifty-foot steel-lined safety booths designed for indoor shooting. He outfitted her with headgear that resembled old fashioned ear-phones. "First, I want you to just stand there and get a feel for the weight of the gun."

Angel felt the steel in her hands. It was heavier than she imagined. She lifted it with two hands, then removed her left and gripped it tightly with her right. She was strong enough to keep it steady, though she was pretty sure holding it steady and pulling the trigger at the same time would be tricky.

"Okay, come over here," Andrew instructed, lining her up in the booth. "Let's see what you've got."

Angel aimed at the target and squeezed the trigger. It sent numbing chills straight up her arm and into her neck. She jumped back from the power of the shot.

Andrew chuckled. "Not bad, except try to keep your eyeballs in your head this time."

Angel had completely missed the target and was taken aback by the force of the gun. She fired a second shot and a third. This time she hit the target and she jumped up and down with excitement.

Andrew smiled. "Good. Very good." He smirked. "I'm impressed."

They practiced a few more rounds with the .22 then with a .38 and a 9 mm. She didn't get a kill shot with any of them, but at least she hit the target every time, and was feeling undeniably proud of herself.

"Now," said Andrew, removing her headgear, "I want you to take some shots without these."

"Why?"

"Because you won't have ear plugs when you have to use it for real and I don't want you freaked out by the sound."

Angel took aim and fired, and the sound instantly numbed her ears. It felt as if she'd sat directly in front of the speakers at a rock concert.

When they got back to the bat cave Andrew asked, "Which gun feels best in your hand?"

"The 9mm," she answered without missing a beat. "It's my favorite."

Andrew collected the other guns, dropped down their clips and returned them to the table of weapons. "Giovanni will undoubtedly issue you several weapons, if he hasn't already."

"He hasn't."

Andrew turned to her and raised his eyebrows. "When he does, I want to inspect them."

"Why?"

"What you're holding right now is a 9mm Smith & Wesson Luger. It's easy to conceal, accurate and reliable. It holds 10 rounds." Andrew took the gun from her, pulled the clip out and showed her. "Your ammo is JHP or jacketed hollow points, which means the cavity at the nose of the bullet is hollow."

"What does that mean?" she asked.

"It means you have all the knock down power you need without having to actually kill someone." He walked to the table and showed her several different types of bullets. "A ball or full metal jacket enters and exits the body, making two holes instead of one. The hollow point bullet, like yours, is less likely to exit the body."

"If someone's attacking me, why do I care whether the bullet exits his body or not?"

Andrew grimaced at her. "I assumed you would prefer to stop them without killing them or accidentally killing an innocent bystander."

"Oh." The whole thought of shooting anyone made Angel queasy.

"Hollow points have less chance of exiting the body and hitting someone else. They also are less likely to ricochet off something if you shoot and miss the guy, which is a real possibility in your case." The sides of Andrew's mouth curled into a grin and Angel rolled her eyes.

"Thanks for the vote of confidence," she said.

As they drove back to her tank, Angel felt liberated with a new sense of power. She could shoot a gun to protect herself and that gave her a confidence she didn't have before. Outfitted with the 9mm Luger, JHP bullets, a Kevlar vest and a brand-new cell phone, Angel climbed into the tank and followed Andrew back to the pub. He told her he wanted to show her something in the storage room and she was hopeful it would somehow lead them to the Tetterbaum tapes.

As she drove, Angel replayed their discussion in her head and tried to push away the sadness she felt over Grayson's death. At some point she would have to confront Giovanni about it, and she needed to be able to maintain her composure when that time came. *There may have been a good reason he had Grayson killed,* she told herself; but the mere fact that any murder could be justified by a good reason stunned her to the realization that something deep down inside her had changed. She was different now, her eyes were opened to a world she scarcely knew existed before, and there was no going back to the blissful innocence of ignorance. She heard Giovanni's voice in her head, reminding her that "family loyalty comes with great responsibility." Her responsibility was to locate the Tetterbaum tapes and find out the truth for herself. Once she knew what was on those tapes, she could then decide whether or not to turn them over to Giovanni.

CHAPTER SEVENTEEN

Half-way up Wacker Street, Angel's cell phone rang and she fumbled it in the seat before finally answering. It was Andrew.

"You've got a tail," he said, and Angel looked back in her rearview mirror. "Two cars back."

"Are you sure?"

"Positive."

"What do I do?"

"Nothing," he answered, "I'm going to turn up ahead and circle back behind them. Stay on course for the pub. I'll meet up with you there."

Before Angel could speak Andrew disconnected the phone and turned left on the next street. She felt a clamminess rush over her. Then all of a sudden, a ringing sound filled the inside of the car. It sounded like it came from all around her, and she quickly realized it was coming through her speaker system. She scanned her console and found the answer button on the steering wheel.

When she pressed it, a thick Italian accent filled her ears. "Michelangela," the man's voice was unfamiliar to her, "there are instructions in your visor. Tell Officer Venturini goodnight."

Then a dial tone and a woman's automated voice that said, "Your call has been disconnected."

Angel grabbed her cell phone, dialed Andrew and told him about the call. "Read me the instructions in the visor," he said.

She pulled down the driver's side visor and a plain white piece of paper fell onto her lap. Unfolding it, her heart froze at the first line. "If you tell him, he's dead."

"What does it say?" Andrew's voice in her ear grew louder but she couldn't form words to answer him. "Angel, what the hell does it say?"

"It says if I tell you what it says, you're dead." There was silence on the other end and Angel imagined Andrew was as shocked by this as she was.

"Listen to me carefully," Andrew instructed, "and do exactly what I tell you."

"Okay," her voice quivered.

"Whoever you're going to meet will search you to see if you're wired. They're going to take your weapon and your phone, so leave them in the car when you go in."

Angel blurted, "I don't want to go."

"Listen to me and don't say anything out loud," Andrew yelled in the phone. "They are probably monitoring every sound inside your vehicle. The moment we hang up, take the back off your cell, pull out the tiny tracking device and put it somewhere on your body."

"Where?"

"Somewhere they won't find and can't remove."

"Like?"

"Put it IN your body, but don't' swallow it." There was a pause and Angel didn't know how to respond. "It's coated so it won't be destroyed by your body's functions, with the exception of stomach acid. Do you understand what I'm telling you to do?"

Angel quietly grimaced. "I think so."

"I'm turning off route now."

"Okay," her voice hollowed out with fear.

"Whoever this is, they're not going to hurt you. They're bringing you in for a meeting. That's all this is. Just stay calm. Okay?"

"Uh-huh," Angel acknowledged almost incoherently.

"Trust me, sweetheart, I will find you, just put the tracking device in right away."

Andrew disconnected and gave his headlights one flash as he turned left. Then he was gone.

Angel followed the directions on the paper which led her to Capilinos on Rush Street. Capilinos was an authentic five-star Italian restaurant known for some of the best Italian cuisine in town. Reservations had to be booked at least six months in advance and even that was a long shot. Olga swore it was over-priced, but Angel loved it the one time she went there with Tony. She parked on the street three blocks up and entered Capilinos through the staff door at the back, just as the instructions read. Just before the kitchen, to the right, was a narrow staircase that led to a rooftop apartment. From the street level, the outside of the building gave the appearance that the restaurant itself was two-story; with a small, covered deck and two tiny, round metal table and chair sets that overlooked the bustle of Rush Street. Now, Angel knew it was merely a mirage.

She climbed up the staircase and stood face-to-face with a large man that looked like he could easily find employment as the head bouncer at any local hot spot. He was six foot four, bald, had a dark goatee, and shoulders that filled the doorway. It was clear by his stature that no one entered that door without his express permission.

Angel cleared her throat and handed him the instructions she had found in her visor. "I'm supposed to meet someone here," she said.

"Turn around, face the wall, put your arms over your head and spread your legs." He ran his hands over her body from her fingers to her toes, including the private areas that were off-limits to strange men. Then he opened the door and pushed Angel through. "She's clean," he announced, and Angel was glad she had left her gun and phone in the car.

Two heavily armed men approached and offered her a chair, which wasn't worth refusing since they nearly lifted her up and set her down into it. She glanced around the room. It was an office, tastefully decorated, if you like deep red tones and dark browns.

"The boss will be with you soon," one of the men said and the big bouncer closed the door behind them.

Angel sat in the round red cushioned chair in front of the giant mahogany desk and studied the room. Deep red velvet curtains covered the windows to her left which looked down on Rush Street and a red velvet loveseat sat against the wall behind her. Black and White framed photographs adorned the wall behind the desk and to her right, and Angel couldn't help but get up and move closer to get a better look at them. Most of the faces she didn't recognize. They were all older men, dressed in dark suits for the most part, some wore fedoras and some held cigars. Angel was certain they were mobsters. She walked behind the desk and saw a picture that made her breath catch. It was her father and Giovanni, shoulder-to-shoulder with their arms linked and big smiles on their faces. A melancholy warmth filled her, and she touched her fingertips to her dad's face in the picture.

"Michelangela," the voice came from the door and Angel spun around, wide-eyed. He approached her quickly, grabbing her face and planting a small kiss on each cheek. "You look even more like your father in person," he said, stepping back and gazing at her. "Come, sit," he motioned her toward the chair, and she lowered herself into it. He sat behind the giant desk and waved his hand for his men to leave them alone.

Leaning forward and locking his fingers together atop the desk, he smiled and shook his head. "The resemblance is uncanny," he said.

"I've been told I have his eyes," Angel spoke quietly.

"And so you have, and his chin and most certainly his smile."

Angel studied the man behind the desk, trying to read him and ascertain motive. He was short, probably no taller than five foot seven, but stocky in a muscular way. He looked to be in his early sixties and in very good physical shape. He had a receding hairline in the front, and with his hair slicked back his widow's peak was pronounced. His hair was gray and hung to his collar in the back, flipping up slightly. He wore a pin-striped, black suit and an olive shirt that made his green eyes pop like they were emeralds. In fact, they were so bright Angel wondered if he wore green contact lenses.

"You must be wondering who I am," he said.

"It crossed my mind," she replied.

"You have never seen me but I have seen much of you through the years." He opened the bottom desk drawer and retrieved a file folder with the label MMM. He handed it across the desk to Angel. "Go on, take a look."

She opened the file and couldn't believe what she saw. There were well over a hundred pictures of her, from every stage of her life. Baby pictures with her mother and her father. A picture of her at the Yankees game when she was five, wearing her dad's ball cap. Pictures of her dance recital in second grade, the school play in fifth grade, her eighth-grade choir concert, and every high school dance she attended. A picture of every boyfriend she had was in the file, as well as a picture of every random date Olga had set her up to take. There were photos of Olga, the Tetterbaums, Andrew, Antonio, Tony, Grayson and Dr. Manzini. She winced at the pictures of her car accident, the paramedics lifting her from the crumpled car into the ambulance, and the body of the John Doe laying smashed on the street. She swallowed hard at the photos of her draped in Grayson's arms on his front porch.

Tightening her jaw and forcing back tears, "Who are you?" she asked, fixing her eyes on his in a stare that demanded an answer.

"Who I am is inconsequential compared to what I am."

"Okay," Angel shrugged, "what are you? Are you my father's Compare?"

He nodded. "You can say that, as I have certainly been your keeper." He stood up and walked to the front of the desk, leaning his bottom against it and crossing his arms. He motioned toward the folder of pictures. "Clearly you can see I have kept a close eye on you your entire life."

"Why?" Angel interjected. "Did my father ask you to protect me?"

He grinned, as if amused by her, and after clearing his throat, he began to pace around the room with his hands clasped behind his back. "Your father hired me for many things but watching over you wasn't one of them. That was something I chose to do for myself."

"Why?"

"Because I knew one day my hard work would pay off." He opened the red velvet curtains and looked down on Rush Street. "And that day is now. Come look," he said to Angel, motioning her toward him. "Your father was a wise man. We called him Solomon, from the Bible, because King Solomon was the wisest man on the Earth, and your father was the wisest in Chicago."

"I know the story," said Angel.

"Your father took the most prosperous territory when he divided Chitown for the bogatas. Rush Street." He said it as if the name itself held power. "More pizzo flows from Rush Street than many of the other territories put together."

"Pizzo?"

"Juice."

"Juice?"

He grinned. "The money business owners pay for our business and our protection."

"Who took over Rush Street after my father was killed?" She followed him back to the desk. "Who has collected the pizzo for the past twenty-four years?"

He sat down in the desk chair and the bright green in his eyes dulled over with hatred. "Giovanni has come here to take the pizzo from us," he spewed.

The way he said Giovanni's name told Angel everything she needed to know about his feelings for her grandfather. She crossed her legs and leaned back in the chair, resting her elbows on the rounded edges. "So, you alone have been profiting from Rush Street for more than two decades?"

"I have kept the business alive, protected your father's interests and secured a secret life for you." He narrowed his eyes, "We have all been profiting from it."

Angel searched his face, wanting to find something likeable about him; but she saw only a snake. She beheld a dangerous, powerful serpent that had always been looking out for himself under the fake pretense of protecting her. She cleared her throat, "So, what do you want from me?"

"Leverage."

She laughed out loud. "I have no leverage."

He jumped out of his chair and to his feet so quickly it startled Angel and her eyes widened. "You are the granddaughter of the Capo Di Tutti Capi." He leaned down in her face. "You can bring an end to the memory of the massacre that haunts that old man. You are the last Maratinzano in existence and you have the power to convince Giovanni to leave Rush Street alone." He circled behind her chair and placed his hands on her shoulders. "You convince him to back off and I will split Rush Street with you." He walked back in front of her and leaned against the desk. "It's enough money that you'll never have to work a day in your life. You can get rid of the pub, which would make your aunt very happy. In fact," he grinned, "I'll buy it from you right now."

Angel stared at him with her brows narrowed and her lips tight. "I am sure my grandfather is grateful that you have protected the family interests, but if he wants Rush Street, it is rightfully his."

He slammed his fist onto the desk. "It belongs to the people who have kept it safe!" He bent down, placing his hands on the rounded arms of Angel's chair, leaning in closely to her face. She could feel his breath on her cheeks as he spoke. "Giovanni is out of his mind. He wants only to kill more innocent people. He has come here to wage war, but you can bring an end to all the fighting before anyone else dies. You can grant your father's soul permission to finally rest in peace, and you can take claim to Rush Street, because it is more rightfully yours than his."

As he leaned back and moved to the other side of the desk, Angel stood up. "If I convince my grandfather to leave Rush Street in your capable care, what will you offer me for the pub?"

A smile filled his face and Angel was certain pure evil dripped from his eyes. "Name your price."

She crossed her arms. "I'll have to think about it." She stretched her hand out and shook his. "It was nice to finally meet my father's Compare." As he walked her to the door, Angel stopped and looked directly in his eyes. "Oh, I should tell you..." she began and then paused.

"Yes?" he uttered with a sadistic smile.

"I'll sell you the pub but not the Tetterbaum tapes. Those have already been confiscated." The smile fled his face and was instantaneously replaced with a red glow of anger that flushed his cheeks.

"Who has them?" he clenched.

Angel feigned innocence. "I gave them to Special Detective Venturini the moment I found them," she lied. "I just thought you should know before we made a deal, but I'm sure that won't affect the price. I mean," she shrugged, "what would you want with Tetterbaum's surveillance tapes?"

She watched as the color ran from his face and actual fear filled his eyes. She could see the wheels in his head cranking out ideas on how to get his hands on those tapes, and her gut told her, beyond a doubt, he was the fifth buyer to whom Mable refused to sell. Now, all she needed to do was find the tapes and find out why he was so desperate to get his hands on them.

CHAPTER EIGHTEEN

Angel walked to the tank with two large armed men on either side. They might have given her a feeling of security had she not been convinced that they would put a bullet through her head if the Compare ordered it.

She climbed into the tank and sped off; hoping Andrew was able to get a lock on her location and would follow. She drove straight from Rush Street to the pub and parked in the back by the alley and the dumpster. She climbed in the backseat, where the tint on the windows wouldn't allow her to be easily seen and waited. Questions bounced through her head. She couldn't understand how her father ever sought counsel with the Compare nor found him trustworthy. He slithered around that office, drooling murky manipulations that made her insides knot. Maybe he held loyalty to her father at one time, but that loyalty obviously didn't roll up to Giovanni. He was hiding something, something big, and she couldn't escape the feeling that she needed to find the tapes to prove it.

When Andrew arrived and they went into the pub, Angel made a beeline for the bathroom where she retrieved the tracking device, that had slipped down into her underwear, and washed it in the sink. She then changed into a new Tetterbaum t-shirt, one that hadn't been puked on and washed her face with cold water and a paper towel. It had been a stressful day and she felt both mentally exhausted and emotionally drained.

She found Andrew in the hallway by the desk and handed him the tracking device.

He smiled. "Lucky little thing," he said to the device. Angel rolled her eyes and started to walk past him when he stopped her with his arm. "I'm proud of you," he said. "Going into that meeting was scary and you did it." He pulled a piece of hair from her face and tucked it behind her ear.

"It's not like I had a choice." Angel started down the hall toward the storage room and Andrew followed.

"So, what did the Compare want with you?"

Angel whirled around, grabbing the 9mm from the back of her jeans and pointing it at Andrew.

He threw his palms in the air in front of him. "Whoa, what the hell are you doing?"

"How did you know I met with the Compare?" she blurted.

Andrew approached her slowly. "Angel, put the gun down and we'll talk."

"No!" she demanded. "Stop moving toward me and answer my question." Rational thought was gone and emotion was behind the wheel now. Angel needed to know if she could trust Andrew and she only knew one way to find out. "Drop your pants," she ordered.

"What?"

"I want to see if you have the AVCG mark."

"Angel, put the gun down and I promise I will answer any questions you have."

Her hand was starting to tremble. "How did you know I met with my father's Compare?"

"I knew by the location. We've had surveillance on that location for a long time. The minute you walked in the building; I knew who you were going to meet." Andrew inched his way closer. "I also knew you would come out alive."

"Take off your pants," Angel stared at him. She wanted to believe him, but she needed proof.

"We all have the tattoo, sweetheart. Anyone alive during the massacre has been tattooed. It was a unifying mark to show we were against one family having power over the next." He took another step toward her. "Your father's ways weren't accepted here."

"You said my father's idea promoted peace between the families."

"It created boundaries and boundaries were needed, but the fact that he took the most lucrative turf for himself caused greater animosity; not to mention that he took out the Galante boss. When he did that, he unified the families against him."

"You told me only the Galante family was against my father and now you're saying ALL the families were against him?"

Andrew nodded. "The Galantes were the family leading the war against your father's re-structuring of territories, initially. But when he killed their boss, all the families turned against him."

"Why didn't you tell me this before?"

"You weren't ready for it," he answered.

Andrew inched closer and Angel tightened her grip on the gun. "Stop moving closer!" she yelled.

"You're aiming a loaded weapon at a police officer. Think this through Angel." Andrew's voice was eerily calm.

"You're not a police officer." She shook her head side-to-side in quick twitches, "you're a Venturini which is why you're working at the pub so you can get your hands on the Tetterbaum tapes."

"Take a breath and lower the gun to the floor," Andrew instructed.

"Did you kill Tetterbaum?" she blurted.

The question abruptly stopped Andrew from moving forward and he hung his head. "You're off base, sweetheart. You have all this information bouncing around in your mind but you're not putting the pieces together correctly."

"Then you tell me, if it isn't to get the tapes, why do you work here?"

Andrew didn't answer. He leaned against the wall and crossed his arms over his chest.

"I want the truth," Angel screamed. "I want the whole truth!"

Andrew spoke low and calm. "I'm going to walk into the storage room where there's no surveillance. You can either shoot me or join me inside, the choice is yours."

As Andrew moved toward her, Angel backed into the storage room, keeping the gun aimed at him. He turned on the light and closed the storage room door. Then he pulled a crate from one of the shelves and sat down. "No, I didn't kill Tetterbaum. Yes, I'm here for the tapes, but as a cop first."

"So, you were placed undercover to find the tapes? How did you even know the tapes existed?"

"This pub has been a mob hot spot for decades and because of its unique history, Tetterbaum didn't pay pizzo. He didn't need protection. No organization in their right mind would pull anything on the Tetterbaums because in an unspoken way, the pub belonged to all the bogatas." Andrew took a deep breath. "And when something attracts that much bogata attention you can bet the police are watching."

"You're not answering my question. How did you know there were tapes?"

"Tetterbaum got greedy. He went to the families and threatened to expose what was on the tapes if they didn't pay him."

"He blackmailed them?"

"Yep, which is why he wound up dead," Andrew answered.

Angel stared at Andrew. "Do you know who killed him?"

"Nope, but I think we can figure that out if you put the gun down and we find those tapes."

Angel's heart was racing. She wanted to trust him, but she wasn't convinced. "What happens to me after we find the tapes?"

"That's up to you." Andrew shuffled his feet and looked up at Angel.

"What does that mean?" Angel was entering panic mode. "What does that mean?" she screamed. "Does that mean I do what you say or you kill me?"

"Sweetheart, you have to make a decision whether you're going to trust me or you're going to kill me because this standoff is wasting valuable time."

He was right, their conversation was going nowhere. She had to focus on the facts and fact number one was that Andrew had done more to help her than anyone else. He knew all along she was a Maratinzano and could have easily taken her out if that was his plan. *Think it through,* she told herself. *Calm down and think.*

It unnerved her to know Andrew was serving up portions of the truth when necessary and not giving her the whole story. Still, he was there with her and for her at every turn. Maybe certain aspects of his police work were confidential, and it kept him from being able to confide in her, or maybe he didn't think she could handle the whole truth at one time; similar to how she felt about Olga. Whatever his reasoning, he was right; she needed to make a choice. She couldn't stand here all night holding him at gunpoint.

Angel exhaled and lowered the gun. "I'm sorry," she whispered.

Andrew stood up and wrapped his arms around her, sliding the gun from her hand and placing it in the back of his jeans. Maybe one day I'll follow that order and drop my pants for you," he teased. "Until then, let's focus on the tapes." He walked to the far, left corner of the storage room. "I have something I want to show you."

He bent down to peer through the shelving when his cell phone buzzed. He answered and Angel could see in his eyes that someone on the other end was telling him something he didn't want to hear. "Get over there right away," he instructed. "I'll meet you there." Andrew disconnected the call and took Angel by the hand. "This will have to wait," he said, pulling her out of the storage room and toward the back door.

"What's going on?" she asked.

He stopped short of the back door and turned to face her. She could see dread in his expression. "There's been a break in," he paused, pulling the 9mm from the back of his jeans and handing it to her, "in your apartment."

Angel took a deep breath. "Is Olga okay?"

"We don't know anything yet. My men are on the way." A deep sour pit hit her stomach and Angel felt like she would pass out right there on the spot. She grabbed her stomach and could feel fear drain the life from her insides. Andrew placed his hands

221

on both sides of her face and forced her eyes on his. "I need you to be able to drive your car there. Can you hold it together and do that?"

Angel nodded.

When they arrived at the apartment, two police cars were already out front, and cops were inside. Angel jumped out of the tank and ran up the steps behind Andrew.

"Any sign of Olga?" she hollered to the cop standing in the doorway.

He shot a glance to Andrew, who nodded, which Angel surmised was giving him permission to speak freely in front of her.

"Near as we can tell sir, a syringe was used to sedate someone and take them offsite," the officer explained.

Angel entered and saw the top to the syringe lying on the floor by the door, next to the potholders. Police tape made little squares around the items as evidence to what may have occurred, but Angel was forming her own theory. She walked into the kitchen and saw the fresh baked bread and manicotti, and tears filled her eyes.

Andrew crept up behind her. "This is good news sweetheart," he said. "Whoever they were, they took her for a reason. If they wanted to kill her, they would have done that here."

"She was baking when they showed up. She probably just took the manicotti out of the oven and that's why the potholders were still on her hands and fell off by the door." Angel's voice was in monotone, as her mind disconnected from her emotions long enough to conduct an analysis of the scene.

"Olga opened the door, at least a little bit, which could indicate that she knew the person who knocked…" Andrew began, but Angel interrupted him.

"Or it shows that she always opened it a crack because she was too short to see through the peep hole."

"That would explain the mark in the center of the door where someone kicked it open," Andrew added.

"What about the syringe?" Angel's teary eyes found Andrew's and pled for information.

"Whoever took her probably assumed Olga would be easier to transport asleep, so they sedated her and carried her out."

"Did any neighbors see them?" Angel asked.

"We're checking for witnesses," one of the officers responded.

"Who called it in?" Angel asked.

"It was an anonymous caller," Andrew said and shrugged. "It happens a lot in this town. People want to help but they don't want to get involved."

Angel glanced around her apartment. It was torn to pieces. The couch cushions were sliced open, and the stuffing was pulled out. The couch was turned upside down and sliced through the back and the bottom. Every mattress was destroyed. Drawers were emptied and tossed across the room. They literally left nothing unturned. Angel walked back to her bedroom and stood in a daze, unsure of whether to scream obscenities or burst into tears. Her computer was shattered, her bed destroyed and the clothes from her drawers were thrown all over the floor.

Andrew followed her down the hall. "Why don't you pack an overnight bag and come to my place tonight until we get this mess figured out." She nodded and he entered his address into the contact listing on her phone. "Plug it in your GPS," he said, and slipped a key in her hand.

"Aren't you coming with me?"

"I need to handle some things here, but I'll be there shortly." He winked at her. "There's food in the fridge and some wine on the counter." She leaned in and gave him a hug. Take a hot shower and go to sleep. I'll tell you when I get home."

Angel opened her closet door and was startled when Midnight popped out from the top shelf, followed by Mo, who peered over the shelf, as if to say, "Is it okay to come out now?" Angel swept both of them up in her arms and hugged them tight, tears running down her cheeks. *If only Olga were hiding in the closet too*, she wished. Before packing her things, she took both cats to her neighbor's door and asked Mrs. Wallace if she could keep them for the night. Mrs. Wallace was a widow who had several cats of her own. She was a wiry woman, thin as a rail, with the roundest brown eyes Angel had ever seen. Of course, they looked bigger through her glasses than they actually were. Angel guessed her to be around Olga's age, though she looked older because her skin hung in layers of wrinkles over her protruding cheekbones.

"Are you in some sort of trouble, dearie?" Mrs. Wallace squinted over the top of her bifocals and stared at the police.

"No," Angel exhaled, "not in the sense that you mean."

Mrs. Wallace leaned in close and scrunched up her face. "Are you going to the slammer?"

Angel couldn't help but crack a smile. "No, nothing like that." Without going into detail, she explained that someone had broken into her apartment and trashed it.

"Did they steal anything?" Mrs. Wallace asked, her eyes widened.

Angel swallowed. *Olga*, she thought, but didn't say it aloud. "Not that I can tell. The place is a mess though."

"Scum bags," Mrs. Wallace scowled. "This city's going to hell in a hand basket."

Angel gave Mrs. Wallace a bag of cat foot, the litter box and both cats and promised she'd be back in the morning to pick them up. Then she kissed Midnight and Mo on their furry little heads and left.

Walking across the lot with a duffle bag in hand, Angel looked over at Bessie parked in her usual spot and choked back tears. *God, please keep Olga safe, wherever she is,* she prayed in her mind, *"and help me get her back."* Angel had just climbed into the tank and started the ignition when the phone rang through the speakers, causing her to jump and drop her cell phone to the floorboard by her feet. She leaned down to retrieve it and hit her head on the steering wheel. Deciding to leave the cell phone on the floor, she pushed the answer button on the steering wheel.

"Hello?" she hollered into the air.

"Michelangela," came the gruff, thick accented voice of Giovanni.

"Yes," she answered, breathless and shaky.

"Where are you? You must come to me right now."

"I can't grandfather, my home has been broken into and…" she stopped herself from mentioning Olga.

"You need to bring me the tapes," he said.

"I don't have the tapes. I haven't found them yet." There was a pause and what sounded like dead-air. "Giovanni?" Angel asked, "Are you there?"

225

"I have been misinformed." There was disappointment in his tone. "Go to Heavenly Towers and use the key on your key ring to let yourself into the penthouse. Tell no one where you are going. I will be in touch soon."

The line disconnected and Angel bent down, ducked her head to the side of the steering wheel and retrieved her cell phone. She started the ignition and punched Heavenly Towers into the GPS. As she made a right out of her apartment lot, Tony dashed in front of her car, slamming both palms on the hood. Angel shrieked.

Tony ran to the passenger side and jumped in. "Drive," he said, but Angel sat stunned, staring at him. Tony raised his voice. "Drive!"

Her foot hit the gas and she squealed forward, heading north toward the pub. "What are you doing here?" Angel was breathless with surprise.

"I told you I'd be in touch, babe." Tony gave a half-hearted smile and focused his attention on the side view mirrors.

"Why do you keep staring out the window and checking the mirror? Who are you looking for?"

"Just drive the car, babe."

"Drive it where?" Angel glanced at Tony and for a brief second their eyes met. She saw fear in his face and felt concern tug her heart. "You can trust me with the truth," she told him. "Whatever it is, I can handle it."

"I need Tetterbaum's tapes," he said.

That wasn't what she expected to come out of his mouth at the moment. *You and everyone else,* she thought. "Why do you need them?"

"Because my life depends on it." Tony looked out the window. "Literally. And so does yours."

"What are you talking about?"

"Remember when I told you I left to save my ass and I came back to save yours?"

Angel nodded.

"Well, I'm back to saving mine again," he said.

"Was that supposed to explain something to me because it didn't," she replied flatly.

Tony told her to take the freeway and head out of the city. "When we were engaged, I didn't know who you were, and then one night my father called me to his office for a meeting and he told me you were Joseph Maratinzano's daughter." Tony ran his hand through his hair. "I gotta tell you, babe, I didn't believe him at first, but he had pictures of you with your dad and copies of your real birth certificate."

Angel's mind hung on the last sentence, and she felt her mouth go dry. The only person she knew of that had a copy of her real birth certificate was Olga.

"I was expected to take care of it but I couldn't," he said.

"You mean you were told to kill me?" Angel couldn't believe she was asking Tony that question.

He nodded. "When I couldn't do it, they sent someone who could."

"And what happened?" Tony gave her a look and she knew the answer. Tony had killed him before he ever reached Angel.

Tears filled her eyes and she reached over and squeezed his hand. "Thank you," she whispered.

"There's more." He took a deep breath and exhaled, and Angel noted in her mind how worn down he looked. "After I killed him, I had to cut a deal, otherwise they'd just take us both out. If I agreed to disappear entirely from your life, they would let me live; and if I found the Tetterbaum tapes and turned them over, they would let you live."

"So, you have to trade the tapes for my life?" she asked.

"Babe, I need to know where those tapes are." His tone pleaded and his expression begged.

"I don't have the tapes," she admitted.

Tony smashed his fist on the dashboard and cursed. "This isn't just about my family anymore. They've got all the families ready to take you out. The only reason you're still breathing is because they think you might be the only one who can locate the tapes."

"Why would anyone think that?" she asked.

"You bought Tetterbaums. The Galante's sent in Grayson to find out what you knew. The Cullato's placed Antonio there to get the tapes from you and sent Markus to take you out when they thought Antonio could get the tapes without your help. The Venturinis have had Andrew in place since before Tetterbaum even made his threats."

"And the Andriachinni's have you," Angel added in monotone. Fear gripped her. *The facts*, she told herself, *focus on the facts.* "Who told your father who I was?"

Tony stared out the window. "Your father's Compare."

Angel felt a pit in her stomach. She knew she didn't like that snake. "And you think he is the one who leaked my identity to all the families?"

Tony shrugged, "It makes sense."

"I met him tonight above Capilinos on Rush Street. He asked me for the tapes."

"What did you tell him?" Tony asked.

"I told him I had already turned the tapes over to Andrew."

Tony grinned, "Good thinkin' babe, that should cause quite a shit storm."

Angel smiled. She was getting pretty good at this lying stuff. She silently scolded herself, *lying is bad; unless it's to save your life, or the life of someone you love, and then it's okay.* The more she thought, the more she realized a blanket of protection could cover a multitude of sins, like lying and even murder.

As they drove, Angel filled Tony in on how Grayson killed Antonio in the cellar near Tetterbaum's surveillance monitors and how she'd found Grayson's body this afternoon in the lake.

"Somebody's orchestrating this whole thing, and one by one, taking us out." Tony's voice was rattled with panic. "It's down to me and Andrew."

"Nobody's going to take you out," Angel said, gripping the steering wheel and hoping she was right.

"He's playing us all against each other." Tony spoke as if he were thinking aloud and the story was just now coming together in his head.

"Who is?" she asked.

"Your father's Compare."

"That snake," Angel spat.

"He gave me the information so I could take out Markus Cullato. He must have given Grayson the information to take out Antonio. Giovanni took out Grayson for him, leaving me and Andrew." Tony exhaled. "I haven't been given any information to take out Andrew, so that probably means Andrew has a contract on me."

"Stop talking like that," Angel scolded. "Nobody is taking you out." Silence filled the tank and fear gripped her heart.

"What were you doing at the lake?" Tony asked, breaking through the silent tension.

Angel shrugged. "I was just thinking."

"Thinking about what?"

"A time when life was a lot easier," she said, exhaling. "A time when I thought I was going to marry you and have babies and a family. A time when everything was normal." Her voice tapered off as she tried to stifle the emotion.

"Babe, I'm sorry I left you, but I didn't have a choice." He took her right hand up to his lips and kissed her fingertips. "I didn't want to leave."

"I know. It's just that everything's different now," she said softly.

Angel's cell phone interrupted the moment and she released Tony's hand and answered. It was Andrew and he was several cars behind. "My tracking device tells me you're headed out of the city and not to my house like I instructed," he said flatly.

"Um, yes, there's been a change of plans," she stuttered.

"Where are we headed?" he asked.

"I'm taking Tony somewhere."

"Tony!" Angel could hear the alarm in Andrew's voice. "When did Tony show up?"

"When I left my apartment," she replied. "He says there's one man he can trust and who might be able to tell us who took Olga." Tony gestured with his hands for her to not tell Andrew where they were headed.

"I'm coming with you. Pull over at the next exit," Andrew ordered.

When Angel got off the phone and told Tony about Andrew, Tony was livid. His face turned bright red and Angel thought he was going to spontaneously combust. "Didn't you hear anything I said? He's probably following us to take me out!" he yelled at Angel.

"I know he's a meat eater and he's probably paid off by the Venturini family to keep some of their indiscretions quiet, but I also know I can trust him. I KNOW he isn't going to kill you." She pulled off at the next exit and put the tank in park. "He's coming with us."

Tony's jaw tightened. He pulled a .22 from beneath his shirt and checked the clip. "If I see one thing I don't trust, he's dead."

Angel swallowed hard. Maybe putting these two in the same vehicle wasn't the smartest idea. It certainly wreaked havoc on her emotions, as at random intervals she wanted to kiss and hit both of them.

Andrew pulled over and ran to Angel's driver's side door. "Leave the tank and get in my car."

"Why?" Tony blurted.

"Because they're tracking this one," Angel and Andrew answered simultaneously.

"Who's tracking you?" Tony's face flashed with angst.

"Giovanni," Angel answered softly. "I'll fill you in from Andrew's car."

Andrew drove and Tony and Angel sat in the back.

"This car isn't outfitted like Angel's," Tony noted.

Andrew looked in the rearview mirror and nodded. "She drives a tank."

Turning to Angel, Tony said, "Tell me about Giovanni." By the time she filled him in on her meeting with Giovanni, they were arriving at the gravel road which led to the lake.

"You sure you can trust the Therapist?" Andrew asked.

"I trust him more than I trust you," Tony quipped. "He's a long-time family friend. He and my dad go way back."

"And what do you hope to find out here?" Andrew asked.

"Anything he knows about the Tetterbaum tapes. If he's heard who took Olga and where they're keeping her. Anything to help bring an end to this." Tony sighed. "He's well connected. He'll have answers or he'll know where to get them."

Andrew's tone was skeptical. "Even if he has information, what makes you think he'll share it with you?"

"Like I said, he's a long-time family friend."

Andrew killed the lights and pulled the car off the road behind a clump of trees. "We'll leave it here and go on foot toward the house," he said.

"This isn't a covert op," Tony sarcastically spewed as they got out of the car and walked to the back, where Andrew opened the hatch, displaying several rifles and guns. "You're just dropping me off at a friend's house for a few minutes."

Andrew leaned into Tony's face, "He's not my friend and neither are you, so I'm playing it safe." Andrew clicked a fully loaded clip into his .22 then threw a rifle over his shoulder. "Angel, you got your 9mm?"

"Yep," she grinned and caught Tony's expression of shock out of the corner of her eye.

"You hate guns," he said to her.

"Not so much anymore. I'm getting used to them."

They crept closer to the house where two large men, armed with military grade Uzi's guarded the front door. Andrew whispered to Tony, "Does your friend always have armed guards at his door?"

Tony shrugged, "I've never seen guards here before." They lowered themselves into the bushes. "Let's cut back and go around the house from the lake side. There's some big windows in the back and maybe we can see what's going on inside to warrant bouncers."

They all agreed it was a good plan and began the trek through the tall weeds. As they neared the lake, Angel's mind drifted back to Grayson and she tried to push the mental images of his dead body out of her head. What was once a peaceful place of serenity was now corroding her senses with sadness and rage.

They crouched in the weeds while Andrew looked through the scope of the rifle. "It doesn't look like there's anyone guarding the back."

"Do you see anyone inside?" Angel asked.

"We need to get directly behind the house to see in the windows. I can't see anything from this angle."

They crept further behind the house where the tall windows were in plain view and the house was lit up. Andrew looked through the scope and cursed. Then he handed the rifle to Tony, who looked through it and mumbled, "Santo cazzo."

"That means holy shit," said Angel. "I remember that phrase." It was one of the first Italian phrases Tony taught her when they dated.

Tony and Andrew shot each other a glance. "You tell her," Tony said.

"Tell me what?" Angel blurted.

Andrew handed her the rifle scope and Angel peered through it. She gasped, "That's Olga on the couch!" She lowered the scope and looked at Andrew and Tony. "What is she doing here? Was Venito the one who trashed my apartment and took Olga? Or maybe Olga just came over for dinner and wasn't even there when my apartment was ransacked?"

Andrew put his fingers over her lips. "Shh," he said, "we already know Olga was taken from your apartment by force."

Anger enveloped Angel. She started to stand up and Tony and Andrew both reached up and yanked her down by her blue jeans. "We have to go get her."

"Not like this," Andrew said.

Angel looked at Tony. "He's right, babe, we have to figure out what's going on and then decide the best play."

Angel raised the scope back to her eyes and watched Olga sitting on the couch. Her heart welled up with emotion and she handed it back to Andrew. "I can't look."

Andrew peered through. "Here comes the Therapist," he said, detailing his movement. "He's talking to Olga."

"Let me see," said Tony, grabbing the scope. "Yep, that's Venito. I don't think Olga's in any harm; they look to be having a friendly conversation."

"That doesn't jive," said Andrew, "we know Olga was taken by force. The syringe was left on the floor."

"Or someone wanted it to look like she was taken by force," Tony mumbled, and Andrew shot him a glance.

"Let me look," said Angel, taking the scope from Tony. Her heart began to pound rapidly in her chest. "Omigod, that's the Compare."

"What?" Andrew grabbed the scope. "No, that's the Therapist."

"No, it isn't," Angel demanded. "That's my father's Compare, the man I met with above Capilinos restaurant."

Andrew looked through the scope again. "Are you positive that's the man who identified himself as your father's Compare?"

Angel nodded. "I'll never forget his face. Bright green eyes, slicked back gray hair that flips up just slightly at his neck..."

Tony cut her off, "She's describing Venito."

Andrew cursed. "Let's get out of here and regroup. I gotta mull through this in my head before we make any kind of move." He looked at Tony. "You don't still want to go inside, do you?"

"Nah, I'll pass," Tony said.

"What about Olga? We can't just leave her there!" Anger flashed in Angel's eyes, and she could feel her face flush.

"Babe," said Tony, "Olga is fine. Venito isn't going to hurt her."

"How do you know that?" Angel moaned.

"Because for all we know they're working together." The words stung her ears and she pushed Andrew for saying it. "All I'm saying is they both have a reason to want to put the screws to Giovanni."

Tony inched his way ahead of them. "I got a bad feeling about leaving your car there too long. Let's get out of here and discuss all this someplace else."

"I can't leave her," Angel cried.

"I know what you're feeling, babe," Tony grabbed her hand, "but sometimes leaving is the only choice you have." That sentence hit home for him, and Angel knew it. She slumped her shoulders and followed.

Andrew led them back through the tall weeds and to the car with Angel in the middle and Tony bringing up the rear.

By the time Andrew dropped Tony and Angel off at the tank, they had developed a plan. Angel was to drive straight to Heavenly Towers and wait for Giovanni, who was probably already there. Andrew was going to lead a search of the room above Capilinos restaurant since they knew Venito wasn't there now; and Tony would take the rifle and survey Angel and Giovanni from the building across the street.

"Just remember to open the curtains when you get into the penthouse," Tony told her. "I won't have a shot if I can't see what's happening."

"You're not going to shoot anyone," Angel argued.

"I'm not planning on it, but if you're in danger, I'll do what needs to be done." Tony leaned down and kissed her on the neck and chills darted up her back. It had been a long time since she felt his lips against her skin.

When Angel arrived at the penthouse level and exited the elevator, Giovanni's men greeted her with a quick pat down. They collected the 9mm from her jeans and took her purse and cell phone. One man waited with her in the hallway, while the other took her belongings inside and gave them to Giovanni. When she was finally ushered in, she was amazed at the size of the suite, surmising it was at least two times the size of her entire apartment. A large dining room table sat directly ahead, with six chairs. To the immediate right sat the kitchen and further to the right was a sitting room and double doors that led to a master bedroom with a Jacuzzi tub. Another bedroom jetted off from the sitting area. Beyond the dining room table was a wall of windows and long burgundy draperies pulled shut. To the left was a living room with a white stone fireplace, a long floral-patterned couch and a big armed chair, where Giovanni sat.

"Come, sit with me," he said, motioning Angel over. Turning to the men at the door he waved his hand. "Ci lasciano ora," he said, and they immediately left. He looked at Angel and smiled. "Where did you acquire your weapon?"

"From a friend," Angel answered, afraid to say his name.

"Is this the same friend who tracks you?" He held up the tracking device that had been removed from her phone.

"Yes."

He nodded and pursed his lips together. "Nobody tracks my granddaughter." He clenched his jaw.

"Grandfather," Angel spoke nervously, "I need to tell you what's happening now because I don't know what to do and I need your help." She could feel the words coming out quickly and tried to calm herself down so she wouldn't ramble at him.

Giovanni's eyes softened and he motioned with his hand. "Tell me."

Angel took a deep breath and began the story. She started with Tony and how he called off the engagement because someone had leaked her identity to his family. She explained every detail, how Tony killed someone sent to take her out, then agreed to leave but came out of hiding and killed Markus Cullato to save her life again; and how his family was forcing him to find the Tetterbaum tapes and trade them for a guarantee of her long-term safety. Giovanni's jaw tightened.

She moved on to Andrew and told him how he taught her about her father and the massacre of her family, and how he helped her with the pub after the car accident; and gave her the gun and showed her how to use it.

Giovanni nodded his head, "I know well of his father Joe Venturini and his influence in the massacre."

"But Andrew isn't his father," Angel protested. "Andrew has done nothing but help me."

When she mentioned Grayson's name, hate filled Giovanni's face. "Grayson was a Galante!" He growled. "We do not tolerate any association with the Galantes."

Angel lowered her head and fought the lump rising in her throat. "I know you killed him. I saw your men take his body from the lake. It's true that he was a Galante and was supposed to use me to get the tapes and then kill me, but he didn't. He was my..." she stopped, once again puzzled to find the right term to define Grayson. She slid off the couch and onto her knees in front of Giovanni. "Grayson killed Antonio Cullato to protect me, and when someone ratted him out to his own family, he tried to fake his own death to escape his bogata for good."

Giovanni waved his hand in front of his face. "Bah," he grumbled, "you trust too many people who are untrustworthy."

She rose from her knees and crossed to the window, pulling back the curtains and opening the doorway to the balcony. "And you trust no one."

"Michelangela," he called after her, "come inside this once and draw the curtains."

"No," she answered flatly, and she could see the shock of her indignation in his eyes. She imagined no one had ever talked back to him.

"Si entra ora," he yelled and his men quickly entered. He pointed at Angel and spoke through clenched teeth, "Portare suo in qui e sedere lei giu'." Both men approached Angel, picked her up beneath her armpits and carried her back inside, plunking her down on the couch. They then closed the patio door and drew the curtains.

"You have got to stop that," Angel spat.

"You are untamed and undisciplined, like your father, trying to change tradition. Look where that got him. Things are as they are and those who try to change the rules end up dead." Giovanni leaned back in the chair. You must learn from your father's errors."

"That's just it…" Angel leapt to her feet, "…my father didn't die because he made errors, he died because he was betrayed and I think I know who was behind it."

"I'm listening," Giovanni said.

"Andrew mentioned that there was a man who had been watching over me my whole life and he called him my father's Compare. When I asked him to set up a meeting with the Compare, Andrew said he wasn't the sort of man you scheduled a meeting with. He said the Compare contacts you. This has bugged me because I always had the feeling that Andrew had never seen him in person either. That was confirmed tonight when we were all at the Therapist's house and the man I saw was the Compare I had met with earlier, but to Andrew and Tony he was Venito Barone."

It was as if fire flew forth from Giovanni's eyeballs and his face lit with anger. "Venito Barone!" he seethed. "What were you doing on the property of Venito Barone?"

Angel knelt next to his chair and touched Giovanni's hand. "Grandfather, you must calm down so I can tell you all the details."

"Si, si," he nodded his head and patted the side of her cheek. "Go on."

Angel told him about receiving the phone call in her car from Venito and meeting him above Capilinos restaurant. "He led me to believe he was my father's Compare and showed me pictures he had taken through my whole life."

Giovanni interrupted her. "You could not receive a phone call in your car, that line is heavily protected. No one has that number but my people."

Angel stared in his eyes. "Then one of your people isn't loyal because Venito called me on the phone in the car you gave me."

Giovanni's jaw tensed and he mumbled words in Italian that Angel didn't understand.

"I have a theory but I don't have proof yet, Angel said.

Giovanni waved his hand as if to say proof was irrelevant. Tell me this theory."

"When I read about my father's murder, the paper said he was killed by a car bomb in an alley off Rush Street. I started to wonder why my dad would have driven alone and parked his car in an alley alone if he indeed was as hated by all the other families as people say he was." Angel stood up and paced in front of the fireplace. "This has bugged me because my dad took great precautions to keep me and my mom safe, so why would he be careless about his own safety?" She snapped her fingers.

"Then it hit me, the only way he would have gone alone is if he knew there was no danger and if he were meeting someone he trusted; like his best friend or Compare." Angel faced Giovanni. "I think he wasn't hated in Chicago for his peace project. I think he was viewed as a hero here because he put an end to the chaos and the fighting. I think Venito Barone killed my father's Compare, and then posed as his Compare to betray my father by spreading rumors to taint his reputation and ultimately setting up his murder." It was a mouthful and Angel took a deep breath. "I think Venito single-handedly fueled the massacre." Angel sat down on the couch. "I think Venito had the Galante boss murdered, and he framed my dad, knowing the Galantes were a bunch of unruly hot-heads who would seek revenge."

Giovanni tapped his fingers against the arm of the chair. "Why? For what purpose? What does he gain?"

Angel narrowed her eyes. "First, he gets the ultimate revenge on you for killing his brother, Lorenzo. Second, he gets the pizzo from Rush Street, which is the most lucrative section."

Giovanni raised his eyebrows and Angel took that to mean she had struck a chord of truth along the way. "Rush Street was allowed to remain in the hands of your father's Compare until which time I either sent someone to rebuild in Chicago or you were of age and interest to take ownership."

"Have you ever met my father's Compare in person?" she asked.

"Bah," Giovanni waved his hand in the air, "I had him checked out but meeting in person was not necessary. He was the trusted chosen of your father, which was good enough at the time. He was loyal to your father for many years."

"His real Compare probably died loyal and Venito stepped in without anyone knowing." Angel got up and paced in front of the fireplace again. "That was the beauty of his plan. He knew no one could identify the Compare because of the stone secrecy of that relationship. Also, no one ever meets face to face with the Compare so he didn't have to worry about seeing people. He could take over his identity from behind the scenes and no one would know the difference."

Giovanni piped in, "Except one person."

They both said it together, "Tetterbaum."

Angel felt wiggly worms in her stomach, telling her they were on the right track. "Tetterbaum figured it out which is why he contacted you and no one else. Andrew thought Tetterbaum blackmailed all the families for money, but he didn't; Venito did." Angel gnawed on her bottom lip. Whoever your leak is must have told Venito that Tetterbaum was going to meet with you, and Venito had him killed before he could give you the tapes."

Angel walked to the window and pulled open the curtains. "We need to leave these open."

Giovanni narrowed his brow. "You have a shooter?"

"Yes, I have a friend across the way with a rifle. If something goes down, he needs a clear shot." Angel picked up her 9mm from the table, slid the clip in until it clicked and shoved it in the back of her jeans. The steel was cold against her skin. "Do you have a gun grandfather?"

Giovanni lifted a .22 pistol from the side of the chair. "Si."

She knelt by his chair. "I have to go and meet up with Andrew and see if we can find the tapes. I was going to request one of your men come along but it isn't safe now." She sighed. "Will you be okay here?"

He smiled at her and patted her cheek. "I am the Capo Di Tutti Capi; you should not worry yourself for me."

Angel studied his face and his tired expression reminded her of Olga. "Grandfather," she spoke softly, "there's one last thing I haven't told you." She took a deep breath. "Venito has Olga."

She saw the hate roll up in his eyes and tension stretch his joules as he spewed forth Italian words Angel was certain were unfit for her ears.

"She's okay for now and we'll get her back," Angel said, trying to convince herself as much as him. "Is there a way I can reach you directly? A number I can call that is safe?"

Giovanni pulled a cell phone from the inside pocket of his jacket. Angel punched the number into her phone and kissed him on the cheek. As she got up to leave, Giovanni said, "What do you expect to find on the tapes?"

Angel grinned. "My fathers Compare, the real one. I think he met with my father at Tetterbaums, which will prove his true identity. I also think Venito was sloppy in the beginning and put out the contract on the Galante boss at Tetterbaums. I think that's why he wants the tapes so badly."

Giovanni's thin lips curled into a smile. "You have your father's smarts."

CHAPTER NINETEEN

Angel eyeballed both of Giovanni's men on her way out; trying to see if she could sense which one was the traitor. She couldn't. She got back in the tank and drove to the pub to wait for Andrew. Once inside, she locked the back door and started to move items from the shelves in the storage room. Whatever Andrew was going to show her before his phone interrupted them; it was located somewhere between the shelving to the left of the door. When she had moved all the storage items from the shelves, she stood back and stared. Nothing jumped out at her. There were no odd markings on the wall. No discoloration and nothing unusual about it. It looked exactly like the rest of the stone walls throughout the storage room.

Angel wasn't strong enough to move the actual shelving but got down on her hands and knees and peered through the bottom shelf, running her fingers along the wall. She started by the door and ran her fingers over every stone. Then she rose to the second shelf level and did the same. When she got to the far corner, she felt it. It was a tiny draft of air seeping through a small section of the wall. She ran her hands along the back wall, which was an outside wall and would more logically have a draft coming through it, but there was no draft there. The air was coming from the interior wall that divided the hallway from the storage room. Angel ran her hand up, but the draft was located only around the cracks of one stone. It wasn't coming in higher or lower or from either side. Her adrenaline ignited at the realization that she was onto something.

The back-door slamming jolted her from her thoughts, and she whirled around to see Andrew staring at her.

"I found the draft," she blurted, holding her hand up next to the stone. "But I think we'll need a crowbar or something to wedge the stone out."

Andrew grinned and held up a crowbar. "One step ahead of you, sweetheart."

They had to dismantle the far section of shelving before Andrew could get a good angle to wedge the crowbar against the stone. He stuck the crowbar in the crevice of the grout and pulled back several times, but the stone didn't budge.

"I thought it would come out easier," he said, out of breath.

Angel's mind was already moving in a different direction. Maybe the air coming through the stone was nothing more than an accidental crack in the molding and not a sign of anything relevant. Her mind manufactured questions. What would cause a crack in the molding in that particular stone but not in any of the stones around it? If it's an interior wall, where is the draft of air coming from?

Angel left the storage room and walked down the hall, stopping at Mr. Tetterbaum's desk. All of a sudden, his words rang through her ears, "It's the best place for me to hear everything that happens in the pub while I manage my receipts."

A cold chill ran up the back of her neck. *The desk*, she said in her mind. The desk sat against the wall that divided the hallway from the storage room. It sat directly on the other side from where the draft seeped through the stone. Angel leaned against the left side of the desk and tried to push it away from the wall, but it wouldn't budge. She went to the right side and tried to shove it as hard as she could, but it was stuck. She stood back and stared at it. It looked like a normal, wooden desk, with three drawers on the left side, a long thin drawer in the middle and three drawers on the right side. The top was shaped like a roll down, but without the roll down lid. It had lots of little compartments for envelopes and pencils and receipts.

Angel lay down on her back on the floor and looked up underneath the desk. She could now see it was bolted to the floor and to the wall, which explained why she was unable to move it. It would be a huge task to unbolt it, but she couldn't escape the feeling that somehow the desk was the key to finding the tapes.

While Andrew was still trying to wedge a stone loose in the storage room, Angel pulled out every drawer from the desk except the bottom drawer on the left side which seemed to be stuck. Then she got down on her knees and pulled at the last drawer with all her might. It would open but wouldn't slide all the way out. She jerked it several times, trying to muscle it free. Finally, laying down on her back and looking up under the desk she saw two tiny metal hooks, keeping the drawer in place. Her heart sped up as she unhooked both sides and slid the drawer out of the desk. Behind the drawer was a hole in the wall. It looked as if one of the rectangular shaped stones had been removed. Angel poked her arm through the hollow drawer space and into the hole and felt a cool draft. She hollered excitedly for Andrew to bring the crowbar and he came running.

"Holy…" he began.

"I know," she said, cutting him off. "We need to unbolt the desk and move it out of the way."

Twenty minutes later the desk was moved and Andrew used the crowbar to remove several stones from the wall so they could poke their heads through the hole. Retrieving flashlights from the storage room, Andrew lay on his back with his head through the hole and shone his light upward, while Angel lay on her stomach with her head through the hole and shone her light downward. On the inside of the wall ran a bundle of wires. They ran from as far down as they could see and ran up the wall past their heads.

"Do you think the wires are leading from the surveillance equipment to whatever device is recording it?" Angel's voice was almost breathless with excitement.

"It would make sense," Andrew muttered, "but how would Tetterbaum have gotten to the recording device if it's hidden between the walls?"

Angel shone her light all around the space. "Maybe it's not hidden in the walls. Maybe just the wires are and we need to follow the wires to find the tapes."

"How are we going to do that? Scale the walls like Spiderman?"

Angel grinned. "You ever been rock climbing?"

Andrew grimaced, pulled his head back in from the hole and shook it. "Sweetheart, I probably can't even fit between the walls and there's nothing to get a foothold or a grip on."

"There has to be a way," she insisted.

"Yes, but this isn't it." Andrew stood up. "We're ignoring an important fact. Tetterbaum was old. The tapes have to be somewhere hard to find but easy to get to."

Angel leaned against the wall, breathing out and letting her mind fill with thoughts. "Has anyone ever seen an actual tape?" she asked.

"I don't know, why?"

"What if Tetterbaum was bluffing? What if he never recorded anything and the surveillance equipment was just to give the appearance of monitoring what goes on in the pub?"

Andrew shook his head. "That's a lot of money in equipment to be bluffing. Besides, he blackmailed the bogatas and got himself killed over it. He had to have had some sort of physical evidence to be a big enough threat to the families."

Angel wasn't ready to tell him her theory about Venito being the one who blackmailed the families. "We don't know which family killed him right?" she asked.

"It's inconclusive. Nobody's taking credit yet," he replied.

"Maybe that's because it wasn't one of the families," she said, laying back down and peering through the hole. "Hold my ankles."

"What are you doing?" Andrew grabbed her ankles and Angel slithered on her back through the opening and then raised herself to a sitting position. "We don't know how far down that goes," Andrew warned.

"Just don't let go." Angel shone her flashlight all along the stone wall above the opening, running her hand along each rock and dipping her fingertips into every crevice. "Andrew," she said loudly.

"Yep?"

"I'm going to stand up, just keep your hands on my ankles."

"No," Andrew gasped, "don't try to stand."

"I have to. Just hold me." Angel bent her knees and slid one leg at a time through the hole, balancing her toes in the opening and leaning her bottom against the back wall to the storage room. She shone the light all over the wall, unsure of what she was looking for, but searching intently, nonetheless.

"Please be careful," Andrew said.

All of a sudden, the light caught something silver above her. "I see something," Angel gasped. "I have to climb up a little higher."

"You can't climb up, there's nothing to stand on and nothing to catch you if you fall."

Angel's hands were beginning to shake. She knew Andrew was the voice of reason, but she felt so close to finding the answers that she didn't want to quit. She stretched her body as high up as she could and shone the light. She could see a metal hook that the bundle of wires wrapped around and then jetted off to the left, back through the stone wall.

"The wires don't go all the way up," she hollered to Andrew. "They go to the left, back inside the pub."

Finally convincing her it was too dangerous to try and climb, Andrew helped pull Angel back through the hole. "Think," he said, pointing to her forehead, "the wires lead to something, something that Tetterbaum had to be able to reach himself." Andrew set the stones back in place to cover the hole. "This can't be the right path."

Angel felt discouraged. "I know the tapes are here," she clenched. "I can feel it."

Andrew kissed the top of her head. "I know you can."

They reassembled the desk drawers and went into the kitchen for a drink and a snack. It was past midnight and Angel was starving. Munching on some chips, she leaned against the stainless-steel preparation table in the middle of the room and faced the row of sinks, industrial dish washer, more stainless-steel tables and the large walk-in cooler. All of a sudden, it hit her. She was facing the kitchen wall that backed up to the back of the bar. She stared at the wall and her excitement grew. She ran to the cooler, threw open the door and stepped inside, analyzing everything in her view, and pulling on each shelf. They were solidly bolted to the walls of the cooler. She came out and closed the door, then moved to the industrial dish washer, opening it and banging on the inside and back walls. Solid.

"What are you doing?" Andrew asked, with a tone half-mocking her.

Angel answered without stopping. "There's an interior wall," she said. "Tetterbaum had the pub renovated years ago and he put in an interior wall here between the kitchen and the bar."

"How do you know that?" he asked.

"Because there's no noise." Angel whirled around and stared at Andrew. "How many times have you worked the bar alone and leaned against the back of it?"

He shrugged and said, "All the time."

"Have you ever heard the noise of the dish washer or felt vibrations from the cooler running, or heard the clanging of pots and pans?"

Andrew narrowed his brows. "No, I guess not."

She smiled. "That's because he had an interior wall built to separate the kitchen from the back of the bar."

"That's probably a pretty normal thing to do," Andrew threw up his hands. "You can't hear the kitchen noise in most restaurants."

"Exactly," Angel blurted. "So normal that no one would think it odd."

"So, you think he hid the tapes in the wall?" Andrew followed her as she darted from the appliances to the sinks, tugging on everything. "I think you've lost all rational thought, sweetheart. Let's call it a night." Andrew reached for her arms, but Angel pushed him away and scowled.

"I know we're close. I can feel it. There's got to be a crawl space or some way Tetterbaum got in. The wires lead back in this direction. We just have to find the opening."

Andrew threw up his hands as Angel dropped to her knees and lay down on the floor, peering up underneath the row of stainless-steel sinks and countertops. She moved down the row, touching everything and tugging at it. *There has to be a way in,* she told herself. She started knocking her knuckles against the floor, listening for a difference in sound.

"Angel, I really think we should call it a night," Andrew pleaded.

She ignored him and continued knocking and listening. When she got to the far corner, to the last stainless-steel table, she heard it. It was a hollow answer to her rapping fingers. Wedging her way across the bottom shelf of the stainless table next to it, she reached over and ran her fingers across the floor behind the steel legs. Her fingertips stopped on a tiny metal lever. She tugged at the lever and then realized it twisted in her hand. *Righty tighty, lefty loosey,* her mind chanted and she spun the lever to the left. A loud clicking sound stopped her and she crawled out from beneath the table. She looked at Andrew and then placing both hands on the stainless table she pulled on it. It immediately tipped toward her on hinges from beneath the floor. Andrew dove to help her lower it to the ground. There, beneath the table was a crawl space, ingeniously hidden and just big enough for a grown man to slide into.

They stepped down into the hole, Andrew first and Angel close behind. It dipped down beneath the kitchen wall and then back up to a room hidden between the back of the bar and the kitchen. The space wasn't wide but ran the full length of the bar and was lined with thin wooden shelves, filled with video and audio tapes of every shape and size. Each tape was labeled with a date, and some held a short description, usually consisting of a bogata family name. The bundle of wires they had seen earlier ran through what looked like a vent opening and dropped down to a device Angel assumed was the recorder.

Angel's eyes took interest in a box of old photographs she found on the bottom shelf, and she knelt down and began to pull out pictures and read the notations on the back.

Andrew looked in awe at the shelves of tapes. "I can't even begin to imagine the amount of evidence that's on all of these," he marveled.

"I don't care about the rest of the tapes," Angel said, "I just need to find one where Venito put out a contract on the Galante boss, or on my father or on his Compare," she said. "All I need is a picture of my dad's real Compare."

Andrew funneled through the tapes. "I bet what's on these could take a lot of people down."

Angel glanced up. "That's why we're not turning any of them in."

"What?" Andrew stared down at her.

"I don't want to cause more violence. I just want to prove my dad was innocent of killing the Galante boss and that Venito is to blame for everything."

"Sweetheart, this is criminal evidence, some of it could bring closure to investigations that have gone on for decades."

Angel lowered her eyes back to the pile of pictures resting on her lap, "I just want to restore my family. I don't want to take anybody down." She could feel Andrew's gaze on her as she filed through the photographs, desperately hoping to find a picture of her father and his Compare.

They worked in silence for several moments, Andrew looking at the tapes and Angel filing through pictures. "Weird," Andrew blurted out of the blue.

"What?" Angel stood to see what he was talking about.

"The tapes start over twenty-eight years ago, most of them audio tapes." He pointed to the handwritten dates jotted on each tape. "And they stop a year and a half ago," he pointed to the date, "the day you came to work at the pub."

"How do you know the exact date I started at the pub?"

"March 3rd," he said with a shrug, "I remember because it was my birthday."

"I started on your birthday?"

"Yep, don't you remember Tetterbaum teased that you were my birthday present?" Andrew grinned, and the memory came alive in Angel's

253

mind. "You were still reeling from Tony leaving so that's probably why you don't remember."

"I remember now," Angel said. "It just feels like that was forever ago." Angel sunk back down to the floor and back to the pile of pictures. "Wait a second..." she stood back up. "...did you say the first tape was over twenty-eight years ago?"

Andrew nodded and handed it to her.

"So Tetterbaum started surveillance on the pub around the same time my father moved to Chicago and he stopped when I started working here."

Andrew squinted his eyes. "Yeah, that's a pretty weird coincidence."

"Somebody put him up to it." Angel snapped her fingers. "The Compare."

"I'm not keeping up here and I'm usually ahead of the game." Andrew raised his eyebrows as if to say *what the hell are you talking about.*

"My dad's Compare hired Tetterbaum to be his eyes and ears so he could know what was happening behind the scenes as my father rolled out his peace project," she explained.

Andrew narrowed his brows with a skeptical expression. "Why?"

"The Compare was a recluse; even Giovanni never met him in person. No one had except probably Tetterbaum." Angel paced back and forth in the tiny area, thinking out loud. "Which meant Tetterbaum was trusted by my father and the Compare, which is how he knew who I was before I even knew. So, when I showed up to work here, Tetterbaum probably assumed I was sent here from Giovanni." She was rambling, but the pieces were falling together in her head so quickly she was getting excited.

"Why would he assume that?" he asked.

"The Compare had Tetterbaum install surveillance as a method of protecting my dad."

Andrew leaned against the shelves and crossed his arms over his chest. "Okay, say that's true, then why did Tetterbaum continue recording everything after your dad was killed?"

Angel bit her lip. "Because Tetterbaum didn't know the Compare was killed too. He probably kept recording, waiting for the Compare to show up again. When he finally realized he was not coming back for the tapes, he contacted Giovanni to give him the evidence."

"This is a lot of speculation," Andrew said.

"But it makes perfect sense now," Angel insisted. "I must have shown up to work here around the same time Tetterbaum contacted Giovanni, so he naturally assumed I was sent here." Angel stopped and stared at Andrew. "Somehow Venito found out about the Tetterbaum tapes and killed him before he could give the evidence to Giovanni." Angel twisted her fingers together. "That leak must have come from whoever Venito has on the inside of Giovanni's organization."

"Either that or the fact that Tetterbaum got greedy and blackmailed every bogata in Chicago," Andrew added.

Angel shook her head. "No, Venito killed Tetterbaum and then HE blackmailed the bogatas himself. I know it."

"How can you know that?" Andrew's skepticism danced in his eyes.

Angel shrugged and sat back down by the pile of photographs she had left on the floor. "I just know."

"Well, that won't hold up in court," Andrew said.

"We're not taking it to court. We're taking it to Giovanni and the other four bosses."

An hour later they climbed back through the crawl space and into the kitchen, reassembling the stainless-steel table and twisting the tiny lever tight. She had found what she was looking for, two photographs of her father, Mr. Tetterbaum and a man she was certain was the Compare; and three tapes, all marked "Therapist", and all dated around the time of her father's murder.

Andrew draped his arm around her shoulder and gave her a smile. "Let's go back to my place and get some sleep. We can go to my bat cave in the morning and see what's on these tapes."

Angel felt tempted, as exhaustion was settling in. "We have to get Tony. He's probably still staked out, watching Giovanni's penthouse," she said.

Andrew nodded.

"And I want to see what's on these tapes now," she added.

"Patience isn't a virtue you possess," Andrew teased.

"No, but I have other virtues to make up for it." Angel tilted her head and gave a flirtatious smile.

Andrew grinned.

CHAPTER TWENTY

Andrew fastened the Kevlar vest around Angel and pulled it tight. "You ready for this?"

"Of course, she's ready," Tony blurted.

Angel exhaled. "I think so," she said.

"Remember," Andrew instructed, "you make the exchange and get yourself and Olga out of the building as quickly as possible." Andrew took her chin and angled her head up so he could look in her eyes. "We have to assume Venito thinks you still believe he is your father's Compare. He thinks you are bringing him the tapes as a peace offering, to cut a deal on the Rush Street pizzo, and to ask for his help in getting Olga back alive." Andrew slid his hands to her cheeks and gently held her face. "Don't tell him you know who he is. Just play along and get yourself and Olga out of there."

"What if he doesn't bring Olga with him?" she asked.

"We've already got that covered," Andrew replied.

"What do you mean?" Angel moved his hands away from her face and threw her hands in the air, gesturing frustration. "What does that mean? Why do I always have the feeling that you're withholding information?"

"Because he is," Tony quipped.

"Not helping," Andrew spewed at Tony, who chuckled.

"Sweetheart, I can't tell you everything we're lining up here. It's too complicated and it will give you too much information to mess up." The second that sentence left his mouth, Andrew knew it came out wrong.

"Whoa," Tony gasped, putting his palms in front of him and backing up. "I wouldn't want to be in your shoes right now."

"That's not what I meant," Andrew said sheepishly.

"Yes it is," Angel snapped. "You think I'm stupid and I'll blurt out information that I shouldn't, so you feed me baby spoonfuls of everything instead of giving me the overall picture to work with." She rolled her eyes and scowled. "I get it."

"It's for your protection," Andrew explained.

Angel stormed across the room and stood staring out the window at the building she was about to enter. She bit her lip. Nerves were starting to wreak havoc on her confidence and her stomach was knotting into uncomfortable lumps of worry.

Tony walked by and slapped Andrew on the chest, "Way to go."

"Shut up," Andrew sneered.

Tony snapped a clip of rounds into the rifle and pretended to take aim. "We'll have you covered, babe," he said, walking over to Angel and giving her a wink.

She nodded. "I know."

"Don't be scared," he said, wrapping an arm around her neck and letting it hang over her shoulder. "I won't let anything happen to you." Angel leaned against him in silent acknowledgment of the fact that she knew, if it were in his power, Tony would protect her. A part of her worried things wouldn't be in his control and that was the scary part.

Andrew interrupted the moment, pulling Angel away from Tony and running a wire up the back of her vest. "As soon as you're out, we'll move in," Andrew explained to Angel, and then looked over at Tony. "You got that hot shot? We wait 'til they're clear before anything goes down."

Tony checked the rifle scope. "I got it."

"Remember," Andrew said, "we'll be listening so if you move from the original meeting place, make sure your whereabouts are loud and clear."

"Venito is going to have me searched and they'll remove the vest and the wire," Angel said.

"Probably," Andrew answered. "But I'm hoping the vest will distract them and they'll miss the wire altogether."

Angel's mind was frozen with fear, but she was also excited to nail Venito. She couldn't wait to set the record straight on everything that occurred twenty-four years ago. Thanks to Tetterbaum, she had all the evidence she needed to clear the Maratinzano name.

Andrew continued talking. "Once you and Olga exit the building…"

Angel cut him off. "You and Tony will get Venito." She touched Andrew's hand, "I know. We've been over this a million times."

Andrew nodded. The fact that he looked nervous was making Angel that much more afraid. Andrew motioned to Tony. "Are the bosses in place?"

Tony pulled out his phone, did some fancy finger movements on the keypad and gave Andrew a nod. "It's show time."

The meeting was to take place in the building directly across the street. To the average person, it looked like an old, abandoned hotel on the south side of town. From the outside, the building appeared dilapidated; but one step through the heavily bolted doors and it was clear this place was a regular meeting hall for mafia members aware of its existence. It was a place only the bosses used and only the big-time meetings were held here.

Andrew had arranged the meeting with the supposed Compare, explaining to him that if he could locate Olga, who had been mysteriously kidnapped, he would give Angel back the Tetterbaum tapes to exchange them for Olga. Venito jumped at the offer and arranged the meeting without hesitation. Now, all Angel had to do was follow the instructions.

She entered through the back door of the building, which led her down a narrow hallway of what used to be hotel rooms. The walls were dingy yellow and the carpet bright red with a three-dimensional square design running throughout. The plan was for Angel to meet the Compare in what was simply called, "The Meeting Room." She was to arrive alone which didn't seem fair, as she was certain Venito would have his armed thugs in tow.

When she reached the double doors marked with a gold-plated sign that read, "Meeting Room," she was amazed to find there were no bodyguards. She pulled open the oversized cream-colored door and stepped inside. The room was the size of a small banquet room, designed to hold no more than fifty people. There were round tables and red cushioned chairs set up. At the back of the room was a long chain of five rectangular tables, with two chairs at each table. The chairs faced outward, overlooking the rest of the room. The walls were golden in color with cream colored crown molding. Three chandeliers hung from the ceiling and were dimly lit. The carpeting was the same deep red with three dimensional squares as in the hallway. Angel stood, taking it all in and wondering why no one was there to meet her.

"Michelangela," came a loud voice over what sounded like an antiquated sound system.

She glanced around the room, locating the speakers in the ceiling. "Yes?" she answered into the empty room.

"Walk through the door to the left of the tables, pass through the kitchen and take the last door on your right. It will lead you to a hallway. Go to room 146."

Angel's heart beat rapidly as she hurried through the door and into the dark kitchen. This wasn't part of the plan and she wondered if Andrew had picked up any of it through her wire. Emergency lighting from the ceiling gave enough of a glow that she could weave her way through the kitchen and find the last door on the right. Her palms clammy with fear, she pushed the door open and entered a hallway that looked exactly like the one she had walked down before. She slowed her pace as she approached room 146, trying to hide the panic she felt certain was seeping through every pore. She twisted the knob and the door opened.

Olga jumped from the bed and waddled quickly to her, hugging her tightly around the waist. "My Angel," she gasped.

Angel threw her arms around Olga but kept her eyes on the rest of the room. "Where is he?" she whispered.

"Merciful Heavens, how should I know?" she sighed. "He's an absolute madman."

Angel's nerves were on high alert as she let go of Olga and dashed around the room, opening the closet, checking under the bed and peering into the bathroom. There was no one else in the room.

"It's a trap," Angel said aloud. "He knows."

Olga stared at her blankly. "He knows what?"

"We've got to get out of here," Angel sputtered, pulling off her jacket and removing the Kevlar vest. "Come here," she said to Olga, draping the vest over her head and fastening it around her."

"It's heavy," Olga moaned.

"I know, but I need to get you out of here." Angel's hand shook as she helped Olga put the jacket on and zipped it in the front.

Angel pulled the 9 mm from the back of her jeans and opened the door.

Olga startled. "Angel May, you have a gun?" She grabbed her chest. "Merciful Heavens, what has happened to you?"

Angel rolled her eyes. There was no time to answer that question. The hallway was clear, and she took Olga by the arm and led her down the hall, away from the kitchen. They followed the emergency exit signs to the far end, but the door was chained shut.

Think Angel, her mind chanted. Then it hit her. "We have to go back the way we came," she said aloud.

"Okay," Olga shrugged, and they headed back down the hall, passing room 146 and through the door into the kitchen.

All the while, Angel's mind was churning to process what was happening. *Maybe he doesn't know I know he's really Venito which is why he took me to Olga first, knowing I would set her free and then meet with him alone. He couldn't have me and Olga in the same room because she knows him as Venito and I know him as my father's Compare.* Angel didn't know if her theory was correct, but there was only one way to find out; and that was to get Olga to safety and come back to meet with him.

Dragging Olga toward the outside door on the back of the building, where Angel had originally entered, Angel whispered in her ear, "Go straight to Andrew and Tony." She pointed to the adjacent building.

"Tony?" Olga gasped.

"Go, hurry," Angel said, pushing her through the doorway and closing the door behind her.

She took a deep breath and headed back down the hallway to the Meeting Room. This time, there were two men waiting for her at the cream-colored doors. She handed them her gun and stood still while they patted her down.

"She's clear," said one of the thugs and opened the door.

Angel entered and saw Venito, sitting at the center of the long line of rectangular tables. She approached him slowly, feeling anger rise and trying to squelch it down with a fake smile. "This was your father's chair," he said. "The Maratinzano table was in the center." He motioned to the left with his hand, "Andriachinni and Venturini to the left" then motioned to the right, "Galante and Cullato to the right." He stared at Angel with a steely glare. "I trust you retrieved your aunt without difficulty?"

"Yes," Angel answered almost breathlessly. "Who kidnapped her?" She tried to feign ignorance but could see the spark of knowing in Venito's eyes. He didn't answer her question.

"And you have brought me the tapes?" He sat back down and motioned for her to sit across from him, but she remained standing. Angel pulled the three tapes from her pocket and set them on the table. "Only three?" he asked.

"They are the only ones that concern you." It took all the self-control she could muster not to jump across the table and strangle him.

"And how did you decide which tapes would concern me?" He folded his hands on the table, making the rings on his fingers stick out, and he stared at her with deadened eyes, like a shark.

Angel drew in a deep breath, aware that the next sentence she spoke may very well be her last; but even if it was, justice had been served. In the building right across the street were all the bosses and Giovanni, watching the real tapes, learning that Venito Barone was the real killer of the Galante boss and the man who single-handedly caused the biggest mafia massacre in history. Angel shifted her weight and pursed her lips together. Her mind told her to stall for time, to allow Andrew and Tony to come to her rescue; but her heart wanted to burst with the truth of what a murdering snake he is.

"Is something wrong Michelangela? I see fear in your eyes." His calm control taunted her and she could no longer contain the rage boiling in her veins.

"And I see an imposter in yours," she seethed.

An evil grin filled his face. "You are a smart young thing, aren't you?" he said and rose from his chair. "But not smart enough." He reached in his pocket, pulled out a phone and pressed one button. Seconds later his thugs entered and stood blocking the doors. "Here you are," he began walking around the rectangular tables to the same side on which Angel stood, "so frail, so weak, unarmed and all alone."

"I'm not frail and I'm not weak," she seethed, glaring at him, "and what makes you think I'm alone?"

"Trust me," he slithered, "whoever you arrived with has already been taken care of." He took his finger and rubbed it up her arm from her elbow to her shoulder. "If you were smart, you would have teamed up with me." He circled around her, talking closely in her ear. "I would have given you more wealth and power than you could ever dream of. We could have run Rush Street together." He stood behind her and ran both hands slowly down the sides of her arms.

She whirled around, pushing his hands away. "I would never be with you. You're a lying, cheating, murderous snake." It felt good to say it to his face. Antagonizing Venito was probably not the smartest move, but it felt good.

He snapped his fingers and motioned for his men and within seconds Angel was lifted from her feet and carried out through the kitchen door, back down the hall to room 146. They dropped her on the bed and Angel shot up to a sitting position. "Why do you work for that weasel?" she yelled, but they just looked at one another and laughed.

They duct taped her wrists together, and then put a piece of tape over her mouth. She kicked and screamed momentarily, but it was no use, she couldn't break free and even if she could, they'd stop her at the door.

"Have fun," one thug mocked as they left the room.

A few seconds later Venito entered with his men in tow. "I can take it from here boys," he said, "but I promise to save you some leftovers."

Angel heard the men chuckle and the door close. Venito approached her and she'd never felt more repulsed. He pushed her from a sitting position onto her back, then sat down on the edge of the bed and wiped the hair from her forehead and cheeks. "You are such a lovely woman," he said in a voice that sounded eerily sincere. "It would be a shame to crush such a beautiful vine," he paused momentarily, lifting her hands to his mouth and licking her fingers, "without tasting its fruits first."

Angel shook her head and tried to scream, but the tape was too tight against her lips and muffled the sound. A pit in her stomach deepened and hardened with a rage unlike anything she'd ever felt. She started to kick her legs but Venito pulled out a small knife. "Hold still," he said and grinned. "I don't want to accidentally cut you."

Angel's eyes widened with terror as fear quickly replaced the rage. He took the knife and cut up the middle of her shirt, slicing it in half and nicking her chin with the blade.

"Oops," he said with a laugh, as a trickle of blood ran down her neck. He grabbed her bra and sliced through the center of it, pulling it to the sides and displaying her breasts. He threw the knife to the floor and pulled at her jeans until they were around her ankles. "Now," he seethed at her, "this is for my brother." His piercing laugh rang in her ears as she closed her eyes and braced for what would happen next.

She didn't hear the shots Tony fired, nor see Andrew enter the room, and put a bullet through Venito's head. She only felt Venito's body lift slightly from her and fall to the floor in a heap. The rest was a blur, a slow-motion haze of movement. Andrew pulled her to a standing position, ripping the tape from her lips, while Tony cut her wrists free and pulled up her jeans. She was in a daze, aware of what was happening but in a surreal place of being unable to respond. Tony took off the flannel shirt that hung over his t-shirt, and he and Andrew maneuvered her arms into it, buttoning up the front. Though they spoke to each other, neither of them spoke directly to her, as if they knew shock had taken her mind to a far away place.

Tony dabbed the cut on her chin with a wet towel and told Andrew it didn't need stitches. Then they set her back on the bed and dragged the thug's bodies into the room, throwing them on top of Venito. Tony collected Angel's 9 mm and shoved it in the back of his jeans, then scooped Angel up over his shoulder and carried her out in the hall, while Andrew locked the door and placed a call advising someone to come clean up the mess. Angel dangled over Tony's shoulder half-way down the hall, before the shock finally wore off and emotion gripped her. She burst into sobs and shook uncontrollably.

Setting her down, Tony hugged her close to him. "He's dead, babe. That son of bitch is dead," he said through clenched teeth.

Andrew leaned down and took Angel's face in his hands. "Look at me, sweetheart. We got there in time. You're okay."

"How did you know where to find me?" she whimpered, wiping the tears as quickly as they were falling.

"Olga," they said in unison. Relief filled her chest. Angel nodded her head up and down, trying to suck in air and push away the memory of the fear she felt. Olga was safe and they had gotten there before Venito could abuse her and Venito was dead. Justice prevailed. Angel forced her mind to concentrate on those facts and she began to breathe easier.

"We've got to take care of one more thing," Andrew added.

267

She knew what he meant. They still needed to expose the traitor in Giovanni's organization. "How will we know which of his men is the traitor?" she asked.

Tony grinned, "I bet the bastard's eyes are gonna pop out of his skull the minute he sees you walk into the room."

Andrew agreed. "Yeah, I think he'll give himself away."

They left the old hotel and walked across the street into the building where the bosses and Giovanni were meeting. Angel paused outside the door and took a deep breath. She looked to Tony, who gave her wink and a grin; then to Andrew who smiled and gave an affirmative nod of his head.

"The hard parts over," Andrew said, "this is the good stuff."

Olga had been sitting in a chair outside the door where the bosses were meeting. She jumped up and waddled over when she saw Angel. She gave her a tight squeeze. "You go in there and show them what my Angel is made of." She patted her cheek. "Your father would be so proud." Olga gave Angel a teary-eyed grin. "Merciful Heavens, you've got me blubbering like a fool," she giggled. "I need a good stiff drink."

"Me too," Angel said.

"Maybe a couple of them," Tony added.

Thunder boomed outside and Angel took in a deep breath and exhaled slowly and deliberately as she opened the door and stepped inside the room. It was important to show nothing but calm and confidence.

It felt as if her world went into slow motion, as Giovanni rose to his feet, followed by the four bosses, all applauding. They had no idea the ordeal she'd just been through and how great the urge to burst into tears tugged at her, but she swallowed back the emotion. Giovanni blinked slowly at her and nodded his head, then drew his fingertips to his lips, kissed them and threw the kiss toward her. A smile inched its way across her face as relief swept her heart. For the first time in her life, she felt she belonged.

She was so caught up in the moment that she almost forgot about the traitor. Scanning the room, she met eyes with each thug from each family, all standing along the exterior walls. Every boss had arrived with at least one man, some with two. Giovanni's men were also present but stood in closer proximity to the table than the others.

Giovanni motioned for Angel to sit in the vacant chair at the opposite end of the table, directly across from him.

"I believe you all know my granddaughter," Giovanni began.

"Grandfather," Angel said abruptly, "Venito is finito," she said with a smirk that made some of the bosses chuckle under their breath. "But there is one more matter we cannot overlook."

"Ah, yes," he uttered with a nod "you are correct." He motioned with his hand and his men stepped forward. "Give me your weapons," he said to them. Both men looked shocked, but one immediately handed his piece to Giovanni and the other paused. *Tony was right,* thought Angel; *his eyes are bugging out of his skull.* When both weapons had been surrendered, Giovanni instructed his men to follow Tony and Andrew for questioning. Andrew escorted the men out but Tony remained at the door, with his eyes on Giovanni.

Giovanni addressed the four bosses. "There is a traitor among my very own. In keeping with our new policy of joint respect, may I have your vote as to the elimination of my problem?" Giovanni cleared his throat. "All in favor say yea." As the Capo Di Tutti Capi, Giovanni didn't need the vote of the bosses, it was a mere gesture to show that from now on each family would be viewed as equally important and stand on equal ground.

A resounding "yea" filled the air and Giovanni nodded to Tony, who then quietly left to join Andrew. Just like that, the fate of a traitor was sealed. With a simple "yea" a life would end and one of them, Tony or Andrew, would be the one to end it. Still, it felt strange to watch five men calmly decide to murder someone, and then proceed on to the next item of business, as if it were perfectly normal. Angel studied their faces and it became undeniably clear, that for them, this was business as usual.

"Michelangela," Giovanni raised his eyebrows, "I do not believe you have had the pleasure of meeting the bosses." He stood and pointed to each one, giving a short introduction. Angel stood and shook hands with Joseph Venturini, Vincent Galante, Charlie Andriachinni, and Carlo Cullato. Irony filled her as she extended her hand in peace to each man, most of whom had, not too long ago, attempted to have her killed.

As they sat back down, Angel shifted in her chair. "Giovanni," she spoke loudly, "with your permission, I have a few things I would like to say." He gave a nod of approval and Angel rose from her seat. Though she hadn't had time to rehearse this speech, she had played it over and over in her mind, unsure if the day would ever come when she would actually articulate the words. She pursed her lips and swallowed hard. "I didn't know if I would live through this day," she confessed. "I realize that may be a normal feeling for some of you, but it's very new to me." Some of the bosses nodded and smiled. "Now that you have all seen the tapes, you know that my father was not responsible for killing the Galante boss or for the massacre years ago. You know that his intent was only to bring peace, that his motives were honorable and that he wanted prosperity for every family, not just his own." Some of the bosses lowered their eyes to the table and others nodded in agreement. Angel made mental note which was which.

She continued, pacing around the table as she spoke. "I know this has been a day of awakening for some of you, but you must understand that I have believed in my father's innocence and fought for it all along." Angel drew in a deep breath. "So, it is a day of vindication for me." She ignored the clearing of throats and continued her speech. "I don't have to tell you that there are many sins in this room; but I am here to tell you that those sins have died with the past." All eyes were on her now. "Aside from the three tapes you watched this afternoon, all the other Tetterbaum tapes and pictures have been placed in a secure location that will not be opened without just cause." Several bosses murmured. "My father has been vindicated. I have murdered the past and am offering all of our families a new day with a clean slate." You could hear a pin drop as they waited in breathless anticipation of what she would say next. Angel looked at Giovanni and raised her eyebrow. "The past will no longer control our lives."

Returning to her seat and folding her hands atop the table, she said, "Now, down to business. I will be taking control of Rush Street which is the territory my father partitioned off for the Maratinzano family." Giovanni looked at Angel and grinned, pride beaming from his eyes. "In addition, I will continue ownership of Tetterbaum's Pub, but all of the surveillance equipment within and around Tetterbaums will be dismantled and removed. From this day forward, it will be nothing more than a pub where each of our families will be welcome to dine at any time."

Silence filled the room.

"One more thing," Angel said, raising her finger in the air. "I know my name is Michelangela, but I'd really like it if, outside of these meetings, you would call me Angel." When she finished, deafening silence filled the room, and she could see the mind of every boss processing her words. Glancing around the table, her eyes met with steely glares from some and curious stares from others; but Angel didn't care. She had made no threats, but rather stepped into a position of power and filled her father's shoes. Their expressions confirmed what she had already come to accept. The Maratinzanos were back and she would be a force to be reckoned with.

When the meeting ended, Giovanni invited Tony, Andrew, Olga and Angel to his penthouse apartment for an authentic Italian meal. "Like mama used to make," he said to Olga, but she threw up her hands and waddled off, mumbling something in Italian.

Giovanni looked at Angel and rolled his eyes, which made Angel grin. "Give her time," she told Giovanni. "Olga's a stubborn one, but she'll come around."

Back at the Penthouse, Angel stood in the doorway of the kitchen, clutching her glass of red wine, and secretly listening to Olga and Giovanni fight over the meal.

"Merciful Heavens," Olga spat. "I can make a better sauce than this."

"Bah," argued Giovanni, "this is mama's recipe."

"Don't you bah me, you old buzzard," Olga argued, ranting something in Italian to which Giovanni responded back in Italian.

Tony crept up behind Angel and draped his arm over her shoulder. He listened to Olga and Giovanni and his eyes widened.

Andrew sneaked up on the other side of Angel and grinned as he listened. "They sound like children," he said.

"What are they saying?" Angel asked.

"I'm not repeating it," said Tony.

"Let's just say it isn't fit for a lady's ears," Andrew added with a grin.

Angel sighed. "Do you think they'll ever get along?"

"Not in this lifetime, babe," Tony quipped.

"I wouldn't hold your breath, sweetheart," Andrew joked, patting her on the shoulder in a teasingly sympathetic way.

Sitting around the table, Giovanni lifted his glass of red wine and stood. "I would like to propose a toast to my granddaughter, Michelangela May Maratinzano, of whom I am both proud and pleased. May we all have her strength, her depth of love and her forgiving spirit." He raised his glass higher, then lowered it back down and took a big sip.

The thunder crashed outside and Angel smiled, basking in the warmth of family. For the first time in years, she felt she was home. The only thing that could have made it better was if her father had been dining with them, but she was certain by the thunder and dazzling display of lightning, that he was watching from above.

After the dishes were cleared and cleaned, Angel stepped out onto the balcony to watch the storm and Giovanni followed her. "I have sent your men to your old apartment to gather your cats and any belongings they can salvage."

"Oh, those aren't men, I mean, they're men, but they're not MY men," she rambled nervously, which made a big smile fill Giovanni's face. "Why are they getting my things?"

He lifted his arms and gestured around. "This is your new apartment," Giovanni said, "that is why the key is on your key ring."

Angel's mouth fell open. "Thank you, grandfather," she said, "but this is one of the premier apartment buildings in the city. I can't afford this every month."

"Bah," Giovanni raised his hand to quiet her, "there is no monthly fee." He leaned in close to her ear and whispered, "I own the building."

"You own the building?" Angel repeated with surprise.

He nudged her with his elbow and put his finger to his lips. "Shh," he said. "I own many things in this city. Someday we will discuss them."

Angel squinted her eyes and smirked at him. "Wait a second, why do you own a lot of things here when you live in New York?"

He gave her wink. "Let's just say this grandfather keeps a close eye on his interests."

Chills darted up the back of her neck. *So even when I thought I was alone, my family was with me all along,* she said to herself.

Angel threw her arms around Giovanni's neck. "Thank you, grandfather," she said. "It's okay if Olga lives here too, right?"

He narrowed his brows and mumbled in Italian, shaking his finger at her. "It is bad enough you have those smelly cats, but your aunt, too?"

Angel giggled. "You know you love her."

"Dios Mio," Giovanni said and made the sign of the cross over his body. "She does not fit with the name."

Heavenly Towers, Angel said the name in her mind and then burst out laughing. "Yes, she does," she scolded Giovanni. "Olga has a good heart."

"If she lives in the building I will have to rename it Towers of Hell." Giovanni's thin lips curled up into a sinister grin and he bellowed out a deep laugh.

"How'd you come up with the name Heavenly Towers anyway?"

Giovanni gazed at her with a twinkle in his eye only a grandfather can possess. "It was built for an Angel," he said and chills danced up her back.

She looped her arm in his and they stood listening and watching the storm. "Your father loved thunderstorms, you know."

"I remember," Angel said.

"He would be proud of the woman you have become." Giovanni patted her cheek and walked back inside.

Angel stood on the balcony alone, letting the wind blow through her hair and unravel her thoughts. There were so many unanswered questions and ends that dangled loosely in her mind; but for now, the questions could wait.

She kissed her fingertips and threw the kiss up into the sky. "I love you dad," she whispered, as the thunder crashed and lightning streaked across the heavens.

The END

If you enjoyed Tetterbaum's Truth, pick up the second book in the Just Call Me Angel series, entitled, Traitor's Among Us.

ABOUT THE AUTHOR

S.R.Claridge, nominated for the 2010 Molly Award, 2013 Pushcart Prize and awarded the 2011 Rocky Mountain Fiction Writers Pen Award, writes full-time and lives in Colorado. She loves autumn, moonlight and Grey Goose martinis with bleu cheese or jalapeno stuffed olives. She believes Friday nights are for indulging in Mexican food and margaritas and Sunday mornings warrant an extra-spicy Bloody Mary. Growing up in St. Louis, Missouri and earning her BA in Psychology from the University of Missouri, Columbia, S.R.Claridge is a mixture of mid-western family values and western wild nights. She loves Jesus, believes in the power of prayer, in the freedom of forgiveness and that life is a gift that should be enjoyed to the fullest. With a background in theatre, S.R.Claridge creates characters with dramatic flair and is known for her intense plot twists and engaging humor. S.R.Claridge would rather walk dangerously where there's a view than sit in idle safety and let life pass her by. Her spirited outlook comes shining through in her novels, as she takes readers to the edge of their seats with bone-chilling suspense.

AUTHOR ACCLAIM

"The Just Call Me Angel series is suspense at its best."
- RipeReviews

"A unique series from a one-of-a-kind author."
- APEX Reviews

"Riveting!"
- TrueBlueEbookReview

"One thrilling moment after another!"
- CanadaReviews

"A best-seller candidate indeed."
- BookWatchMagazine

BOOKS BY S.R.CLARIDGE

Tetterbaum's Truth *(book 1 in the Just Call Me Angel series)*
Traitors Among Us *(book 2 in the Just Call Me Angel series)*
Russian Uprising *(book 3 in the Just Call Me Angel series)*
Death Trap *(book 4 in the Just Call Me Angel series)*
Loose Ends (*book 5 in the Just Call Me Angel series)*
Divine Intervention (book 6 in the Just Call Me Angel series)

Petals of Blood *(short story; Pushcart Prize Nomination 2013)*

House of Lies (*Political cult suspense)*

No Easy Way *(debut novel; nominated for The Molly Award
from the HODRW 2010)*

The Candy Shop *(Suspense Thriller)*

Men-Take-Pause

'Twas the Night Before COVID

** S.R.Claridge has ghostwritten
ten novels.

www.GlobalPublishGroup.com